Praise for Camilla Gibb's

MOUTHING THE WORDS

"Gibb scales her story small, twists her sentences into prickly, unsentimental assaults and ends up with a portrait of terrible, comic humanity." —*The New York Times*

"Gibb's prose is elegant and sings with an almost Victorian delicacy and sophistication: Dickens, interrupted." —*San Francisco Chronicle*

"Beautiful and compelling ... an insightful and humane exploration of the space between reason and imagination." —*The Times* (London)

"A novel of astonishing power; this book is a journey of such searing pain and courage that my mind was driven back to Dante."
—*The Baltimore Sun*

"Suggestive of Wilde at his spirited best. Gibb's narrative of a troubled childhood leaves you poised—sometimes within a single sentence—between laughter and heartbreak ... a compelling journey ending in an admirably unsentimental redemption." —*The Globe and Mail*

"A startling debut ...You won't find a more passionate voice than ... in ... the pages of ... Gibb's bristling debut novel ... If it weren't for Gibb's smart, punchy prose—a smashing combination of the heartbreaking and the hilarious—this might have been a sad story.... Instead, she challenges both the reader and narrator, eliciting an examination of the self—the good, the bad, the pleasure, the pain, and the unrelenting humor that exists in all of us." —*Vogue*

"Lock the doors, take the phone off the hook ... for an inspiring and incredibly moving story that deserves your full attention." —*The List*

"Her tales of growing up in Canada with neglectful parents are both funny and alarming ... Gibb seduces the reader with sparkly prose and charming storylines before drawing us onto a heart-wrenching roller-coaster ride through one breakdown after another." —*The Guardian*

The

Petty Details of

So-and-so's

Life

CAMILLA GIBB

DOUBLEDAY CANADA

Doubleday Canada and colophon are trademarks.

NATIONAL LIBRARY OF CANADA CATALOGUING IN PUBLICATION DATA

Gibb, Camilla, 1968–
        The petty details of so-and-so's life

ISBN 0-385-65802-8

        I. Title.

PS8563.I2437P48 2002   C813'.54   C2001-904044-X
PR9199.3.G53P48 2002

Jacket image: Tomek Sikora / The Image Bank
Printed and bound in the USA

Parts of earlier drafts of this novel first appeared as the short stories "On All Fours in Brooklyn," in *Carnal Nation: Brave New Sex Fictions*, and "ID Me," in *Canadian Forum*.

Quotes from Rimbaud are taken from *Arthur Rimbaud: Seasons in Hell*, translated by Wallace Fowlie, Phoenix Books (University of Chicago Press), 1966.

The author wishes to thank the Toronto Arts Council for support.

Published in Canada by
Doubleday Canada, a division of
Random House of Canada Limited

Visit Random House of Canada Limited's website: www.randomhouse.ca

BVG   10  9  8  7  6  5  4  3  2  1

"I will make gashes on my entire body and tattoo it.
I want to be as hideous as a Mongol.
You will see, I will howl in the streets."

– Arthur Rimbaud, *A Season in Hell*

# The Extinction of the Question Mark

A photograph. A single photograph. White borders blackened with the grease of family fingers groping at the only remaining evidence of themselves: a picture of a man kneeling on all fours in the dirt. He is drunk, he is thin, he is tired. He is Oliver Taylor, a man gazing at a camera like a bewildered animal caught in headlights, looking feral and fetal and altogether strange. It's the middle of winter, but he seems to have adapted to the bitter cold. A white shirt hangs off his otherwise naked frame like a vestigial remnant of some earlier evolutionary stage; a time when business meant business and men wore suits.

*They* know he came from elsewhere—emerged, devolved, transmuted from some earlier incarnation of himself—because they remember when he lived in a house with a wife, two children, and a cat, and ate roast beef on Sundays and rice pudding for dessert. His wife was called Elaine, the cat called Frosted Flake, and they were those children—Emma and Llewellyn—Em and Blue for short.

They liked their roast beef bloody and dripping, and Elaine made the rice pudding with rich, flesh-toned condensed milk because that's what Oliver's mother had done during the war. Which war, Elaine never told them, even though they always asked. "The war during which your granny"—that mysterious entity who lived on the other side of the ocean—"used condensed milk," she'd answer obtusely.

Emma and Blue grew up feeling as muddled about the history of the world as they did about their own ancestry. Having learned the futility of asking questions at such a young age, it's a wonder the question mark didn't become extinct. They fabricated answers to unasked questions in the rank and damp of the basement where they played "I'll show you mine if you show me yours." They shared secrets and understanding as they crouched by the furnace with a face like a monster in the bowels of their house in Niagara Falls.

It was there that nine-year-old Blue pulled up his sleeve to show Emma the initials he'd carved into his arm with a homemade tattoo gun made from the broken needles of Elaine's old Singer. Emma had turned away when he'd started to pull the needles downward through his skin the day before. She'd wanted to cry out but she didn't dare because they were already in trouble. They often were. It was the middle of a Tuesday afternoon and they were hiding in a place infinitely superior to that space between a Formica-topped desk and a doll's chair one was supposed to occupy in grades three and four.

Blue preferred wearing graffiti to scribbling it on bathroom walls. Emma preferred darkness to daylight. They both preferred being in the basement to most places above-ground, but it was there, on that day, that Emma stared at Blue's baby-boy bicep and realized for the first time that she and her brother didn't wear the same skin.

She'd thought they were identical. She'd thought they were both gap-toothed and lonely and saw all the same things, even though her eyes were grey and his green. She had no idea that while she was staring at the horizon like it was icing on a cake at the edge of the world, Blue was squinting in order to avoid staring directly at all that he saw.

But they had always been different. Emma was a round little pudgeball with the type of cheeks peculiar mothers fantasized about biting. She did somersaults on sticky sidewalks, pale limbs over paler skin; she was a tangled, translucent mass, a "Holy Christ, here she comes." Her brother, on the other hand, was long and lean and getting longer every day, emerging from baby fat into boy-body with alarming speed. He had muscles as tough as straw, and was unconsciously troubled by his limitless potential for physical growth. He was cautious, doubly so, enough for both of them, his posture hunched and timid, his movements measured and deliberate against the clumsy backdrop of his sister tumbling head, belly, then knees over heels.

"It's my first tattoo," he declared proudly, speaking as if he'd just adopted the first strange animal in a bestiary he was planning on housing. Because theirs was a world without questions, Emma didn't ask the obvious. She simply nodded and put her hand to his forehead to see if he had a temperature. She spent that night, and many nights that followed though, wondering if her little brother was afraid of forgetting his name. She wished she could forget hers. She was, after all, named after her mother's childhood pet—not a movie star or a war hero or a favourite aunt, but a bouvier—a four-legged furry thing with a tail like a sawed-off carrot.

In secret defiance Emma had actually changed her name. She was Tabatha—daughter of the good witch Samantha—a pretty little blonde girl who lived in a happy suburban home where mischievous witches and warlocks turned up unannounced for tea and inadvertently distressed her poor mortal father with trickery designed to embarrass him in front of curtain-twitching neighbours.

CAMILLA GIBB

She sensed Blue's motivation to identify himself was different. Perhaps he was afraid of getting lost in the street. She pictured some kind stranger, a Jimmy Stewart look-alike in a suit and a white hat, approaching her brother and saying in a voice out of a black-and-white movie: "Why, you look lost, son. What's your name, boy?" Blue would pull up his sleeve to consult his bicep then and the Jimmy Stewart look-alike would exclaim, "What the dickens?"

If it were the fear of being lost and not found that compelled him to etch a deep, dyslexic "LT" into his arm, she would have suggested a different set of initials. Ones that would lead you back to a house with a swimming pool, or a family with twelve kids, or a mother who would buy you skates and take you to hockey practice. Initials you might want to have monogrammed on a set of towels that belong in a house with a finished basement on some street with a name like Thackley Terrace.

Instead, there they were with Elaine and Oliver, all crammed into a tiny three-bedroom house in Niagara Falls, across the street from a restaurant offering french fries and chow mein available twenty-four hours, even though a big CLOSED sign hung across the door at night because of lack of business. The house, a decrepit building that they'd bought for next to nothing, stood on the tawdry main street, sandwiched between a hardware store and a used-clothing store. In its previous incarnation, their house had been a pet food store, evidenced by the basement full of dog food that was part of the bargain. Before that, as Elaine and Oliver deduced on the basis of what lay behind the cheap drywall, it must have been a porn shop. The building was apparently insulated with mouldy copies of *Penthouse*.

Oliver painted the storeroom window over with red paint, until Elaine pointed out the obvious—it looked like they were advertising themselves as a whorehouse when they turned the living room light on

4

at night. He remedied this by covering the red paint over with thick lashings of industrial grey, creating the feeling that the world outside was perpetually overcast. Oliver liked it that way because it reminded him of his childhood spent in a grungy two-up two-down with windows clouded over with bacon grease on one of Glasgow's dodgiest streets—where that mysterious entity called Granny still lived.

In the porn-pet-shop-cum-house, there were three tiny bedrooms lined up in a row off a narrow corridor, at the end of which was a damp brown bathroom. The upstairs had obviously been a boarding house because each of the bedrooms smelled like dead bodies and old cheese and there was a fridge in one of them and a cooking element in the closet of another. But Emma and Blue each had their own room for the first time in their lives and this was better than anything that had ever happened before. Even better still, Elaine allowed each of them to choose a colour for their bedroom walls. Blue, of course, chose his namesake, and Emma asked for the colour of the sun, wherein a long debate ensued between Elaine and Oliver about just what colour that was. In the end, Oliver painted Emma's bedroom a colour that turned out to be more custard than sunshine. Emma helped her father, pointing out all the spots he'd missed and getting underfoot and nattering on inanely while he strained his neck to paint the ceiling.

"You're getting in the way," he finally said, irritated.

She opened the door of the closet then and sat on the floor, out of Oliver's way, but still in full view of the change of seasons. When she leaned back against the flimsy, fake-wood panelling at the back of the closet, though, she discovered a hole the size of a saucepan lid. Curious, she reached inside and wrapped her fingers around a hard, mysterious object. She tugged and pulled and finally yanked a grey bone longer than her leg out from the noisy clatter behind the panelling.

"Daddy! Look! A dinosaur bone!" she shrieked.

"What on earth have you got there?" he asked, puzzled.

"I told you—a dinosaur bone!"

"Fancy that," mused Oliver, putting down his paintbrush. He crawled inside the closet with her and said, "I wonder if the rest of its bones are here." He reached down into the hole and said, "Yup. There's definitely something here, all right," and told her to wait while he went to the basement to get a crowbar.

He ripped the panelling down and there, amidst dust, used condoms, and fossilized chocolate, were several large teeth. "Dinosaur teeth!" Emma squealed in delight, picking them up in her hands.

Oliver chuckled and said, "Doubtful, but interesting nonetheless." Later that day he drilled a needle-sized hole through one of the molars and strung it on a piece of string so that Emma could wear it around her neck. She wore it proudly, even though a boy at school called her a cave woman, in the hope that if she rubbed it the right way, she would be teleported into a secret world where animals larger than trucks ate clouds for breakfast. She and her dad could travel back in time and discover lost cities and people who spoke languages before English was ever invented. Worlds far more interesting than Niagara Falls.


They had moved to Niagara Falls in 1974 because Oliver had lost his job as an architect in Montreal the year before. Something about him losing sight of the third dimension. He'd sneezed so hard on his way to work one morning that the world in front of him had suddenly collapsed. It was flatter than anyone before Copernicus had ever even imagined: far too flat to even consider continuing on his way to the office.

"Oliver? Don't you think it's a little arrogant to think you have the power to change the shape of the earth?" Elaine had to ask when he showed up at home only an hour after he'd left. He just shrugged and went to bed for the next six weeks.

Perhaps that was the beginning of the end, it's always been hard for Elaine to say, because ends by definition shouldn't have beginnings. Something definitely changed from that day on, though. She'd long ceased imagining him as a lover, but an architect missing a third dimension was really pushing the limits of shared reality.

What Oliver didn't confide was that in place of the third, he'd discovered an altogether different dimension. Fair enough, he'd never be able to design buildings according to other people's conceptions of space any more, but his new sight brought him the remarkable ability to see things lurking in places where other people didn't see them. A gift. Superior insight, he congratulated himself with a smug grin.

"Elaine, my real talents were wasted there," he declared when he woke up after his six-week nap.

"Really," she droned sarcastically. "And how might they be more meaningfully employed?"

"As an inventor," he said.

"You're not serious."

"Damn right, I am."

"And what, exactly, are you planning on *inventing*?"

"Don't worry, Elaine. You always worry. There's divinity in these hands," he said, raising his palms in front of her face. "I'll let them guide me."

"Did you suddenly get religion, or something?"

"Just a little perspective," he said.

She sighed. "Will you do me one favour?"

"What is it?"

"See a vocational counsellor."

"What on earth for?" he barked.

She winced. "If you really are entertaining a career change, it might be helpful to talk to someone about it."

"But I know exactly what I'm going to do. I've found my calling."

"Just this one favour, Oliver—could you do me this one favour? I promise I'll respect whatever decision you make after that."

He stared at her blankly.

"For me?" she pleaded.

"All right," he conceded. "But my mind's made up."

"All right," she sighed, diffusing what she knew could have otherwise mushroomed into something large and toxic. She was relieved that he was simply out of bed.

The vocational counsellor quickly dispatched Oliver for a psychological assessment. He spent what he said was a useless hour and a half staring at ink blots, but was pleasantly surprised by the report sent by the psychologist the following week. It was full of words: *superior IQ*, *delusional*, *overinflated sense of self-worth*, *self-aggrandizing*, and *paranoid tendencies*. The report offered more of a career-related prognosis than definitive clinical diagnosis: Oliver Taylor was an employer's worst nightmare.

"It simply means I'm of much more use on the planet when I'm marching to the beat of my own drum," he said proudly, taping the assessment to the fridge. He repeatedly punched it with a firm finger, demanding each member of his family acknowledge the scientific proof of his superior intelligence. He'd stopped reading the report after *superior IQ*, completely failing to register that the words that followed were suggestive of dubious character and unstable mental health. Oliver Taylor was thirty years old and had just received the last pay-cheque of his life

Elaine had always known Oliver was *different*, and that was precisely why she had married him. Her path down that slippery slope toward him had begun in 1967, when she was at the zenith of her adolescent life as an angry young woman. As the end of her senior year approached, it became obvious she wasn't going to be asked to the prom at her Boston high school. Since this was a stigma akin to having leprosy, her parents decided to intervene in the hope of preventing her from being banished to some remote colony where she would spend the rest of her days losing bits of her body and soul.

They weren't sure if she even had a soul, though. She had what they termed "socialist leanings," a tendency which was so thoroughly offensive to their class pretensions that she had, for the last two years, dined alone with her books in her room, and spent the summers wait-ressing while her parents holidayed at the cottage in Maine. *She* knew she had a soul—just one the world around her considered alien. She'd hitch a ride on a satellite one day and wander the universe in search of like aliens. Until then, she had her books, and an industrial-sized lock on her bedroom door.

When Peter Wainright asked her to the prom then, she was deeply suspicious. The prom was at the end of June, and dates for the great event had been secured as early as January. It was the third of June when he asked her, so she knew she couldn't be his first choice. But she was *a* choice, and although this mystified her, she couldn't help but feel flattered.

On the fateful day, she had thrown her bookbag down on her bed after school, and in and amongst the dog-eared textbooks, feminine hygiene products, chewed pens, and lint-covered lip glosses was a postcard of the Great Wall of China. On the reverse it read:

*Dear Elaine,*

*It's taken me such a long time to work up my nerve to ask you, that you probably already have a date for the prom. If you don't—I'd be honoured to take you.*

*Yours sincerely,*
*Peter Wainright*

She stared at his minute, precise scrawl, thinking, Surely, this must be a joke. Peter Wainright was the son of Dr. and Mrs. Derek ("Tilly") Wainright, the snooty couple with whom her parents played bridge every other Sunday afternoon. Dr. Wainright was a plastic surgeon, and Mrs. Wainright was just plastic, and Peter was apparently going to dental school in the fall, presumably because, like every other boy in her year who was off to dental school in the fall, he'd failed to get into medical school. Despite all that was not in his favour, Elaine actually thought Peter Wainright was all right. Still, this surely had to be a joke.

"What do you make of this?" she asked her older brother Sam.

"Well, I might be stating the obvious, but it looks like Peter Wainright is inviting you to the prom."

"For real?"

"Well, what other kind of invitation is there?"

"Maybe it's a hoax."

"You read too much," Sam groaned. "I'd say you better say yes. Might be your only chance of being normal."

She dared to brush by Peter Wainright's desk the next day on her way to her seat in calculus class. She peered down at his notebook and flushed red at the sight of his handwriting—as minute and meticulous as the letters on the back of the Great Wall of China. She sat nervously in front of him, wondering if her hair looked like a battered meringue from behind, and scribbled a note to him on the last page of her notebook.

*Dear Peter,*

*Thank you for your invitation to the prom. ~~After seriously weighing the options of my various offers~~, I have decided that I would, indeed, like you, above any one else, to take me. I'll be wearing pink and I'm allergic to roses.*

*Yours sincerely,*
*Elaine Howard*

As soon as the bell rang, she bolted from the room, dropping the note on Peter's desk as she ran past him. In her haste she dropped her calculus text with a humiliating thud, but was far too embarrassed to turn around and pick it up. Peter retrieved the book from the floor and followed her to her locker, where she was rummaging clumsily in search of nothing in particular.

"You dropped this," he said.

"Oh? Did I?" she said, feigning surprise. "Silly me."

"Thank you for your note."

"Note? Oh yes," she said, as if she'd forgotten having dropped off her unabashed "yes" five minutes earlier.

"So, I'll pick you up at seven?"

"Oh. Yes, fine. Thank you," she nodded and returned to the catacombs of her locker.

"I'll be seeing you, then."

"See you!" she chirped inside the dead space of her locker. She didn't dare look at him. She was sure she was turning green. She leaned further into her locker and breathed deeply, and then quietly threw up into her running shoes.

After a jocular exchange full of "Haar yes," and "Of course, sir," between Peter and her father in the foyer, Elaine and Peter drove off in his father's white Buick.

"First stop, Mike's place. Then we pick up Mary-Ann," Peter announced. Elaine froze. Mike was Peter's best friend, and Mary-Ann, his date, the type of girl who was a cheerleader with all the sickening potential of being chosen prom queen.

In fact, when Mary-Ann plopped down in the back seat, all flounce and ringlets, she said as much. "Petey! You know, if you guys don't make me prom queen, I'll have to burn the hair of the girl who wins!"

She turned to Elaine then and commented on her dress. "Interesting" was the word she used. "Did you make it yourself?" she asked patronizingly. Elaine nodded, and Mary-Ann said, "Oh, good for you! I'm just *useless* with a needle and thread."

It went from bad to worse. Peter and Mike took turns dancing with Mary-Ann all night and Elaine spent a great deal of time staring at her shoes (which she hadn't, incidentally, made herself). Peter kept coming up to the table and asking her if she was all right, bringing her a glass of punch each time. Halfway through the night, she was sitting alone at a table with six glasses of punch lined up in a row, none of which she had touched. Mrs. Petrie, the gym teacher, must have felt sorry for her, because she pulled up a chair beside Elaine and asked her if she was having a lovely time.

"Terrific," Elaine said drolly.

Mrs. Petrie looked sympathetic and said, "I wouldn't worry, dear. They haven't got half your intellect," nodding her head in the direction of the two boys flanking the now near-hysterical swirling blonde. "You got accepted to Harvard, didn't you?"

"Yeah, so?"

"Well, that's better than any of them could do."

"Well, I'm not going."

"You haven't accepted?"

"I never wanted to apply in the first place. I just ghost wrote my mother's application. It wasn't me. It isn't me. I'm getting the hell out of Boston."

"Where are you going?"

"Canada."

"Canada?" said Mrs. Petrie with such surprise you'd think it were a penal colony.

"Montreal. McGill." Montreal was only six hours away, but it was about as far away from the sordid demonstration in front of her as she could imagine.

"Well, that's brave," she commended her.

Not really, thought Elaine.

Despite feeling self-righteous and determined, Elaine did still, of course, secretly hope that Peter was just being coy and saving the last dance for her. Anticipating this as the night wore on, she excused herself

13

from Mrs. Petrie and went to floss her teeth in the ladies' room. "Shhhh," she heard as soon as she walked in, followed by a succession of hiccups and muffled giggles. A bottle of cherry brandy crashed to the floor inside the cubicle behind her and Mary-Ann let out a high-pitched screech: "Oh shit, Peter! You've stained the front of my dress!" Mary-Ann burst out of the cubicle then and ran to the sink beside Elaine, hitching up her dress to her navel in an effort to get it under the tap. Elaine was staring into the mirror as Peter emerged, his reflection slightly drunk and stupid.

"Hi," he waved lamely at Elaine's face in the mirror.

"Hi," she waved back, mockingly.

"Peter, you could at least help me!" shouted Mary-Ann, frantically scratching her nails into the fabric of her dress.

When Peter didn't move, Elaine said, "It's the least you could do," and gave him a patronizing glare designed to make him feel like a pathetic fool.

"Elaine—" Peter stammered, indeed feeling like a pathetic fool.

"Fuck off, Peter," she said simply.

Peter and Mary-Ann both looked shocked. "*Such* unladylike language," Mary-Ann chided. "No wonder your father had to pay someone to ask you to the prom."

"Mary-Ann!" Peter cringed.

"Oh," Mary-Ann crooned with false pity. "You didn't know your daddy paid Peter to ask you? Come on, darling. You didn't really think Petey Wetey was interested in you, did you?"

Elaine called Sam from the phone in Mrs. Petrie's office. "Come right away," she said. "They're a bunch of cretins."

"He could have at least driven you home," Sam said in the car after he picked her up on the corner. "I mean, jeez, Dad paid him enough."

"You knew?" she screamed. She sank back into the plush burgundy seat in defeat. She closed her eyes and erased the world in front
of her, imagining Montreal instead, a city of exotic light at the end of
this tunnel of horrors. The rest of the world and all the people in it
could go straight to hell as far as she was concerned. She locked her
bedroom door until late August, until it was time to pack nothing and
leave for university.

"I want to be a writer," she told the shaggy-haired Scottish boy in the
smoky coffee shop the following November.

"Cool," he said. He fingered a Rizla intently and rolled a perfect
cigarette, which he then offered to her. She took it from his wide,
black-ink-stained fingers and said a shy thank you. She liked his deep
blue eyes and his throaty, smoke-laden laugh. She liked that he was
here in this café every afternoon, looking moody and making a single
cup of coffee last for hours.

"So let me see what you're writing," he said after he'd lit her cigarette.

She looked sheepish and said, "It's really rough."

"I like it rough," he teased.

"Where do you come from?" she asked him.

"Oh, the wilds," he said, his eyes widening. "The land of bracken
and heather and haggis."

"Scotland?"

"Right y'are, missy," he growled in becoming brogue.

"And what are you doing in Montreal?"

"Ahh. I'm escaping a terrible past," he said flirtatiously.

"Are you on the run?" she asked, hoping for danger.

"I am."

"From the law?"

"From all laws that say a man must live out the expectations of his parents."

"What did your parents want you to be?"

"A military officer like my dad, married to a wee hen from the Hebrides who would serve me tea at six, and wouldn't often have an opinion—unless, of course, she agreed with me."

"I'm on the run from that law, too," Elaine confided.

"Did they want you to be a schoolmarm and give it all up to marry a doctor from Philadelphia?"

"How did you know?" she said, rolling her eyes.

"I could tell, missy."

"Could you?"

"You've got the look of a dreamer about you. A bird like you would bite through metal bars if she were trapped in a cage."

Elaine smiled. She'd never thought she had the look of anything in particular about her, except perhaps that of an alien. Certainly nothing with a bite strong enough to chew through metal.

His name was Oliver. He'd been sent to live with his uncle Hugh in Montreal a couple of years before and was now studying architecture just a few buildings away from where Elaine was studying English. He didn't want to talk much about his past. "As far as I'm concerned," he said, "my life didn't begin until I arrived in Montreal."

"Are you happy here, then?" she asked him.

"Yeah," he said, sounding a little surprised. "Not forever, but for now, yeah."

On cold afternoons throughout that winter she let him read her rough drafts, and rather than respond in words he would doodle in the margins, framing her stories with colourful gnomes and one-eyed animals. He made her laugh, and each time she laughed the vice grip around her heart loosened another notch. In a matter of months it was beating regularly, without restraint. When he'd worn down every one of her defences with fun and flattery and long dreamy rants about how he was going to paint billboards in New York City and she was going to write a famous novel and they were both going to be fantastically rich without having compromised their "socialist leanings," she said yes to his repeated proposal of marriage.

"But I'm never living in the U.S. again," she declared, standing flanked by pasta and Cream of Wheat in the middle of the last aisle in a supermarket.

"Oh. But *New York*," he said longingly, tossing a carton of eggs carelessly into their basket.

"That's my one and only condition."

He thought about it for a minute. "Would you ever consider Niagara Falls?"

"The Canadian side?"

"Sure." It didn't matter to Oliver—the Falls paid no attention to the border—they were the simultaneous wonder of New York State, Ontario, Canada, the U.S., and the world. They *were* the world, in his mind, or at least the central destination of its people, and he fancied himself at the centre of the universe. "Let's have our honeymoon there," he said excitedly.

"Kind of clichéd, don't you think?"

"Charmingly so," he agreed. "We'll sleep in a heart-shaped bed and go bowling. What do you think, missus?" he asked, picking up a honeydew melon from a pile and bowling it down the length of the aisle until it crashed into the heel of an innocent senior citizen pushing a cart full of Pablum.

"Sorry!" he called saccharinely when she turned around in fright. "That would have been a strike," he muttered to Elaine, grabbing her hands in his and kissing her hard on the mouth. Their kisses were always hard, and she liked their determination.

She moved into his rundown apartment with sloping floors after the honeymoon. First there were termites, and then there were two babies, and all of sudden, there they were with Oliver punching his finger against the fridge declaring himself a certifiable genius and prophet of invention. His inventing would never prove to be a big money-maker, and his big dreams would never provide the warmth to heat them adequately through harsh Montreal winters. Elaine began to wonder when exactly they were going to start living the life of artistic expression and political integrity they'd once imagined.

It was after the first baby was born and named after Elaine's favourite family pet and the world became all crap and diapers and cracked, chapped nipples, that Elaine knew they were never going to start living. All they had done was come full circle; managing to create a pathetic imitation of the very type of domestic arrangement they had sought to avoid. Oliver went to work in the mornings and drafted plans for tall buildings and Elaine stayed at home with Emma, and then Emma and her baby brother Llewellyn, and watched as the dream of writing a famous novel shattered into tiny fragments.

Oliver was totally unrealistic. When the baby girl was born he brought her an enormous box of assorted chocolates and tried to cram the bonbons into her mouth when Elaine wasn't looking. He read to the baby from a dusty old encyclopedia and got frustrated when, instead of listening, she threw up in her lap. He asked her if she could remember her dreams and she looked at him with her wide eyes and burped. When Llewellyn arrived, he'd already long given up even attempting to pretend to be a parent.

Oliver was prone to Big Ideas and Pronouncements. The fantasy of their life was constructed on these BIPs. Oliver could make tangible shapes out of dust spiralling in a sliver of sunshine that pierced a dirty window. He could look at the clouds and say, "Elaine, that quadrant of blue is exactly the colour of the water that will lap against the shore of an island that our descendants will name after us one day."

Oliver's inventing was going nowhere, but he was sure it was all a matter of location, location, location. Montreal was too Old World, too European, he declared. What he needed was the contagious spirit of American entrepreneurialism to spur him on. In the middle of a blistering snowstorm, six years into their mostly miserable marriage, Oliver begged Elaine to pack up and move to Niagara Falls. "We always said we'd do it one day, Elaine," he encouraged.

"But we said *when we retired*," she disparaged.

"What the hell are we waiting for? The kids'll love it. All those positive ions: they'll grow up full of good air and promise."

Elaine didn't have the strength any more to start kicking the bricks out of his foundations and topple the grand scheme of the moment. By the time Oliver had declared he was going to be an inventor and set himself free from the conventions of nine-to-five, she had already given up. So in the middle of the worst blizzard to have blighted Montreal in decades, she resigned herself, with the faint hope that a change of scenery might do them all good.

They packed up the contents of the apartment above the Portuguese bakery on Rue St. Dominique into a blue minivan and a rented U-Haul. When everything from their four-room flat was crammed in, there was little space left for actual human bodies.

"They'll have to take the bus," Elaine declared with a shrug. "They'll manage."

Emma thrust a protective arm around her little brother, who, although only a year younger than her, was still saying little more than "mumble," "wumble," "bambam bolly." "Booly boo?" he asked his sister.

"Of course," she nodded and squeezed him reassuringly.

Elaine made two huge and humiliating signs reading: "Niagara Falls or Bust," hung them around their necks and ordered them not to let go of each other's hands. On the bus, they sat behind a kindly grandmother-type, the sort with an endless supply of Kit Kats. She sucked the chocolate off the wafer sticks noisily and then let the wafer dissolve in her mouth because, as she explained to Emma and Blue, "When you get to be my age, you've got to save your teeth in case you ever have to bite a mugger."

"Biteamugger, biteamugger," Blue repeated with a giggle.

"He's a sweet little boy, your son," the sticky-mouthed granny said between the crack in the seats.

"He's not my son," Emma said. "He's my brother. And I'm only five years old."

The granny laughed, "Goodness, me. Seems my eyesight's really going! I thought you were his teenaged mum and the two of you were on the run from the law or something! Here—have some more Kit Kat," she said, shoving a soggy bar through the crack between the seats as if to say, "And we'll just forget about my little mistake then and carry on."

"We're going to Niagara Falls," Emma said flatly.

"A good thing too, because that's where this bus is going," the granny chuckled. She then leaned back into her seat, suddenly nodding off in the middle of her chocolate high.

A whaling, high-pitched whistle squealed over the quiet *rurr* of the bus. The ridiculous noise was apparently coming from the sleeping granny's left nostril. Blue attempted to whistle and started to giggle uncontrollably. Emma clasped a loving hand over his mouth to shush him and leaned forward to listen more carefully. The granny's nose was whistling a song: *Summertime, and Niagara is sleazy—*

Emma already knew that she would prefer the winters, when the place was whitewashed by wind and ice. She imagined the Falls frozen into the most gigantic icicles on the planet, she and Blue tobogganing down their slippery slopes on their bellies.

When the bus pulled into a station, Emma worried that this might be the end of the line. Blue had kerplunked in his pants by this point, and was squirming uncomfortably beside her. He was still holding her hand. When he felt her grip tighten with worry he began to blubber. She offered him false comfort as sweat bubbled on her forehead. The bus hurtled forward again and she breathed a sigh of relief.

This was their first journey, and like every other journey that was to follow, Emma was never certain where to get off. She hoped that one day, when Blue could speak, he'd be able to tell her.

# The Language of Home

Emma's sixth birthday party. The obligatory snapshot. The children from her grade one class are lined up in a row along the corrugated tin fence in the backyard and none of them look remotely happy. The girls wear long skirts and look like they're picking cake out of their hair, and the boys stand with their legs apart and their eyes cast downward. Emma is not wearing a skirt and Blue's hair is far too short for 1975, and the two of them look pale, nervous, and embarrassed.

Oliver and Elaine had tried, but the games were all unusually complicated and the loot bags were filled with articles for personal grooming instead of technicolour jawbreakers, Good and Plenties, and cinnamon-flavoured toothpicks.

Emma had just begun to realize that their father was different from other fathers. Having a father who was different wasn't all bad. Having an inventor at home was something to brag about in the school-yard and Emma had learned such useful skills as how to distinguish an eighth-inch drill bit from a sixteenth before she had finished first grade. She, in turn, had taught the difference to Blue because Oliver constantly lost patience with his son.

She remembers their father poised with a hammer at Blue's temple. After arriving in Niagara Falls, Oliver had had the ingenious idea of financing his creative endeavours by selling "antiques" to tourists. A sandwich board dominated the front lawn and invited curiosity and ridicule. The "Emporium" was the garage. The "Antiques" were chairs and tables Oliver whacked together out of scrap and then set Emma and Blue to work distressing with toy hammers, barking orders like, "Bash the fuck out of it, you two layabouts!"

At Emma's sixth birthday party he offered a prize to the child who could do the most damage with a hammer in half an hour. Much to Elaine's embarrassment, Emma, with her considerable experience, won the prize, propelling a whole garage full of children into tears of envy and defeat. Emma had refined her technique: the trick was in the breathing. She'd inhale deeply as she raised her hammer and exhale like a burst balloon upon contact, a method that seemed to produce the biggest dent with the least effort.

While Emma was quite content banging inanimate objects, Blue developed an unfortunate habit of employing his toy hammer as a defensive weapon against smaller children and the occasional animal. "Boys will be boys," Oliver had initially shrugged, but when Blue took a swipe at Elaine's fat red goldfish, Oliver raised his voice and said, "Llewellyn. Now you've *really* crossed the line."

Blue's eyes welled up with tears and he stammered out an apology, saying he should have taken the fish out of the tank first, rather than trying to hammer its head in through the glass. He was sorry about the mess of water soaking into the carpet. Oliver unhooked his hammer from the wall of the garage and then held it against Blue's temple. "How would you feel if I put this through *your* head?" he threatened.

This was typical of Oliver's parenting: arming his children with weapons and telling them to shoot, although they didn't know where they were supposed to aim or why they should do so except to please him. So they aimed, and invariably pointed at the wrong target and ended up with their own heads on the chopping block. It became safer to take aim at themselves in the end. Before he did, and before they hurt anyone else.

Emma could never pinpoint the moment when she began to realize that being an inventor wasn't the only thing that set their father apart. She didn't know what the difference was, but whatever it was, it certainly did invoke fear. Emma's classmates were scared of her father and didn't want to come over to the house after she'd turned six. But Emma thought fathers were perhaps built to bully—that it was part of the paternal mandate to reduce children to tears by calling them stupid or lazy, which their father did, not infrequently. It was certainly embarrassing, but it was understandable because it was familiar, and people become fond of the familiar, no matter how strange.

It was the night after Oliver threatened Blue with the hammer that they built their bubble in the basement. Emma lay in bed looking at the iridescent stars on the ceiling, worrying about her baby brother. She knocked the secret knock on their adjoining bedroom wall and awaited Blue's reply. The silence from his bedroom was loud enough to make her wonder if the hammer was lodged in his mouth. She crept to his room in her fuzzy Minnie Mouse slippers and checked for him under the duvet, under the bed, and in the closet. No sign of little life. She tiptoed past her parents' bedroom and down the stairs at the end of the hall. In the green-tiled kitchen, over the drip drip of the tap, she heard the muffled sound of crying coming from the basement. She found Blue down there crouched by the furnace, next to an industrial-sized bag of Purina Puppy Chow, sobbing into his flannel-covered arm.

She knelt down beside him and made like a mama bird and wrapped him in her wing. He had language now, but they didn't speak. Even when he did speak to her he didn't use the language of the rest of the world. It was still all "boo" and "booly boo" and "bambam bolly" when it was just the two of them.

"I know," she said, in response to his silence. "He doesn't hate you. But we could pretend we're orphans."

The following week, Oliver told his son he was going to build him a bicycle. Blue didn't know what to make of this, at once elated by and wary of his father's gift. He was beginning to get a sense of Oliver's rhythm. Whenever Oliver knocked him down he would pick him up a week later with some promise: a trip to the butterfly conservatory, a ride on the *Maid of the Mist*, a hamburger with fries and a chocolate milkshake. Those days were the happiest for Blue, even though he knew they would be short-lived.

Oliver did build him a bicycle—a fast but strange-looking beast over which he took much abuse from the other kids on their street. His dad had built it for him, though, and he was so proud that he would pedal furiously past the taunting and teasing with a baseball cap pulled down so far over his eyes that he could only see the pavement beneath him, never the road ahead. He heard Oliver shout, "That's my boy!" as he watched him tear off down the street. As Oliver's boy, he flew without restraint, holding on to the handlebars for his life.

Oliver did take him to the butterfly conservatory. They stood side by side in a lush, tropical jungle amidst four thousand dancing wings. Oliver narrated the visit with a thousand and one handy facts about butterflies drawn from a colourful pamphlet. Blue would never cease to be amazed that monarchs know each other and the world without a map. He imagined them congregating in late summer for a family picnic in a favourite tree—drinking themselves stupid on nectar before making their way en masse to their villa in the Mexican forest. Is that where we go when we die? he wondered. To Mexico? He imagined old people in their beds falling asleep at night and waking up wearing cocoons instead of pyjamas. Leaving their beds as butterflies bound for the heavens of Mexico.

Oliver did take him for a hamburger, fries, and a chocolate milkshake, but on one of these occasions, Blue received a brutal blow. Oliver was delivering a sermon over a bottle of ketchup when Blue excused himself to go to the bathroom. Blue stared at the big man standing at the urinal beside him. The man stopped peeing, but continued to stand there, running his hand up and down his ridiculously long cock. Blue had never seen anything like it—he'd only seen his father's penis once and it was nothing like this man's, which was more like a baseball bat.

"Pretty big, eh?" the man said, pumping the thing up and down. It frightened Blue into wide-eyed silence. The man's breathing made him uneasy. He wanted to shout for his dad, but instead he just said a meek "I guess so."

Oliver walked in then. "What's taking you so long?" he said, coming around the corner.

The large man stopped his pumping, stuffed the baseball bat back into his jeans and walked out of the room. Blue, standing there with his own little penis in his hand, didn't know what to say. He'd been too scared to let go.

"What are you doing, Blue?" Oliver shouted. "Playing with yourself? What are you—a faggot or something?"

Blue had heard the word once before. He had only grown just past Oliver's kneecaps when Oliver refused to take his searching hand any more on the way to the liquor store. "Men don't touch other men unless they are ho-mo-sex-uals," he had said, pronouncing each and every syllable like a sneering British broadcaster. "Don't want people thinking we're a couple of faggots now, do we, Llewellyn?" Oliver had said, slapping him on the back.

"No, sir," Blue had coughed, just about choking on a caramel.

Blue didn't know what he'd done wrong in the washroom that day but he knew he'd done a bad bad thing. He sat in terrified silence beside his father all the way home. "What were you staring at that man's prick for, Blue?" Oliver began, after an interminable silence.

"Nothing," Blue mumbled through his tears.

"Do you know what faggots do to each other?" his father asked him. "They bugger each other. They stick their pricks into dirty bums, Blue. Like dogs."

Blue was so mortified that the hamburger in his stomach began to moo and the milkshake started to sour, and he would never again eat at McDonald's. Never again in his whole life. He had a secret so shameful and dirty that he couldn't even tell Emma. "He hates me," he told her in the basement. "He just does."

In their basement bubble, Emma and Blue learned how to hold each other's breath, becoming indistinguishable on the same oxygen. They began to take frequent refuge in the dank and musty grey space where they inhaled deeply, and got so dizzy that all they could hear were hearts pounding in their ears. When they could hold their breath no longer they grabbed each other's hands and pulled each other up, their heads spinning so wildly that they lost their balance and collapsed against each other, more often than not, crashing back down onto the cement floor. They called this "the hugging game."

When Emma crashed down on top of Blue she would rub her torso against him and press her pelvis into his. When fate toppled them the other way, it was Blue's turn. They were entangled and inseparable: horizontal and upright, they were constant and complex companions. They held hands in the schoolyard, at least, they did until Emma was in grade six and Brenda Tailgate told her she must be a pervert because sisters were supposed to hate their brothers. But until that day, she didn't let go of her baby brother's hand.

In the world above the basement, Oliver had started to renovate. "I'm going to build you your dream home, Elaine!" he announced one day in mid-manic upswing at the dinner table.

"What exactly does that entail, Oliver?" Elaine asked suspiciously.

"You tell me," he said. "You want a swimming pool—I'll give you a swimming pool. You want a greenhouse or a fireplace—I'll give you a greenhouse or a fireplace."

While Oliver sincerely thought this would please her, all Elaine could imagine was living in the middle of a construction site, picking nails out of her cornflakes, shaking sawdust from her hair. She could picture them walking the plank over a cavernous hole in the garden where the swimming pool Oliver had promised would forever remain a pit of despair. Elaine picked up the dishes and started washing them in the sink.

"Your mother's got no vision," Oliver said conspiratorially to the children. "She can't picture it. What do you think, kids? A big old fireplace?" Emma and Blue nodded eagerly. "A swimming pool?"

"Yipeee!" Emma said, grabbing Blue's hand and throwing their arms up in the air. They loved these moments when their father came to life. Lightning streaked across his face and his eyes wandered like he was watching a meteor shower that was setting the world on fire. They were enraptured and terrified: fully aware of the fact that wherever lightning strikes, things are likely to burn.

"What's that?" Elaine said, her back to them as she stood at the sink.

"Nothing, dear," said Oliver. "Just garnering a little support over here."

"Oliver—don't do that. Don't make them choose sides."

"I'm not making them choose sides. I'm just showing them how to dream."

"Perhaps you could teach them something a little more practical," she said angrily.

"Elaine, you know," he sighed, shaking his head, "you're just not the woman I married."

"Well, unfortunately you *are* the man I married."

"What's that supposed to mean?"

"I mean, when are you going to grow up?"

Dad isn't a grown up? Emma wondered.

"You're the most irresponsible person I've ever met," Elaine snapped. She thoroughly resented being the sole wage earner. Since they'd arrived in Niagara Falls, Elaine had been working two jobs: substitute teaching whenever she could, and booking tours of Niagara Falls for busloads of tourists who would have been millionaires if they got paid to complain. She'd begun to wonder if she wouldn't have been much better off doing what her parents had wished and marrying some bug-eyed dentist from Philadelphia. Even if he did have a personality as dull as a used drill bit, she could at least have been able to afford to keep her kids' teeth clean.

Oliver paused. "What happened to your dreams, Elaine? Where did they go?"

He sounded wistful, and that made Emma and Blue feel sorry and sad.

My dreams? Elaine thought. How dare he? Perhaps she could just declare she was going to write a novel and go to bed for six weeks in order to dream up a plot. Maybe Emma and Blue could quit school and support them. Her dreams? She didn't have the time or the energy now to write much more than a shopping list. "Life, Oliver. Life got in the way," she finally said. "It does. For most people, anyway."

Oliver took up full-time employment in the garage after that, engaged in the puttering and putzing that apparently constituted the process of giving birth to great invention. When he did come into the house at the end of each long day, Elaine expended so much energy yelling at him that she had little left for Emma and Blue. The world above the basement became full of noises like crash, fuck and hiss.

It was never entirely clear to Emma and Blue what their parents were fighting about. Money was definitely part of it. Emma knew this because Blue started looking for pennies on the street on their way home from school. "It's our nest egg," he told her wisely when she asked, repeating verbatim something he had obviously overheard.

"What's that?" Emma asked him.

"Our protection," he nodded. The little boy, who only a short time ago had stopped talking baby babble, was obviously sucking up critical life lessons like a sponge. A good thing too, because Emma wasn't taking notice—she was busy daydreaming, preoccupied with the adventures of Tabatha the baby witch, trying to figure out how to disappear from one room and appear in another rather than deal with the here and now of how to survive life as Emma.

She and Blue spent most of their after-schools and evenings whispering in the basement, or sitting on the ugly orange carpet in Blue's room, engaged in their respective silent passions. Emma would sit with her legs crossed and her back against the radiator and read book after book from the school library. She read about dinosaurs and Lilliputians, and journeys to the centre of the earth, space-time travel, and ancient pyramids full of hidden treasure. She'd morph into characters contained in pages she wished wouldn't end.

Blue wasn't a reader, but they did share one book between them —a scrapbook that had been sent with a package of mouldy gingersnaps one Christmas from some relative Oliver denied having. *Imagine you were a woolly mammoth*, Emma wrote on the first page of the scrapbook.

"Write: 'And you had fur instead of skin and you were on display in the museum,'" Blue said with excitement.

Emma loved the ideas they came up with, loved the way they looked on the page. She sucked on the letters like lollipops, while Blue became obsessed with trying to draw pictures to accompany the wild words. Pictures were his thing. He would tear images from magazines Elaine had brought home from the doctor's office, and glue them into haphazard collages on bristol board. He had a box of art supplies under the bed that included broken, discarded, and lost bits of things he found at the bottom of drawers and under the sofa, and pine cones and chestnuts he'd picked up on the way home from school. He was in the habit of painting things blue after his nickname.

Elaine showed some sign of life when Blue presented her with a collage for Mother's Day. He'd torn up tiny bits of glossy paper into squares and assembled a face with long auburn hair, and mysterious eyes, and lips curved into a beautiful smile. He'd taken bits of Elaine's broken jewellery and given the face earrings and a tiara. "It's you, Mum," Blue said, as she unwrapped it.

While Elaine was touched, she worried that this was an early indication of the same creative predisposition that had driven Oliver to spend increasingly more time in the garage. "It's beautiful, Llewellyn. It looks like Picasso. But don't let it overtake your ABCs, okay?" she said, and then gave him one of those rare hugs that he and Emma so often daydreamed about.

His creativity worried Elaine enough that it kicked her into action and she started taking her children to the public library on Saturday mornings. Emma was fine to wander around on her own, but Blue, because of his habit of tearing pictures out of books, needed constant supervision.

When Elaine asked Blue what he wanted for Christmas that year, Blue said, "I want to see Picasso."

"I think he's dead, Llewellyn."

"I mean his pictures."

Elaine sighed. "I'll make you a deal. If you have a decent report card next June, then I'll take you to see some Picasso at the end of the school year."

Poor Blue. He tried so hard to read over the next six months that the blood vessels in his eyes burst. The pages he read stuck together as their lines melted and books he touched ceased looking like books at all. Despite all his effort, his report card proposed remedial English for the following year.

Elaine blamed Oliver, or rather, Oliver's neglect. He had at least tried with Emma—reading *MacBeth* and *Aerospace Construction for Beginners* to her when she was tiny. He hadn't even offered Blue language, and now, as Blue got older, he barely spoke to him at all. Oliver finally consented to a few afternoon efforts at male bonding, but the pressure was so enormous, and Blue so desperate to impress, that they were destined to fail. He was too little to handle the unwieldiness of the circular saw, too fearful to ever go near a hammer again, and too worried that he'd disappoint his father to try his hand at much. Finally, Oliver, totally exasperated, said, "All right, Llewellyn. Is there anything you *can* do?"

Blue hesitantly picked up the pencil beside Oliver's plan for an underground wine cellar. He stared at the blueprint for a moment and then started scribbling on the page. Oliver looked horrified. "Blue. What are you doing?" he shouted.

"But now it looks real," Blue said, putting down the pencil. Sure enough, Blue had added a third dimension. The plans were suddenly intelligible—at least they would have been to anyone with a grasp on reality.

"You've desecrated my work!" Oliver yelled at him. "You've obscured it with graffiti!"

"But it makes sense now," Blue said, confused.

"You're telling *me* what makes sense? Who do you think you are?" Blue's eyes welled up. "Jesus Christ, stop being such a pathetic little mama's boy, Llewellyn," he snapped in disgust.

Before Elaine had stated the inevitable—that there'd be no seeing Picasso—Emma had stolen two books of prints for Blue from the public library. These were not the first books she'd stolen. One by one, she'd been accumulating an arsenal of Nancy Drews. This time, not only did she steal the glossy volume on Picasso she'd been eyeing for Blue, but on a whim, she also grabbed the book of Aubrey Beardsley prints lying next to it. It was full of black-and-white prints of people without legs pulling off each other's heads, and she knew Blue would love its bold lines and graphic images.

Blue was captivated for most of a summer. He filled in the white spaces between the thick black Beardsley lines with bold swipes of yellow, red, and blue paint. He drew butterflies in the margins. Monarchs bound for Mexico. Then, working his way through the volume on Picasso, he stopped dead at the paintings Picasso had done during his Blue Period. "Em," he said, pointing to a face made up of blue squares. "But this looks like me," his voice caught between fascination and terror.

"I guess so," she shrugged.

"But I've never met Picasso."

It must have unnerved him more than Emma initially realized, because from that day forward, Blue stopped tearing up bits of paper. His next artistic effort would be the initials he carved into his skin. What Emma didn't know then was that it was Oliver, not Picasso, who had implicitly conveyed the idea that creation was necessarily painful. He dug as deep as he could stand it with the needle, and ripped, rather than drew, those initials into his skin.

Although Emma and Blue were eventually forced to stop holding hands at school, they were always aware of the precise whereabouts of the other. They met at the corner store three blocks from school every day in order to walk home together, well out of eyesight of cool Brenda Tailgate. For two blocks it was safe to hold hands.

With his hand safely in the grip of his sister, Blue would natter on about how Joshua, a boy in his grade four class, had peed all over his hands, or how he had a new best friend called Stewart who had a hockey card for every one of the Boston Bruins. Emma would tell him that Sandy, the girl with eyebrows that met in the middle, was wearing a bra, and that Mrs. Daniels, their art teacher, had let out a fart when she bent over to pick up a piece of pottery that Gary, the hyperactive boy, had thrown on the floor.

"Do you think these pants make me look fat?" she asked him.

"But you are fat," he responded, in all innocence.

"That's why boys don't like me," she sighed.

"But I like you," he had said in his wide-eyed way.

"I know, Blue. But it doesn't count."

Elaine wordlessly handed Emma a book at the end of that year called *Dr. Nelligan's Diet Book for Girls*. She had offered her daughter the first silent lesson of being female: dieting was the road to love; thinness, in a mad, mad world, was the answer. The world was becoming like this—less and less spoken, much more in books. The world above the basement had grown quiet since Oliver had started to sleep in the garage on a camp cot from the army surplus store.

"Dreaming is an essential part of any creative process," Oliver had said, defending his self-imposed exile to the end of the garden. "I simply need my psychic space to be free of distraction in order to invent." Distraction obviously meant human contact, particularly that with the members of his immediate family who seemed to him more wanting and needing than other human beings. "Look, Elaine. Just give me some time and space. I'm on the verge of something big."

"You're *always* on the verge of something big, Oliver."

"Well, I'm on the verge of something *really* big this time."

"Another flying what's-it?" she asked.

"You're taking the piss, aren't you?" he said, annoyed. "That airborne radio receiver had revolutionary potential. Do you hear me? *Revolutionary.* You just couldn't see it. You don't have any vision. Or any faith, for that matter."

"What are you working on now then, Oliver?" she asked without the slightest bit of genuine interest.

"If you're really curious, I'd be happy to show you. Hey, I've got an idea," he said, raising an eyebrow.

"When have you ever *not* had an idea?" she muttered to herself.

"Why don't we have a date? Come to the garage on Friday night. We'll have a bottle of that Chianti you like and look over the plans."

"You mean the big something is still at the paper stage?" she asked, rolling her eyes.

"Oh, please, Elaine. It's a final draft," he pleaded.

"Why don't you just show me when you've actually built the thing. I don't believe in make-believe any more, Oliver."

"When did that happen?"

"About seven inventions ago."

Elaine hardly needed Oliver to share a bottle of Chianti. For the next couple of months she drank one by herself nearly every night while Oliver whittled away in the garage in silence. They didn't hear much from him except for the occasional torrent of profanities from the end of the yard when he inadvertently hammered some body part. There was a small mountain of empty takeout pizza boxes growing at the entrance to the garage, reassuring them that Oliver was still, in fact, alive.

Blue took to retrieving the discarded pizza crusts out of the boxes and eating them for breakfast: a scavenger in search of familial debris. The foraging was necessary, because with Oliver retreating, Elaine, too, despite her presence, was becoming just as remote and inaccessible. It was as if they'd each taken on new lovers, and forgotten about all that came before and between: their children, reminders of themselves and the mess they'd managed to create together.

The first time Emma and Blue really understood the seriousness of Elaine's drinking problem was when she tumbled down the stairs one late afternoon and ended up with a face full of splinters

"Living this close to the States seems to have driven her bonkers," Oliver had said, having just entered the house for what seemed like the first time in months. He'd responded to Blue's desperate cry that Mum had cracked open her skull. Oliver heaved Elaine up off the floor and carried her to the couch and then went straight back out to the garage, leaving Emma and Blue staring helplessly at their scratched and bruised mother.

"Pour me a Scotch, sweetie," she said, gesturing to Emma. "It'll help take away some of the pain," she winced, running her fingers over her face.

"Mum?" Blue asked with a frightened look in his eyes.

"What is it, sweetie?"

"Why does Dad sleep in the garage?"

"Because he's an *eccentric*, Llewellyn, that's why," she said, unable to hide her irritation.

That was generous on her part. She would have liked to have said: Because he's a lazy, self-absorbed bastard and he's losing his fucking mind. As time went on, she simply drank deeper and stopped referring to him. When she was forced to acknowledge the existence of the man at the end of the garden in some way, she called him "your father," as if to deny any association with her.

After spending months in the garage thinking about his inventions, Oliver had still failed to get the voice-activated circular saw, or any of his other ideas, past the paper stage. No one could see how desperate he was becoming. If he failed as an inventor, he was finished. Paralysed by lack of progress, he was spending much of the day masturbating compulsively in his camp cot. He'd stopped taking garden hose showers and his hair had turned completely grey. He pissed in a bucket, and defecated at night in the flower bed, covering up his fecal lumps as instinctively as a cat—anything to avoid contact with Elaine.

He was sure he repulsed her, and so he became repulsive. He was certain that she was determined to see him fail. And he was bound to fail: she, like his parents, expected things from him that he'd just never be able to deliver. It was no wonder. He'd constructed the entire idea of a life on the basis of promises, but he'd forget what he'd pledged as soon as the wind changed the direction of his mood. The whole idea of life consequently and constantly changed. He would decide they should all go and live on a desert island, and he would drive them through cruel waters on a leaky boat to get to some weedy shore where, as soon as they'd reluctantly disembarked, he'd tell them he was off to find a better island. Oliver the adventurer: explorer, inventor. Oliver the adventurer: sociopath, madman.

"You're all right, Oliver," he would tell himself. "You're just a man who marches to the beat of his own drum. A genius. Bound to be misunderstood." He repeated such things to himself, likening himself to assorted fearless eccentrics of history, while he paced around his place of exile.

In his less resilient moments, Oliver would sink down with his head in his hands, lamenting the truth that he'd failed as a husband and a father. Then he'd quickly slap himself out of tears and start wondering why they were all hounding him. Their voices travelled through the back door of the house. Their wanting and needing were like hypodermic needles pushed deep into muscle in order to stifle movement. They're trying to slow me down, he thought, fastening the lock across the garage door.

It was when the statement addressed to him from the Bank of Nova Scotia arrived that Elaine finally stormed out to the garage and confronted him. She slid the paper under the garage door and screamed, "Oliver, I need you to explain this!"

"I have a new bank account, Elaine. And *that* is none of your business."

"None of my business?" she screamed. "Since when have our financial lives been separate?"

"Since three o'clock last Tuesday afternoon," he said.

"But where did you get the money to open this account, Oliver? There's ten thousand dollars here."

"From the Bank of Montreal," he said matter-of-factly.

"You mean from our account?"

"Yes."

"*Yes?*" She was aghast. Oliver had just drained the entirety of their savings and opened a new account under his name, and his name only. "But why on earth would you do this?" she asked him.

"Protection," he muttered.

"Protection?" she yelled. "If you're looking for protection, Oliver, this isn't going to get it for you. I have half a mind to go straight to the police."

"You can't go to the police," he protested. "I'm your husband."

"But this is robbery!" she screamed. "Oliver, I want you out of there. Out of this garage, just out—away from this house!"

"But it's my house, too," he said quietly. "And besides, where would I go?" he whimpered, though well out of earshot of Elaine who had by this time run through the back door of the house and picked up the phone to dial the police.

"He's not done anything illegal, ma'am," the officer on the other end of the line said.

"But he has done something insane!" Elaine shouted, the rest of her drink sloshing out of the glass in her hand.

"But not criminal."

"You don't call robbing your wife blind *criminal*?"

"I don't know what I'd call it, but I don't think it's us you want. Try the mental health authorities," the officer said, and hung up.

Twenty-four hours later, she had a call from Dr. Eisenbaum. Elaine had ferreted out the psychological report on Oliver that had been prepared some years before and tracked down Dr. Eisenbaum in Montreal. He didn't remember Oliver exactly, but he did agree that there was at least one architect at McQuinn and Associates who he'd been asked to see for a psychological assessment some years earlier.

"That would have been my husband," Elaine said. "I have the report right here. Signed by you in February 1973. 'Superior IQ, delusional, overinflated sense of self-worth, self-aggrandizing, paranoid tendencies'—does that ring any bells?"

"Far too many, I'm afraid, Mrs. Taylor," said the doctor. "Listen. Is he in any danger of harming himself or your family?"

"He's done plenty of harm already."

"Physical harm?"

"Well, no," she had to concede.

"Then there's really nothing anyone can do. You can encourage him to see a psychiatrist, but you can't force him to do anything against his will."

By the time Elaine went out to talk to him the next morning, Oliver, it seemed, had disappeared. The garage was locked and there was no response from inside. Elaine picked up a brick and threw it through the small window and stood on a rotting stump of wood in order to peer inside. Oliver was definitely gone. She enlisted Blue's help then, giving him a leg up so he could cram his prepubescent body through the small window and open the door from inside. How Oliver had managed to lock the door from the inside and escape would remain a mystery.

"Dad's a real Houdini!" Blue said in delight.

"Your father," Elaine said, "seems to have more than just one screw loose."

The inside of the garage smelled rank with dirty human. "Pee-yu," Emma said, pinching her nose.

"Pee-yu, it stinks. What a bunch of lousy Chinks," Blue chanted.

Elaine slapped him on the back of the head then. "Blue, that's a nasty little rhyme." He had absolutely no idea why what he'd said was nasty and Elaine, having already downed a glass of Scotch that morning, and underestimating her strength, had slapped Blue so hard that he fell to the floor. It was Emma who helped him up and held his sobbing face against her chest. Elaine, although she apologized profusely, said it was all Oliver's fault for creating such a mess in the first place.

Emma looked around the garage in silence. Her father had obviously spent months engaged in some strange tasks. The entire ceiling was covered in pennies glued in methodical order. He'd arranged all the tools on the wall into circles: hammers and saws and screwdrivers forming the spokes of wheels going nowhere. Emma looked in a bucket on the floor then and screamed. There was a mass of grey hair floating in oil in the bucket. It seemed Oliver had cut off his hair, and had been trying to preserve it somehow.

"That is *just* disgusting," Elaine said, gagging. "Don't go near it, Llewellyn!" she shrieked.

"But it's just his hair," Blue shrugged.

The police weren't willing to do a missing person's report, but because Elaine managed to imply murder when she mentioned there were body parts in buckets in the garage, they said they'd be right over.

"Hair," an officer noted. "His own, I imagine, but we'll take it in for testing."

"I'd just be grateful if you could take it away," she shuddered.

We found bits of my dad in the garage," Blue whispered to his best friend Stewart in the playground the next day.

"Gross," said Stewart. "Like his legs and stuff?"

"His hair."

"But my mum has a piece of my hair from when I was a baby."

"Well, my dad's hair was grey."

"Oh," Stewart nodded like he understood, and then said, "But I don't get it."

"Neither do I," Blue had to agree. "I guess that's why my mum called the police."

"Holy drama, Batman," said Stewart.

# Kiss

It was under the front porch that Emma and Blue had their first kiss. She and Blue were coughing on a stale cigarette stolen from Elaine's purse a month before, when Emma suddenly mashed her mouth into Blue's. Then she snapped back and shrugged her shoulders, saying, "Huh. I don't see what the big deal is about."

"Me neither," said Blue, although he was more than a little bewildered by the abrupt smack on the lips. They'd been rubbing bodies in the basement since he was little, but this was different somehow. It had a guilt-free air of purpose and finality. She was thin now, and in the grand scheme of the mad, mad world that meant that kisses were just around the corner.

In fact, it actually took Emma more than a year to work up the nerve to kiss anyone again, and when she finally did, it was only under duress. In grade seven, Fraser O'Donnell, who she thought was a geek, but a cute geek, asked her to slow dance with him at the end of the first in a series of awkward junior high school parties. She'd never danced to a slow song before and there she was with a boy's head on her shoulder, looking over at her almost-best friend Charlene Boysenberry who was moving around in slow circles with bad-boy Dillon and mouthing: "Do this," as she rubbed her hands up and down Dillon's back.

"No way," Emma mouthed back at Charlene.

In the alarming glare of the gymnasium lights, after seven whole minutes of "Stairway to Heaven," Fraser said, "Uh, thanks," and then popped the big question: "Hey, like, you wanna go around with me?"

"Sure, I guess so," Emma said, looking at her shoes.

"Well, I guess I'll be seeing you then," he said, leaning over and giving her a peck on the cheek.

"Sure, see ya," she said, still standing there staring at her shoes.

He walked off with his hands in his pockets and Charlene came running up to Emma and squealed, "Score!"

"Charleeeene," Emma protested.

"Did he ask you to go around with him?"

"Yeah. So?" she shrugged.

"I knew it!" Charlene shrieked.

"It's no big deal," Emma said, taking a stab at sounding dismissive.

"Oh, yeah," Charlene groaned, rolling her eyes. "Like, Miss Snotty-big-tits Brenda Tailgate doesn't even have a boyfriend. She'll be so mad!" she giggled. "So, is he a good kisser?"

"How should I know?" Emma said defensively.

"Well, didn't you?"

"No. Gross."

"Well, you're going to have to kiss him."

"What for?"

"Else he'll think you're a lezzy," she declared.

Ugh. Emma was now obliged by the perverse protocol of junior high to let him be a disgusting boy. But only the once. She and Fraser walked home together awkwardly after school the following Thursday. They sat in the park on swings opposite each other as he blathered on about his drum set and the band he was going to form. Emma stared at her hands and picked at her cuticles. Fraser asked her if she wanted to do backup singing on one of the tracks he wanted to lay down. "You know, you look a little like Karen Carpenter," he said, nodding his dopey head.

Emma wasn't sure if that was a compliment, but she blushed anyway, and that was when Fraser made his big move. He stood up, stumbling over his big flat feet, and lunged across the sandbox with his tongue outstretched. He plunged the purple splatter into Emma's mouth and she felt the horrific sensation of peanut butter over bristly taste buds. She thrust out her arms like an automatic weapon and pushed him and his purple peanut splatter about seventeen feet across the park.

After that, Fraser did start calling Emma a lezzy. In fact, so did Charlene. "I don't know if we can be almost-best friends any more," she said one day after school. "You're ruining my reputation."

So for the next three months it was Charlene and Fraser holding hands in the schoolyard, Charlene rolling her eyes melodramatically every time they walked by Emma and claiming that Brenda Big-tits was her new best friend.

But Emma didn't care. She had Blue. And Blue had her. With Oliver's disappearance, they'd lost whatever had remained of Elaine. It seemed he had dragged Elaine's entrails with him: she was the vessel of their mother, but with the contents poured out. She put a brown casserole dish into the oven every morning before she went to work and didn't return home until late. She slammed the door when she got back, gave her children a refrigerated glare that collapsed into a frown, and made her way straight to the liquor cabinet.

Emma and Blue, hungry for her, buzzed around like flies. She greeted their frenzy with bitter silence and switched the lights off in her head. She was too tired, too angry to be Mother, but they gravitated toward her, sticking against her flypaper skin, flailing their limbs, struggling frantically.

"Ma?" pleaded Blue.

"Llewellyn, not now," she groaned, putting her palm to her forehead and squinting under a headache as dense as concrete.

"But when then?"

"If you could think of anyone other than yourself, not ever," she snapped.

"But all I—"

"I don't want to discuss it."

"Discuss what?"

"Jesus, Llewellyn, stop playing games. Just ... leave your mother in peace, will you? I've got enough problems as it is."

The fantasy of being orphans was only appealing when they actually had parents. They needed her now—more than they wished to— but the more they needed, the less she had to give.

Emma and Blue gradually learned to stand at greater and greater distances. Emma filled the tumbler with two cubes of ice and three fingers of Scotch, and wordlessly handed it to her mother. Blue just slept most of the time. This was the new language of home.

"I saw Dad today," Blue said one day after Elaine had slammed her way back into the house. It had been about eleven months since Oliver had done what Blue saw as his Houdini-like disappearance from the garage. Elaine had no observable reaction. She sat back in the comfy chair and raised the glass to her lips and asked Emma and Blue whether they'd finished their homework.

In bed that night Emma stared at the stars on the ceiling and wondered what her mother had done with that piece of information. It seemed to have gone in one ear and straight out the other. Maybe it was living like a rotting rodent in the pit of her stomach. She was beginning to think Elaine might have animals living inside her—blood-sucking, flesh-eating reptiles that were turning her brittle and cadaverous.

Emma rapped the secret knock on her bedroom wall and listened for the hinges on the door to Blue's room.

Blue sat waiting for her on the cement floor of the basement and yawned. He was wearing what Emma saw as his embarrassing Smurf pyjamas.

"You really saw Dad?" Emma whispered.

"I think so."

"Did he have any hair?"

"Yeah."

"But where did you see him?"

"At the schoolyard."

"He came to your school?"

"Hmm."

"Did you talk to him?"

"No. But I waved."

"Did he wave back?"

"Kinda."

"I wonder if he came to my school, too," Emma thought aloud. "Did he look okay?"

"I guess so. He looked, you know, like Dad."

"Just the same?"

"Yeah. Like Dad before he slept in the garage, except old."

"Mum thinks Dad is mentally ill," Emma said. "Did he look mentally ill to you?"

"I don't know. What does mentally ill look like? I told you—he looked like Dad," Blue shrugged.

"Do you think he'll come to your school again?"

"I don't know," Blue said, frustrated now with all his sister's questions.

Emma kept a lookout in the schoolyard the next day, wondering if it was her turn to see their father. She hoped it was, but at the same time she didn't want her father to see her being taunted in the schoolyard now that she had a reputation for being a lezzy. Junior high school sucked. She wished her dad would come roaring by in an expensive European car and pick her up and take her out for ice cream. She didn't care that all the other kids would tease her, call her a daddy's girl or a loser because it was uncool to have parents, let alone have parents who picked you up at school. She might have felt that way about Elaine, but Elaine was still technically more of a parent than Oliver. She did at least live in the same house. Elaine was Elaine, but Oliver wasn't always, necessarily, Oliver.

She kept a lookout for the rest of the school year, but if he came by, which Emma was sure he must have, she never saw him. She felt like she and Blue had their very own ghost, their ever-present invisible father. She couldn't tell anyone. It was bad enough they called her a lezzy—she didn't want to be called a lezzy who saw ghosts.

# Seasons in Hell

Elaine had wanted to scream when Oliver left, one endless, blood-curdling wail that would put every banshee in history to shame. She'd hoped for months, she'd even prayed to a god she didn't believe in, that Oliver would emerge from the garage an even partially reformed man, one who'd seen enough of a light to renounce the descent into madness in favour of a more reasonable existence.

She had wanted to scream, but instead, she did the middle-class thing she'd inherited from her parents and swallowed it down with a litre of toxins, keeping it inside where it could fester and poison everyone around her in ways much more insidious and enduring than a single howl.

She wouldn't have had children if it weren't for him—she shouldn't have had children period. She should have moved to France and become a poet with a pension and eaten baguettes for dinner and had a string of exotic lovers half her age. Instead, here she was in a lonely town full of strangers with a mortgage to manage single-handedly and two children too many. Emma and Blue were heading into the crushing horror of adolescence, she could see it all too plainly—Emma who would always struggle to find a place of acceptance, Llewellyn who didn't have the smarts to do well at school. She could see they both had their father in them—Blue more physically, Emma more emotionally. In neither case was the prognosis good.

But nor was hers at the moment. A few too many fantasies of driving the car over the Niagara Escarpment had forced her to seek out help. The doctor she saw was an octogenarian with a hearing problem who had handed her a prescription for Valium like she was a 1950s housewife. The drinking made her drunk, but the Valium made her stop caring. Her children had no idea just how thick the wall that separated their mother from them had become. Their tears, their moroseness, their pleading, their sulking, none of it could put a dent in this lead-filled barricade.

She had, of course, heard what Blue said. He'd seen his father at the schoolyard that day. It was possible, she supposed, but unlikely. She decided not to attach any meaning to it, and took the bottle upstairs with her to her bedroom to say a quiet hello to the face of misery in the mirror. But Oliver was everywhere in that room. He was in their wedding photos, in the paint on the walls, in a framed antique map of Scotland above the bed. She pulled a book from the shelf: Rimbaud's *A Season in Hell*. Oliver had underlined passages, passages she hadn't read since those early days in a Montreal café. They were only poetry then, but now they seemed like prophecy.

"There are countless hallucinations. In truth it is what I have always had: no faith in history and the forgetting of principles. I will not speak of this: poets and visionaries would be jealous. I am the richest a thousand times over, let me be as avaricious as the ocean."

Had Oliver been speaking of himself? Had he always been haunted? A few stanzas later he'd underlined: "Then trust in me. Faith relieves and guides and cures. Come all, even the little children—and I will comfort you, and pour out my heart for you—my marvellous heart!" So there it was: Oliver asking Elaine to put her faith in a madman. Elaine accepting, and now, a season, several seasons in hell later, here she was.

She flipped to the last page of the book. On the inside of the back cover she'd long ago taped her favourite photograph of Oliver. She pried the yellow tape off with her fingernail, liberating a wild-haired man in a poncho, and laid it on her pillow for a single drugged night before putting it an envelope the next awful morning and addressing it to Llewellyn. For one day, although which day, she didn't know.

# Greetings

A couple of weeks later a postcard came flying through the letter slot and landed belly up on the hall carpet. Oliver's handwriting, and on the reverse, the CN Tower and the words "Greetings from Toronto" emblazoned in red on the blue sky above.

"I can't make it out, Blue," Emma shook her head. "Something about the beach. I don't know," she said, passing it to her brother.

"Yeah," he nodded.

"What?"

"The beach. And this says, 'In case,' and he signs it 'Take care.'"

"Take care? Is that all he says? How are we supposed to do that?"

"I don't know, Em. At least he sent a postcard."

"Yeah, well big fucking deal. So he's moved to Toronto to have a whole new life. Thanks for letting us know."

A condo on the beach, a car, a dental plan, maybe even a cleaning lady, Emma thought. And we're stuck here in this crappy town with no money and no dad. How could he just go and dump us like this? He could at least give Mum some money for child support. But the real question underlying her anger was the one she kept asking Blue: "Why does he come and see you but not me?"

"You're going to have to ask himself yourself, Em," Blue said. It wasn't as simple as she seemed to think it was. It wasn't pleasant seeing Oliver. It was ugly, sad, and strange: it caused gut rot so painful that it felt like someone was rubbing the insides of his intestines down with sandpaper.

"Fucking bastard," she said angrily. "I don't want you to tell me when you see him any more, okay, Blue?"

"Sure. Whatever."

"You know what I mean?" she said in lieu of saying: because it hurts too much. She didn't know what parents were really good for, but they were at least supposed to be around. Without contact, without even the desire for contact, you might as well forfeit the title. If Oliver was no longer technically a father to her, then she was no longer technically his daughter. It was simple. It was logical. It was impossible. She would fell the remaining stumps in the landscape of the familiar, Elaine largest among them, unearth her butchered roots and pack them into a knapsack. She'd carry herself over some mountain and fall into the depths of some thick, foreign forest, where the trees had stood tall and firmly rooted for generations. She would attach herself like lichen on a host.

She thought Blue was with her there, same soil and roots. But Oliver had been like glue between them. In his presence, they had shared a problem, but in his absence, while they shared certain memories, they shared increasingly less experience. The glue had begun to loosen, unhinging a static photograph of them as identical twins.

"I guess so," Blue shrugged. He didn't see new forests though. He saw the sad image of his sister standing at a distance, giving a lame wave and a weak smile as she abandoned the sinking ship that was family as they had once and only known it. "I guess so," he repeated, as he stood there alone on the deck, the only remaining child left on board. Elaine didn't want to know; now Emma, too, wanted to be left out of it. His job would be to continue to hold on for life; keep his bruised feet rooted on a bloodied and precariously tilted deck, carry on through the icefields and into the depths until he saw Elaine to safety, and could give Oliver a respectable burial at sea. Emma would just have to learn to be a good swimmer. There wasn't much else he could do.

# Boys and Girls

On her first day of high school, Emma showed up with her formerly auburn hair dyed black, and wore a corset that suffocated her under her baggy, patchwork overalls. When they did roll call in homeroom that morning, Emma didn't answer. She had decided that life would be different from now on. In high school she would be an altogether different person with an unpronounceable name and a mysterious past. Tabatha had been a secret: Oksana, she would share with the world. Tabatha had had parents, but Oksana would be simply singular—without attachments to the past.

"Taylor, Emma," her grade nine English teacher called out. "Taylor, Emma?" he repeated.

"She's there," Charlene said, pointing spitefully at Emma.

"Are you Emma Taylor?" Mr. Flick asked.

"Well, actually, I've changed my name."

"Officially?"

"Yes," she lied. Imagine that I have. Imagine that I am actually Oksana Vladivostok—the only surviving member of Russia's royal family, the great granddaughter of King What's-his-name, a revolutionary girl who narrowly escaped execution by hiding in the womb of an unsuspecting woman in Montreal called Mrs. Taylor. Or a mole who had been programmed to attend Eton and Cambridge and get a top-secret job with MI5, working for a certain Mr. Philby, but everything had gone so horribly wrong that she ended up at McArthur High in Niagara Falls rather than Eton.

Whatever it was, the whole plan had gone so awry that revealing herself as Oksana at fourteen wasn't going to put her in any danger. In fact, in the best-case scenario, it actually might spare her the fate of Emma.

"What will we call you then?" Mr. Flick asked with annoyance.

"Oksana Vladivostok," she stated. Mr. Flick smiled and the entire class burst out laughing, Charlene's high-pitched squeaking audible over all the others.

"Perhaps you could spell that for me," Mr. Flick said sarcastically.

"Sure. O-X—no. O-K—"

"Well, which is it then?"

"O-K—"

"Okay, Commie girl," Wayne shouted from the back of the room.

"O-K ... go on," Mr. Flick prodded.

Emma Taylor was inconsequential. She was a fly on the wall of a house in Niagara Falls—the eldest child of two non-existent parents, one missing in body, the other in soul. Oksana was different. Perhaps she would even be removed from McArthur High and sent to some boarding school for Russian defectors, where she would study Latin alongside other reformed moles, anorexic gymnasts, and closeted ballet dancers.

Emma spent most of that fall behind her locked bedroom door, writing poetry in front of a window propped open with a carrot. Her hands were stiff with cold and tired as she wrote painful poems about dead cats and other roadkill. She spent hours in the bath on Saturday mornings, reading biographies of famous women writers who had tied stones into their long skirts and thrown themselves into rivers, or given their children glasses of milk before they stuck their heads in ovens.

It was two years now since Oliver had disappeared from the garage and puberty seemed to be making her hallucinate. She was sure she saw him sometimes, although Blue was the one he talked to. Oliver would turn up every couple of months at his school and wave to him through the fence. It changed Blue. He didn't play hacky sack or throw a tennis ball at the school wall like other boys did during recess, at lunch, and after school. He stood alone and simply stared at the fence, his eyes running back and forth like they were punching keys on a typewriter.

"What are you waiting for?" the other guys would taunt. "The second fucking coming?"

It *was* sort of like looking for God. His thoughts were like prayers and he would tune out the sounds of the schoolyard and concentrate hard and wonder if he could will his father into appearing. Oliver's visits did become more and more frequent during Blue's grade eight year and Blue thought it must be because his concentration was getting better.

But he never approached his father. Blue stood rooted in place like a river too fast and deep ran between them. It was as if they saw each other through water: a swift current distorted their features; Oliver looked like waves of sand had run over his face and eroded his expression. He began to speak to Blue, his lips parting in slow motion and bubbles of air without sound floating up into the sky.

Blue mouthed back slow-motion, water-laden words. "I can't hear you," he said.

"No one can," Oliver mouthed back.

Blue had always been a boy of few words and ever since being banished to remedial English he'd been called "dumb," stuck in what other kids charmingly referred to as "the retard class." "You look like a gaping fucking fish," one of the guys laughed. "Who the hell are you talking to?" Blue didn't care: he was learning to speak without sound, finding a way to communicate with his father—the man on the other side of the fence who no one but him could see.

Emma was a person of few words herself, but unlike Blue she'd adopted a waif-like and distressed posture early on; after *Dr. Nelligan's Diet Book for Girls*, she'd shed pounds of innocence and adopted an appearance that made people think her mysterious or badly nourished, but not stupid. But, six blocks away from Blue, at McArthur High, her classmates were persecuting her as well.

"Suck my cock, Vladivostok," boys in the schoolyard taunted. "You fuckin' Commie."

The kinder-whores dressed in tube tops and high-tops preferred calling her "Princess Commie Big Shit" and they still weren't relenting on "Lezzy."

Still, being a Princess Commie Big Shit Lezzy was at least better than being a boring old Emma Taylor in her mind, even if it meant everybody hated her. Everybody, that is, except her brother and her new best friend, Max.

The first time Emma saw Max she didn't know whether Max was a boy or a girl. Max had a blonde brush cut and wore army fatigues and looked like her earlobes had been repeatedly punched with a staple gun. She wore steel-toed boots, had an all-purpose jackknife chained to her studded belt, and rarely looked up when she shuffled past people. Maxine was her name, but since she thought she was a boy, she went by the name Max.

If Emma thought she had it bad, Max had it far worse. The kids at school didn't know what to call her: it was more often "faggot" than "lezzy," but most often "freak." And when Maxine and Oksana became friends, they started to call them both lezzies.

Oksana would lie with her head on Max's belly in the park and read aloud from a copy of the *Scum Manifesto*, which Max had given her. Max would listen, staring at the sky and blowing smoke rings over Oksana's head in the heat of the late afternoon.

"Why the fuck do they call us lezzies?" Max asked angrily one day. "I mean, I'm a guy and you're a Russian princess. There's nothing lezzy about us."

"'Cause they're a bunch of fucking mutants," Emma said.

"High school sucks."

"You said it."

"Life sucks."

"Sure does."

Elaine actually took notice of Emma's new friendship and asked her, "Who's that strange girl I see loitering in the front yard?"

"That's Max. Maxine."

"Well, you've changed since you started hanging out with her— and not for the better."

"What do you mean?" Emma mumbled as if she had a mouth full of mashed potatoes.

"You've become rebellious. That girl looks like she needs a bath. I don't know if she's quite right," Elaine said, as she plopped down a plate of takeout Polish cabbage rolls in front of her alien children one interminable Saturday night.

"I don't care, Mum. She's my friend, okay? At least I have a friend."

"What's that supposed to mean, Emma?"

"Nothing," Emma muttered into her paper plate.

Elaine let it go. She remembered fourteen all too well. All she could hope was that Emma would outgrow it before she made the same mistakes she had. But Emma was cursed with a disposition similar to Oliver's. She hoped the repugnance of Oliver's hair floating in oil in the garage was enough of a warning, but she felt compelled to say, "You might think it's great to hitch a ride on a magic carpet, Emma, but those things don't come equipped with brakes," as if Emma were privy to her thoughts.

"*What* are you talking about?" Emma asked, rolling her eyes.

Emma spent the rest of the night writing angry rants about school and mothers and men and everything else she could think of that she hated at fourteen. Snow was drifting through the open window as Emma smoked a cigarette. She smoked Camel Lights because they were Max's brand, just as she carried a jackknife in the pocket of her long black skirt now, and slathered her lips obsessively with Carmex. She was a girl who wanted to be just like a girl who wanted to be a boy. It was all very confusing.

Blue was certainly confused. His sister looked a little weird these days. All blood-red lipstick and long black clothes and a permanent sneer on her face. She was even bitchy with him on occasion, but whenever she snapped at him she sobered quickly, and melted back into the girl Blue remembered, wrapping her arms around him so that he was buried like a baby animal in the arms of a black-robed witch.

"Fuckin' lezzies," Emma's sort of ex-boyfriend Fraser and his posse of pimpled pinheads shouted as they passed her sharing a cigarette with Max in the alley beside the school.

"Fuckwit," Max shouted back. "I'm not a lezzy. I'm a guy."

"Yeah, right. Good one. Like you gotta dick, right?"

"Bigger than yours, pencil prick," she snickered under her breath.

"Whad'ya say, bitch?" Marco said out of his dirty, pubescent, peach-fuzzy mouth. "You're fucked, man."

"A lot more often than you," jibed Max. "Had more girls than the whole lotta you," she boasted.

"It's true," Emma said in her defence. "No one's gonna put out for a limp dick like you, Marco. Max is a regular Don Juan."

"Yeah, well, no one else would fuck a retard like you, anyway," he said, wandering off in pathetic defeat.

This took Emma aback. If Max did have a dick, then he really was a boy, wasn't he? Or she? But if Max was a girl with a dick, what the hell was she? Or he? Emma did and didn't want to know.

She rapped her knuckles on the bedroom wall that night, asking Blue to meet her in the basement in five minutes.

"Blue, this is gonna sound strange, right," she began, flushing with embarrassment, "but I need you to tell me what makes a boy a boy."

"What are you talking about?"

"I don't really know."

He looked exasperated. "Sounds like you've been smoking too much pot."

"Me? No way. What do you know about pot, anyway?"

"Oh, you know, I toke here and there," he said in a boyish macho way.

"You do? But, Blue, you're only thirteen years old."

"I'm almost fourteen," he defended

"But where do you get pot?"

"Guys from your high school."

"They come to your school?"

"They trade it for hockey cards and stuff."

"What kind of stuff?"

"Ah, forget it."

"No, I'm serious, Blue. I wanna know."

"They give it to us if we watch them jerk off," he shrugged.

"You're kidding."

"You wanted to know."

"Fucking pigs," Emma said with disgust.

"Don't you dare tell Mum."

"But, Blue, that's really warped."

"I don't care," he muttered. "At least I don't hang out with her-maphrodites."

"Is that what they say about me?"

"Kinda," Blue winced a little guiltily.

"But what the hell is a hermaphrodite?"

"Fuck if I know. Some kind of lezzy fag or something."

"Seriously?" she moaned, her eyes welling up with tears.

"Oh, don't let it upset you," Blue said. "You know they're just idiots."

"I know, but still ..."

"Don't worry, I don't believe them."

"But do you stick up for me?"

"If I was bigger, I'd punch their fuckin' heads in. But seeing as I'm not, I've just gotta ignore them." *Wimp*, he could hear his father saying. *Sissy. Mama's boy. Afraid to get a little blood on your shirt?*

My tough little man, Emma thought, and burst into tears.

Blue pressed his forehead against hers. When they'd been at the same school he'd held her hand and followed her around so she wouldn't feel like she was alone. They used to tease her, tell her she had hairy legs and was a loser. He wanted her to feel like she had a best friend. Later they called her a lezzy and she thought boys didn't like her because she was fat. But he liked her and he was a boy. They kissed under the front porch so that she'd know boys did want to kiss her even though she knew kissing your brother didn't count. Now she was looking skinny and strange and hanging out with a lezzy faggot. He didn't know what else he could do. He didn't know how else to protect her.

For the last dance of their grade nine year, Max dyed her hair black and wore a white polo shirt reeking of Stetson. She and Emma got modestly drunk beforehand on the tequila they drank out of a Mason jar marked "Black Currant 1975," while crammed into a phone booth at the intersection down the road from the school.

"Look, the lezzies are here in drag," mocked a pack of puke-skinned boys as they walked up the stairs to the gym.

Mrs. Salerno, the gym teacher, stood there like a soldier, saying, "Spot check for alcohol, drugs, and weapons."

Emma was alarmed. "When did this become a prison?" she asked Max.

"When Mrs. Salerno decided she didn't like me," Max groaned, standing with her legs apart and putting her arms in the air so Mrs. Salerno could do her customs-official number.

"Forget it, Helen," Emma heard Max mutter to Mrs. Salerno under her breath.

"I think we've got one here," Mrs. Salerno said, gesturing to her colleagues. "Feels like she's packing a pistol."

Emma watched in horror as Mrs. Salerno started unzipping Max's pants. "Hey! You can't do that!" Emma shouted, but then her jaw dropped as something blue and rubbery fell to the floor.

"Oh my God," Mr. Mackenzie, the chemistry teacher, said, stepping back from the object on the floor.

Emma inched forward and stared at it, thinking, What the hell is that? "Don't worry, it's not loaded," Max said, rolling her eyes.

"I don't know what that is exactly," said Mr. Mackenzie, remembering he was supposed to be an authority, "but I'm sure it's against regulations."

"I don't know if you actually have school rules about this," said Max.

"That's enough, young lady—person—whatever you are," he shouted. "I think you and the Russian girl should just leave."

"Oh, don't worry. I'm outta here," Max said, jumping down the stairs three at a time. "Like forever!" she shouted. She only turned around when she'd reached the bottom of the stairs to ask Emma if she was coming. Emma hesitated, and then bolted down the stairs after her, although she knew the era of Oksana and Max was all downhill from there. There were just too many things she didn't understand. Being a Russian princess wasn't all rubles and romance—it clearly had its dangerous side.

Max wouldn't be allowed back to McArthur for grade ten and she'd have to take Oksana with her wherever she was going. Emma dreamt that the two of them had gone backpacking through Europe and Asia in search of ancestral roots, sharing a toothbrush, a pack of Camel Lights, and a couple of trashy novels, wandering deep into the heart of Communism. Being Emma again was infinitely lonelier, but it was safer, English-speaking, more familiar.

# Bald

Blue turned fourteen that summer. On his birthday he locked himself in the bathroom and took Elaine's electric, pink lady razor to his head. He cringed at the sight of his mutating face in the mirror and decided to rid himself of all hair. He was going to hide: be like Casper the Ghost, friendly, but invisible.

The razor's vibration tickled above his upper lip. He contemplated getting rid of his eyebrows next but moved straight up to his hairline and peeled a highway through the centre of his head. His scalp was some shade of grey, almost green in fact, ghoulish. As his hair floated down into the sink he wondered if he should keep it. Preserve it in oil for some unknown purpose. Be a man, like his father.

Shaving his head was the culmination of the worst week in a lifetime of bad weeks. On Monday, he'd felt an ache for the ages in his stomach. On Tuesday, his intestines were on fire. On Wednesday, the toilet was full of blood; he stared at the rectal red in horror, wondering if words were sharper than razor blades, deadlier than bullets. He thought he must be dying.

"Don't you fucking tell Mum," he said, as he and Emma took a taxi to the emergency room paid for with money stolen from Elaine's purse.

I'd never, Emma thought. She'd be useless in a crisis, she was disastrous enough in the day-to-day.

After an interminable wait, he was finally seen by a doctor. Emma remained in the waiting room, peeling off most of her fingernails and then part of the rubber sole of her shoe.

In the examining room, the doctor, whose name Blue blanked out, asked him to describe his symptoms. He depressed Blue's tongue, poked cold metal in his ears, pulled syringes full of blood out of his arm, made him crap in a cup, and finally, told him to take off his underwear and roll over.

"But why?" Blue demanded, not moving.

"Because we need to do a rectal exam."

"Why?" he repeated, nearly shouting.

"First we need to rule out hemorrhoids or see if there's any rupture. If not, then we'll need to take a tissue sample."

"But why?"

"We need to locate the source of the bleeding."

"But why?"

"Because we want to help you," said the doctor, his voice now showing signs of agitation. "This can be a sign of serious illness or injury. It's a good thing you're here. Now, if you could turn over, we could proceed."

Blue sat rigid, motionless. No one was going anywhere near his bum. Oliver had told him bums were dirty holes reserved for faggots and dogs. In their last underwater exchange, Oliver had driven a nail the size of a railway spike into Blue's head. "You're not a fucking faggot, are you?" he'd mouthed at Blue through the fence.

He'd heard this several times in his life, but this time the silent words exploded like bombs in his ears. He wasn't a faggot, but he was feeling guilty. Earlier that afternoon Blue had stood behind the tennis court watching Jake the Snake jerk off. Blue hated Jake, hated all the guys from high school and their stupid dicks, but when you're nearly fourteen and a pothead, and your mum doesn't give you an allowance because she's bringing you up on her own without child support and she's yammering on about a second mortgage, it's either that or stealing in order to get your drugs. Oliver must have seen him.

Blue could feel Oliver's venom and rage through the fence and he was so humiliated that he imploded inside. In the hospital it occurred to him that that was the source of bleeding. Oliver had broken him. He had stood in front of the spectre of Oliver, his head hanging down, tears as thick as molasses creeping down his face. "No," he had mouthed back helplessly.

"There are other ways," Oliver had sneered. "You could get a job, for example." And then he shuffled off to wherever he had come from.

The doctor tried to coax Blue, placing a hand on his arm and asking him to cooperate and turn over. "No," Blue protested.

"It'll be all right. There's nothing to worry about."

"No!" Blue shouted.

"Look, we can't help you unless you're willing to cooperate," the doctor said. Then he picked up the phone and called for help.

Two nurses, one male and one female, were called in to roll over the increasingly hysterical boy. He lashed out with epileptic strength, flailed his arms and legs like he'd just been attacked by a shark, while their grips on his arms tightened. One of the nurses pinned Blue's arms above his head, the other laid his arms across the back of Blue's calves.

They spoke quietly to Blue, despite the aggression of their actions, confusing and terrifying him.

They lifted his torso up and thrust him into a straitjacket. Armless, he used his mouth and bit down hard into the female nurse's arm. "Jesus Christ, he's drawn blood," she said. "You're going to have to sedate him," she said, not letting go.

The other nurse jabbed a needle into his bum. "It's a local anesthetic. You won't feel a thing," he said to Blue. Blue hammered his forehead against the cot. The nurse with the bleeding arm stuffed a pillow under his face. "Just keep breathing," she told him.

The entire lower half of his body was disappearing. They'd cut him off from the waist down, sawed off his legs, he was sure of it. He'd seen it happen in *Gone with the Wind*. He'd seen someone saw off the gangrene leg of a soldier. They were doing whatever they were doing now to the dismembered lower half of his body. He'd have to spend the rest of his life in a wheelchair—that is, if this didn't kill him.

Emma waited for well over an hour until someone came and told her what was going on. "We're going to keep him here overnight," a nurse said.

"So, it's really serious?" Emma asked her.

"I'll let you speak to the doctor," she said quietly.

Emma waited some more, becoming even more worried. "We just want to do a psychological assessment," the doctor told her.

"But it's not a mental thing!" Emma stammered. "It's his bum! And a fever."

"It looks like salmonella," the doctor said. "*That* he'll get over. It's his reaction I'm concerned about. He refused to let me examine him."

"He's just scared," Emma defended.

"Well, we had to restrain him."

"Oh my God."

"He's calmed down now."

"Can I see him?"

"Of course," he said gently. "You can sit with him while I sort out the paperwork."


Blue was lying on his side in a cot wearing a straitjacket. "Blue," Emma said, fighting back tears. "What did they do to you?" He just sobbed. Emma crawled onto the cot and wrapped herself around him.

The doctor came back into the room with his clipboard. "I need someone to sign a consent form," he said. "Your brother's a minor. Can we call in one of your parents?"

"No!" Blue shouted. No one was ever to going to know about this. Especially not Elaine. She wouldn't want to know. And if she did know, would she call him a faggot too? Would she tell him he was useless, just like his father? He'd rather protect himself and her by denying his mother's existence. His sister tacitly agreed.

"Uh," Emma stammered. "It's tricky. I mean, our parents are dead."

"I see," the doctor said, taking this in. "Do you have a legal guardian? Someone who takes care of you?"

"Well, actually, we sort of take care of each other."

"I see. And how old are you?"

"Eighteen?" Emma said without much conviction. She knew he knew she was lying, but she supposed he must have appreciated that she had a good reason for doing so because he let her sign the admittance form, just above the line that read, "False claims are punishable by fine and/or imprisonment."

"But I don't want you to leave me," Blue said.

"It'll be okay," Emma tried to reassure him. Then she turned to the doctor, "You're just going to ask him some questions, right?"

"Yes. Actually, not me, but Dr. Sears. One of the staff psychiatrists. And we'll just keep you under observation for the next day or so," he told Blue, trying to be reassuring.

"But you're not going to do any more examining are you?" Blue asked, clearly afraid.

"Shouldn't have to. We should have the results of your tests back later today."

"Can you stay with me a little longer?" Blue asked Emma weakly.

"Uh," she hesitated, looking for the doctor's permission.

"That'll be fine. Dr. Sears will probably be down in about an hour so your sister can stay with you until then, okay, son?" the doctor said, putting his hand on Blue's shoulder.

Blue looked green with fear.

"Do you think we could take this off now?" Emma asked, pointing at the straitjacket.

"Sure. He's been sedated, anyway."

"Jesus," Emma muttered, picturing a rabid dog, raging and frothing at the mouth, seized and anaesthetized.

She went to get herself some coffee, and by the time she came back, Blue had fallen asleep. She sat beside his sighing body until Dr. Sears arrived.

"So this is Llewellyn?" Dr. Sears asked, entering the room. She was tall, thin, and graceful, with a comforting smile.

"Yeah. My brother."

"Well, we're just going to wheel him up to the psychiatric ward. He'll be quite groggy for another hour or so."

"Do you think ... um ... he's got some kind of mental problem?" Emma asked her.

"Dr. Menzies was just a little concerned about the severity of his reaction to being examined."

"I think he's just really scared," Emma said. "He's not usually explosive."

"So you've never seen him have this kind of outburst before?"

"No," she answered definitively, although she didn't really know.

"He must be very upset about something," Dr. Sears commented. "Has anything happened recently? Has he encountered any violence?"

Emma shrugged. Had he? Was it Jake the Snake and his hell-hound friends? Was it some dare or deal or weird fucking boy thing? Christ. Could it have been something to do with Dad turning up at his school?

"How long ago did your parents die?" she asked.

"Oh, I guess about six months ago."

"Car accident?"

"Yeah."

"Well, I imagine that must have been quite traumatic for the both of you."

"Yeah, pretty much," Emma shrugged.

"Well, then. You don't need to worry. We'll take good care of your brother. Why don't you call and see how he's doing in the morning."

Big trouble was brewing like a pot of poisonous soup on a stove. Elaine called Mrs. Brown, the mother of Blue's only friend the next day in order to ask her son to pick up some cigarettes for her on his way home from his sleepover. Emma had told Elaine that Blue was staying over at Stewart's house because it was his birthday.

But Mrs. Brown said, "No, your son isn't here. I haven't seen him in weeks. Seems he and Stewart had a huge fight over some hockey cards or something."

"So it isn't Stewart's birthday, then?" Elaine hissed, glaring at Emma, who was doing her best to avoid eye contact.

"No, Stewart's birthday isn't until October," replied a perplexed Mrs. Brown.

Elaine slammed down the phone. "Now, you just better tell me what is going on, young lady!" she shouted. "What's Blue gone and done now?"

*Saved by the bell.* "I'll get that," Emma said, running for the door.

"We're Jewish," Emma immediately said to the two women standing there, thinking they were going to try and give her a copy of the *Watchtower.* Emma was starting to close the door when one of them stuck her hand out and introduced herself.

"That's nice," was all Emma could say as Ms. Glendon, a public health nurse, introduced herself and the other woman, a social worker named Ms. Frank.

"We just want to ask you a few questions," Ms. Glendon said. "Do you mind if we come in for a couple of minutes?" she smiled.

"Who's at the door?" Elaine yelled from the kitchen.

"Religious fanatics!" Emma yelled back over her shoulder, and then, turning around, she smiled at the women apologetically. "It's not a very good time right now," she whispered. "Why don't I call you," she said, reaching and taking the card Ms. Glendon was holding.

"Are you living here alone, Emma?" Ms. Frank asked her.

Oh Christ, Emma thought, she knows my name. "Uh, not exactly. I mean, I live with my brother. Usually."

"You're awfully young to be living on your own."

"I'm eighteen," Emma shrugged.

"Tell them we're Jewish!" Elaine yelled from the kitchen.

"Who's that?" Ms. Frank asked.

"Oh. That's just the neighbour. She's a little nuts."

Emma winced as Elaine came storming toward the door. "Look, we're Jewish. Do you get the message?" Elaine said abruptly to the two women.

"Right," said Ms. Glendon. "Well, thank you for your time," she said, stepping backwards. "I'll look forward to hearing from you tomorrow," she nodded at Emma gravely.

"Sure," Emma said. "And God bless you," she called cheerfully after them, closing the door.

"Fanatics," Elaine spat, shaking her head. "Listen, young lady," she said, turning to Emma. "You tell me where Blue is right now or I'm calling the police."

"I'll just go get him," Emma said, grabbing her coat.

"From where?" she shouted. "Is he in jail or something?"

"No, Ma," she said. "He's fine. He just went to see Dad last night."

"See him where? The gutter?" she scoffed.

"We knew it would make you mad, so we didn't tell you."

"I don't like being lied to, Emma."

"I know. I'm sorry. Look, I'm just gonna go meet him at the bus station. You can yell at me some more later."

And that she did, at Blue and Emma both; right down to the last inch of her bottle of Scotch. Blue preferred silence, rather than having the truth, whatever precisely that was, be known. He'd given the psychiatrist just enough words to prove himself sane. He'd consented to the proviso that if he felt the need he wouldn't hesitate to use their out-patient services. He had no intention of doing so. Instead, Blue

shaved his head, thinking he could disappear. But he could never disappear. He was growing at an alarming rate and being bald made him
larger still. By fourteen and a half he was looming above his sister who
appeared to have stopped short when she was twelve. He just kept on
going, his skin stretching like the bum end of a roll of Saran Wrap over
a much too large piece of meat. It hurt him to grow like that—ached
and itched and didn't make any sense when he was sure he was meant
to be little bigger than a clam. The more he wished to hide, the more
his body betrayed him, growing upwards and outwards as if to mock his
tiny core.

By the time he was fifteen and could see the top of everyone's
heads, he realized he'd have to find another way of becoming a different boy. That's when he decided he would drop out of school. "You
*could* get a job," Oliver had gaped. As far as Blue was concerned that
was parental consent, so as soon as he could he said, "Fuck this noise,"
and "*Hasta la vista.*" It felt nobler than he made it sound. He figured he
was being responsible.

"Because Dad said I could," Blue shouted when Elaine went
ballistic.

"Your father has no right—" she continued yelling, but Blue
walked straight past her, out the door, and into the street, leaving her
anger to bounce off the walls and come hurtling straight back at her.

Blue got a job as a busboy in a fancy-ish restaurant, scraping bird shit
off patio furniture and occasionally stealing tips as compensation.
Pulling out chairs for women with peroxide-blonde hair and men with
thick rugs on their heads who wrote off lunches during which they
talked about their affairs. Blue continued living at home and spent
most of his money on dope. He wondered where he would next see

Oliver. He wanted Oliver to see him: he hoped his father would be proud to see that he'd left the schoolyard and found a grown-up way of earning his keep.

While Blue was spending his money on dope, Elaine was spending hers on Scotch, and Emma was praying some strange and miraculous occurrence would happen and transport her out of her horrible life. Oliver, she supposed, was busy schmoozing his way through life with monopoly money. Maybe he was standing on a street corner begging for funds in exchange for ideas. "I'm an ideas man, Emma," she remembered how he used to say. "It's just a question of hooking up with the right company. I should get paid for my ideas."

Emma could picture it. Oliver in a windowless room on the twenty-eighth floor of some high-rise building in Toronto being paid to spend the day thinking his great thoughts. "Take a dictation, will you, Margie?" he would shout into a speakerphone. "Immigrants," he would start. "The solution is finally within reach …"

She'd had no exchange with Oliver. "Do you still see Dad sometimes?" she asked her brother.

"I thought you didn't want to know."

"I don't really. But I do want to know why he comes to see you and not me. I don't get it."

"Maybe you remind him too much of Mum," Blue shrugged.

"But I'm nothing like Mum. Fuck. Am I?" Nothing could be worse than being a brittle and bitter alcoholic with a bad perm and no friends. She'd rather be an earthworm, created out of some dismembered bit of her own body.

"Kinda," he shrugged.

"Like the way I look?"

"Yeah. And sometimes the way you act."

"What do you mean?" she asked defensively.

"Ahh, forget it. I don't mean anything." He had been plucking at straws. Oliver continued to seek out his son because there seemed to be no end to the things he wanted to say to him. Insults, criticisms, cruelties. Without them, Blue wouldn't know who he was. Emma was actually much more like Oliver than Elaine. Oliver had removed himself and they were all supposed to keep on living. Emma was quite capable of doing the same.

# Caterpillar Princess

Emma and Blue had started to live separate lives, half-lives with uncomfortably sticky edges. When Blue dropped out of school, Emma started to seek refuge in anonymous public spaces. She would pace around parks, determine their geographic centre and lie there for hours at a time even if the ground was covered in dog shit, even if there was frost on the grass on which she lay.

Once a week, she took the black-robed shell that housed her molten interior to the public library. The library tamed her angry soul. She sat in lumpy chairs and went through trashy novels like cotton candy—sickly sweet, all fluff and melt, immediate gratification subsiding into craving for substance leading to yet again more sickly sweet.

On the heels of another predictable ending, she would look up at the acoustic tiles of the ceiling and connect the dots. But on the heels of one particularly trashy ending, somebody sneezed. She looked up at the sneezer with disdain, her routine interrupted, but the boy-man of indeterminate age sitting across from her was so absorbed in his *Scientific American* that he didn't look up. She kept staring. She coughed. Still nothing. She was determined to provoke him. He was determined to remain unaware. He was so clean-looking that she was sure he must squeak. Must get straight As. She noticed drool coming from the corner of his mouth and a vein pulsating on his forehead.

The following Saturday, he was sitting in exactly the same chair. She plopped herself down dramatically in the opposite chair and cranked her Walkman up to its most deafening level. She pretended to read but she must have been singing out loud because when she looked up, he was mouthing something at her.

"What?" she shouted. She couldn't hear a thing outside her ear-phoned world.

"I said, do you fancy yourself a Caterpillar Girl?" she heard the boy-man saying in an English accent as she pulled her earphones off.

"Do I what?" Emma asked.

"It's The Cure, right?" he said.

"Yeah. So?"

"Do you fancy yourself a 'Caterpillar Girl'?" he repeated.

"I don't know what you mean. What do you mean, 'fancy'? A fancy caterpillar?"

"Fancy, as in 'take a fancy to.' Like."

"You mean do I *like* caterpillars?"

"Not to worry. Sorry to have disturbed you," he said somewhat sarcastically, and went back to his reading.

Emma put her earphones back on and stared at the cover of the magazine he was reading. Stared through it to a place she couldn't see. Are you there, mister? she silently wondered.

He was there again the following Saturday. Reading the *New England Journal of Medicine* this time. Emma couldn't resist sitting down across from him and asking him if he fancied himself.

"Do you mean in some kind of autoerotic way?" he asked her.

"Yeah, sure," she smirked.

"I'm not a wanker, if that's what you're trying to ask," he laughed.

"No, I'm sure you're not," she said.

It sort of started from there somehow, with him saying a lot of things Emma didn't really understand, and Emma telling jokes that fell like lead balloons, but neither of them budging from their chairs. Emma didn't know whether he was a loser or whether he thought she was, but there seemed to be a strange tug of war going on between them, as if they were both pulling on a piece of fishing line. It was unclear which one of them was holding the rod and which one was caught on the hook. Neither of them wanted to move too abruptly and have the line snap back in their face.

Over the course of several Saturdays, Emma found that, despite her resistance, her angry poetry was starting to yield to even greater clichés—ones about (God forbid) longing and love, although she used every other word possible. Weeks passed in this way until the boy-man, whose name was Andrew, asked Emma if she wanted to come and see a band playing at McMaster University, where he was a physics student.

"Sure, why not?" Emma shrugged, cool and cavalier, although saying yes propelled her into an epic clothing crisis for the rest of the week where she tried on every item in her closet and thought she was fat— fatter than fat, obese, criminally so—despite what the mirror said, *the lying mirror.*

She applied toothpaste to the zit that emerged the morning of their date and thought about cancelling because of it. Fortunately, he didn't seem to notice. He picked her up in a battered Suzuki jeep without any heat, and they drove to Hamilton, where they spent the night dancing and drinking beer. Emma thought the beer tasted like piss and would have said as much if she weren't so determined to look cool. She plugged her nose and swallowed it instead.

He escorted her out of the hall some time after midnight and she promptly threw up all over his shoes. She sat in the passenger seat beside him with her head between her knees the whole way back to and beyond Niagara Falls. They pulled into a circular drive in front of a huge house that seemed to stand alone in the middle of a wooded park overlooking the Niagara Gorge. He left his vomit-covered shoes on the front porch and then, once they were inside, Emma threw up on the Persian rug in the front hall. "Not to worry," he assured her. "There are plenty of others." He hoisted Emma over his shoulder and climbed the stairs with her alternately groaning and apologizing.

They slept in a four-poster bed in their clothes and she woke up in the night and listened to his breathing, inhaling the sweet smell of alcohol leaking from his skin. He was nothing more than a gentle body in sleep, nothing to be afraid of, and she gingerly traced her finger down his tanned, hairless arm.

Emma woke in a huge room with dark wood panelling and plush mahogany drapes. "Who lives here?" she whispered to the boy-man lying next to her.

"I do," he said matter-of-factly.

"Alone?"

"For the time being," he acknowledged somewhat sadly. "It's the house my mother grew up in. She inherited it after my grandparents died. My parents are only here during the holidays. They teach in Montreal and my sister is away at school."

"But doesn't it give you the creeps living here alone?"

"Sometimes," he nodded. "It's a little big. A little empty."

"My house is like a shoebox," Emma said. "There's nowhere to hide. That's why I come to the library all the time. To have some privacy."

"That's funny," he said. "I go for company."

"I would love to have all this room to be alone."

"Trust me, the novelty wears off. It gets lonely. But you're welcome here. I mean, to spend some time here if you want. I wouldn't mind trading you."

He couldn't possibly mean that, she thought. Trade me for what? And have me here? Throwing up on Persian rugs and breaking mirrors and clogging the bidet? I'm not the most domestic of creatures. Boys had never been particularly nice to her. She knew it was because she wasn't pretty, didn't have big tits, and didn't wear inviting makeup and a Wonder Bra like the other girls at school. They still called her a loser and when they really want to be cruel, a dyke. She hadn't outlived her reputation as the girl who preferred hermaphrodites to boys.

"What's this?" he asked her, fingering the tooth around her neck.

"Dinosaur tooth."

"Is that right?" he laughed. "And where does one get a dinosaur tooth?"

"There's only one way," Emma told him. "Your father has to reach through a hole in the back of your closet and find it for you."

"Can your father find one for me?"

"I don't have a father any more."

"Is he dead?"

"Vanished."

"Vanished? How does a father vanish?" he asked her.

"Poof," she said, and gestured with her hands—up in smoke.

"Is that why you always look so sad?" he asked her.

"I don't know," she said, her eyes filling with tears.

Saturdays were fast becoming the days when the world was different. Imagine if I actually lived here, she thought, looking at the walls of books in Andrew's house. Imagine if I'd grown up here. Supposing I'd grown up in a rich, literary household rather than a silent and broken home—I'd be nothing like Emma Taylor at all. The books in Andrew's house were worlds away from the sickly sweet trash she was used to tearing through. They were denser, heavier, older, and the more famous they were, the longer they took to read. Everything was slower, calmer, and quieter here.

She read books on a long divan in front of French doors through which sunlight streamed and imagined she was the long-lost daughter of Bavarian aristocrats who had searched for her for years and finally brought her home. There were no neon lights in this wilderness. She imagined herself a caterpillar girl in a garden full of vegetables and knew she was falling in love.

Andrew played the piano in a room in the near distance. Late in the afternoon he would find Emma lying in the very spot he had left her hours before, engrossed in the pages of the same book. Emma stretched her limbs and smiled at him and asked him to tell her about Truth. Andrew had introduced her to this big, elusive love of his life. He'd been reading about the properties of quarks named Strange, Charm, Up, Down, Beauty, and the as-yet-undiscovered sixth partner in all this—a little girl named Truth. Andrew wanted to spend his life in heroic pursuit of this elusive quark. He wanted to be the Little Bo Peep of the subatomic world. He dreamt of Geneva, where he hoped to one day smash atoms in a particle accelerator that straddles the border between Switzerland and France.

Emma had no trouble inserting herself into his fantasy. She wondered if they would give her a job sweeping nuclear dust off the accelerator floor. She would be the Border collie guarding the five other sheep in the pen if he asked her to. She wanted to smell him, dusty, in bed beside her every night. That's all she wanted. We don't even have to talk, she thought to herself. Even if he just crashes into bed late in his lab coat and dirty shoes—I really don't care—just as long as I can wake up to the smell of him every morning.

"I suppose it would be time for tea," she said playfully. She liked his strange rituals.

"Why, yes," he said. "Spot on. I think you are instinctively British."

Emma pulled open all the cupboards in the kitchen looking for teacups like the ones on "Coronation Street." She found them—all gilt-edged and frilly with saucers to match.

"Shall I be Mother?" Andrew asked, gesturing to pour.

"As long as that doesn't mean I have to be Father," Emma laughed, but her smile turned down as she realized the seriousness of what she'd just said. If Oliver could see her right now, he'd be shaking his head. Thinking: Christ, Emma, who do you think you are? What kind of pretence have you got yourself caught up in? Whose house is this? Looks like it belongs to some mercenary bastards who inherited a whack of cash from some decrepit aunt and haven't had to work a fucking day in their lives.

"Oh, don't, Emma," Andrew said gently. "You were looking so happy. You've started to look so much happier than when I first saw you come into the library. You were so foul-tempered then."

"I'm happier now, especially on Saturdays," she brightened, adding shyly, "thanks to you."

"It's funny," said Andrew, relieving her of embarrassment, "but so am I."

CAMILLA GIBB

Saturdays soon rolled into Sundays, and then began on Fridays, and Emma started taking up more room. Moving from the divan through various rooms, cautiously at first, but with an increasingly greater sense of courage. She wanted to take steps in the shoes of every person who lived in this house; there were so many of them that Emma could be distracted from being Emma for a good long time.

In Andrew's parents' room she became his father—a caricature of the distinguished archaeologist. Pipe-smoking, professorial, scatter-brained, and obsessed with detail. She would comment on the furniture: "I say, old chap. I do believe that is a Ming vase. Notice the detailing around the filibuster and the Cornish hen."

Andrew easily fell into the game. "Why, Russell, that is a remark-able discovery. And to think I have lived my whole life with this treas-ure right under my nose and never been aware of it. How careless of me never to have noticed the mushrooms on the hedgerow. I do believe they are *psilocybin cubensis*," he would muse, stroking his imaginary, yet ample beard.

In the kitchen Emma played Andrew's mother. "Mary," she would gesture to her servant. "Do find me the egg beater so I might whip up a lovely Stilton soufflé for my charming family."

"Here you are, madam. I just polished it this morning." Andrew would curtsy, handing Emma a piece of fine silver.

"Be a dear, will you, and wash the fiddleheads."

In Andrew's sister's room Emma became a very spoiled daughter. With all the pink in her room, Emma could not imagine her to be anything but. "Andrew, do get rid of him, will you?" she would say. "He's such a dreadful bore even though he does have pots of money. I can't bear to hear him ask me to marry him and wave that horrendous crown jewel in front of my face one more time. And by the way," she said, her expression brightening, "what's happened to that chum of yours from the academy?"

"Becks, you *are* difficult to please," Andrew would chide. "I don't think I can afford to lose any more of my mates to you. You have your wicked way with them and then—off with their heads. You're like a praying mantis, devouring your lovers in turn."

"Poor Andrew," Emma would say. "At least I have love and admiration, which is more than I can say for you, dear brother."

Andrew didn't respond to that and Emma feared that she had perhaps taken the game too far. She ran out of the room and into the next one. The guest bedroom. Of course, this was the room of ghosts. There has to be one, doesn't there? The Dead Baby Brother's room—the stillbirthed, or murdered, or simply self-suffocated little boy whose presence would forever linger and haunt. The parents, who had decorated the boy's room while he lay in utero, still, twenty years later, could not bear to use the room for any other purpose than to hold a space in which the Dead Baby Brother's name could never be mentioned.

"Andrew?" the Dead Baby Brother would call out.

"Tiny Pip?" Andrew would ask cautiously. "Can it really be you?"

"It is I. Your Dead Baby Brother."

"Oh, how I have longed for you my whole life, Tiny Pip. Spoken to you as if you were alive. It is as if a part of me has always been missing. Thank God, at last, you have spoken. Now I too may die in peace."

"Rush not toward my light, brother. Live long and prosper. Be fruitful, fanciful, and multiply. Fare thee well, dear brother," he said waving, fading, fading, fading from sight, leaving Andrew open-mouthed and saddened. Emma had obviously hit a nerve. There were secrets somewhere in this house.

⌒

"And you?" Andrew asked her later in his bed. "Where are you?"

"Me?" Emma stared at the ceiling. "Where am I? Here am I," she said, arching her back and raising her face to his. "The Caterpillar Princess," she whispered. "At home among the cabbages."

When Andrew's family came home that summer, Emma quickly got the sense that they wouldn't appreciate her caricatures of them. They were all terribly, terribly serious, and she was altogether intimidated. Annelisa wasn't quite the domestic and culinary character Emma had imagined, but rather, an acerbic and aggressive woman with clear and determined aspirations for herself and her children. Russell was not a doddery professor, but a slightly lecherous, although relatively benign, and obviously unhappy middle-aged man. And Rebecca was far from a spoiled debutante: she was a recovering anorexic prone to violent mood swings.

Andrew was no longer as playful. He was serious and scholarly in their presence. Emma could still feel him solid beside her though, even if he didn't laugh much any more.

There were dinners, usually cooked by Russell, during which they all engaged in intense debates about political issues. Emma would mostly sit mute, feeling completely inadequate. She tried to look attentive, but she often failed to understand what made them so excited. She couldn't help flinching when Annelisa tore, as she habitually did, into Russell in opposition to his views.

Andrew's family overwhelmed Emma: she mistook the ideas, the opinions, the words, the information passing loudly over a single meal for anger. She heard her father—*Pretentious bloody gits. Noses up their arses*—but at the same time she heard Andrew. "It's just conversation," he reassured her. "You know, discussion."

Perhaps Emma just wasn't used to conversation. There certainly wasn't anything like it in her house. Before Oliver left, the soundscape had been dominated by Elaine and Oliver snapping at each other, and Oliver ranting on to himself. After he left, it was even less human: just "hush hush," "ring ring," and "clink clink." The language of home had become one of silence: shadows orbiting around planet Elaine.

"If you could just make a little more effort to contribute, you'd see they weren't so bad," Andrew encouraged.

And so she ventured, beginning tentatively. When they talked about disarmament one night she dared to say, "I agree." Annelisa cast her eyes over Emma and actually looked pleased. When they talked about the situation in Burma one night, Emma said again, "I agree." When they talked about soil erosion, or toxic waste, or the way to achieve peace in the Middle East, she nodded, "I agree."

"You seem to agree a lot," Annelisa observed one night. "Is there anything, Emma, with which you don't agree?"

"Uh," Emma stammered. She wasn't used to having all eyes upon her, inviting an opinion. "I think that television's probably not a good influence on children."

"Well, that's a start," Annelisa mused. "Any specific reasons why?"

"Violence."

"Profound," Annelisa muttered sarcastically.

"Annelisa," Russell interjected in Emma's defence. "I think you're right, Emma," he said, mustering support. "Although there is some debate as to whether watching violence actually breeds violence."

"I think it must," Emma said.

"Well, how do you solve it then? Ban depictions of violence on TV? Monitor everything your kids watch? Throw out the television?"

"I'd probably throw out the television."

"But then kids would grow up without a set of common cultural references," Russell continued.

"I hadn't thought about that."

"Well, what do you think about it now?"

"I think I don't know what I think."

"Indeed," muttered Annelisa.

"She thinks I'm dumb," Emma said to Andrew later that night. "She thinks I'm a complete moron."

"She doesn't, Emma," Andrew tried to reassure her. "You're not dumb. You're just not used to having discussions. What did you talk about at home? I mean, with your parents?"

What did we talk about? she wondered. We didn't. We got talked at, and when we were old enough, we talked back. But even that was rare. We listened for noises. We didn't know when things were going to blow up. We tiptoed. We choked.

"It's okay to ask questions, you know? I mean, if you don't know what someone's talking about, you can tell them. You can say, 'Actually, I'm not familiar with that situation,' or, 'What are the implications of that?' or, 'I'm not sure whether I agree or not because I've never really considered it a realistic possibility,' or you can say, 'It's something I've always wanted to know more about,' or, 'What is the historical background to that particular issue?' or turn it on them, and ask, 'What's your experience?' or, 'Has this issue concerned you for long?' Or just throw out something that they'll respond to, like, 'You seem quite passionate about this issue,' or, 'That's very interesting,' or even change the subject and say, 'That reminds me of the time ...' or, 'What I think is even more interesting is ...'"

Emma just stared at Andrew. Where the fuck did he get all those words? All those questions? They seemed to come naturally to him, an endless stream of conversational openers and possibilities. "That's very interesting," she said to him.

"Isn't it?" he grinned.

So Emma began asking questions, even though she didn't really know what she was asking questions about. It didn't quite work at first.

"I disagree. The Americans shouldn't even think about stepping into the middle of that mess," Annelisa said, arguing with Russell.

"Have you always felt that way?" Emma asked, as she'd practised.

"Um. Sorry, Emma? What do you mean 'always'? They only announced the possibility of their intervention this morning."

Emma blushed.

"It's as simple as $E=mc^2$," Russell said.

"You seem to have quite a passionate view on the subject, Russell." Emma felt she was gaining new ground.

"Well, not exactly passionate," Russell coughed. "Pretty straightforward, really. I mean, it's obvious if you sit down and add up the figures."

Stupid, Emma, she chastised herself. Andrew made it seem so easy.

"No, Annelisa. Hess was really a minor player by that point. Hitler just kept him in the public eye out of personal loyalty. Payback for the early days."

"Oh," Emma brightened. "He was the guy who wrote that book, right? You know, Andrew, you gave it to me."

"You mean *Siddhartha*? Emma, that was Hermann Hesse. They're talking about Rudolf Hess, Hitler's deputy führer."

"Right," Emma nodded. What a humiliating exercise this was, still, although there were more misses than hits, she was encouraged by the fact that even when she missed, people actually replied. The question mark had returned to her and she discovered it had a purpose she'd never known. Questions had the power to take you places. With the return of the question mark Emma's world was becoming infinitely bigger.

And then Russell turned to her with a question. "What are you planning on studying at university, Emma?"

Emma gulped. No one in her own family had ever taken much interest in what she was going to do with her life, in fact, she'd never even really considered that life was anything more than all days past culminating in today. "In university?"

"Yes, you're not far off. You'll make the most of it if you go in with a clear idea of what you want to study. You can do a general liberal arts degree, but I don't think that's the way to go."

"No, of course," she agreed. She was making a huge mental leap, right over the question they didn't even ask—whether she even *wanted* to go to university. "I don't know if I know yet," she finally replied.

"Any ideas?" Russell encouraged. She looked blank. "What excites you?" he continued. "What do you have big questions about?"

"Hmm. Well. Why dinosaurs disappeared. Whether they've discovered all the great tombs of ancient Egypt."

"Archaeology," he nodded, flattered.

"Yes," she said, much to her amazement. There it was: her daydreams, the dinosaur tooth around her neck, her fascination with ruins and other lives all captured in a single word, a respectable word with a future. She felt an enormous sense of relief and looked at Russell with a smile of gratitude.

Russell dragged dusty book after dusty book off his shelves and said, "Thought these might interest you. This one's a little old, but most of the superstructure was unearthed by 1923 so the basics are here." And so she read about burial customs and Mesopotamia and the discovery of stone tablets with the oldest alphabets in the world. She was enchanted, and that wonder showed in her face. Annelisa even started to look at her slightly differently, as if she were worthier somehow.

It was becoming clear that by going to university she would be making a choice between slamming the door every morning and drinking herself to sleep every night and arguing with people at the dinner table. Argument would never be easy for her: this new language, although it had started to become intelligible, would never feel warm or familiar, but it was a passport to somewhere else where life looked like an elevator ride—push a button and reach a destination—rather than an endless ride on a merry-go-round in a decrepit playground. No matter how awkward, it was the way out of Niagara Falls. She'd be a pioneer of sorts—taking the well-worn path of relatives not her own to a place she might actually find belonging.

# Beach

"It's like she thinks she's found a prince and she's gone off to live in his castle," Blue said to his mother. Ever since she'd met Andrew, she'd become all big-lady speak, started using words like "consternation" (which sounded like a painful crap to him) and "immaterial" (which made him think of Madonna) and talking about going to university.

"Your sister's just got class pretensions," Elaine said drolly. Elaine was actually in shock, stunned by Emma's pronouncement that she was moving into Andrew's house. It wasn't the move but the way Emma explained it that bewildered her. Neither Blue nor Elaine could believe how pompous she had begun to sound.

"The environment is just more conducive for what I want to accomplish," Emma had said.

Pardon? Who do you think you are? Elaine thought, before saying, "You do what you need to do." Fly, my little chickadee. See how far it gets you. But at some level, Elaine was relieved, unburdened. She started to talk to Blue like he was an ally. "Your father and I built our lives on the idea of rejecting that sort of bourgeois existence," she said to Blue. "I had no idea Emma was that way inclined."

"I think she caught it, this bourgeois thing, whatever the hell that is exactly, from Andrew. I don't like him," he said. Andrew reminded him of an android: a big boring brain housed in a casing without soul or fire. Blue saw his sister running, separating, detaching herself. Orbiting around some idealized planet. Leaving Oliver in the dust. Leaving Blue to sweep up.

Blue couldn't help noticing that this was the first time in years Elaine had mentioned Oliver without lambasting him. She sounded wistful, almost affectionate. Blue might have been the only person on earth who knew where Oliver was. Only Oliver wasn't technically Oliver any more: he'd cut up all the ID he'd ever owned and was changing his name more often than most people change their clothes. He wasn't exactly living on the street—he was squatting in abandoned warehouses on the shores of Lake Ontario, never staying anywhere for long. He was living among stray dogs and rotten fruit and had given up on the basics like personal hygiene.

"How is your father, anyway?" Elaine asked for the first time ever.

Blue was so shocked by this that he didn't immediately answer. "Ma, you didn't really mean to ask me that, did you? I mean, you don't really want to know, do you?"

"Just curious," she said. "I know you see him."

"Yeah, well ..."

"It's all right, you don't have to tell me anything."

"Well, he's not too good."

"All right, don't tell me," she said then, realizing that she couldn't really bear to know.

It had taken some time for Blue to locate Oliver. He had only one clue: "the beach" Oliver had mentioned on the back of the postcard from

Toronto. He could picture the waves of Lake Ontario lapping against his father's face and eroding his features. Dead fish sticking out of his pocket and seagull feathers in his hair. With this image in mind, Blue had started taking the bus to Toronto every weekend and combing the shore. He started in Etobicoke, at the city's western edge, determined to make his way east across the entire width of the city until he found his father. After two months of carrying an old picture of Oliver around, he finally found someone who thought they recognized the sunburnt man holding a chainsaw in the photograph. A photo taken in their backyard the summer that Oliver had declared he was going to fell the land.

"The *land?*" Elaine had mocked. "It's a patch of grass, Oliver. Who do you think you are? Davy Crockett?"

"It's *our* patch of grass, Elaine. And I'm going to clear it."

"For what?"

"You'll just have to trust me."

"Right," she had said, slamming the back door as she marched into the house.

"Will you take a snap of your old man?" he had asked his son then. "For posterity?"

"I know this guy," a waitress in a nearly deserted coffee shop nodded. Blue was sitting in the shop, which was located in an industrial wasteland, warming himself on the way toward Cherry Beach. "He's a semi-regular," she said. "Takes his coffee black. One day you can't shut him up, the next day he pretends he doesn't know you. He's working on some big project for the government—inventing some kind of security system or something. I don't know."

It was the word "inventing" that triggered Blue. "I gotta find this guy," Blue told the waitress.

"He owe you money or something?"

"No. He's my dad."

"You're kidding "

"Nope."

"Well, you look nothing like the guy. You're a real cutie," she said flirtatiously.

"So, how often does he come round?" Blue said, trying not to turn red.

"Once, maybe twice a week."

"Anybody else around here know him?"

"Nah. The guy's a loner."

"Well, thank you," he said to her. "I really mean it."

"Sure thing. Any time. Come back and have a beer later, or something. I'm here until six."

"Yeah, maybe," Blue blushed, reaching for money to pay for his breakfast.

"It's on me, okay?" she said, putting her hand on his.

"But—"

"Really," she insisted. "It's not every day a guy finds his dad, eh?"

"Well, I haven't found him yet."

"All right. Close, though. So when you really find him, I'll give you extra bacon with your eggs."

"Thanks," he said, sliding off his stool and walking out the door. He turned around and looked back through the glass once he was outside.

She waved and pointed to her name tag. "My name's Faith," she mouthed.

"Lou," he said, pointing at himself.

After a day of wandering around Cherry Beach, Blue did return to the coffee shop. He was grateful for Faith's face, not exactly familiar, but less foreign and less hard than all of the others he had passed that day. "I just wanted to say that if you do see my dad, don't tell him I was in here looking for him, okay?"

"Sure," she shrugged. "Is he in trouble?"

"No, not really. I just think it might freak him out if he knew I was around. I don't want him to take off. It's taken me months to get this close to him."

"What's he running from?"

"I don't know exactly."

"My dad took off, too," she nodded. "What a dickhead. My mum was pregnant with my sisters then—she had twins actually. I was a twin but the other one died."

"Sorry," said Blue.

"Nothin' to be sorry for. It's just the way it goes."

"Pretty freaky though when it's your twin. I mean, like the other half of you."

"Nah. I think that's just sentimental. Twins only feel like twins because people treat them like twins."

"You don't think they have some kind of special psychic connection or something?" he asked hopefully.

"I think they think they do because people always tell them they're so alike," she stated matter-of-factly.

"Well, sometimes I have that with my sister—only she's not my twin."

"Why do you think that is?"

"Dunno. We invented this whole kind of language when we were kids. We used to make up words and speak in fragments but we understood each other perfectly. Sometimes we didn't even have to speak at all."

"So you're a mind reader?" she said coyly, raising her eyebrows.

"Nah," he laughed, and looked down at the countertop, embarrassed.

"Come on," she provoked. "Try." She leaned down with her elbows on the countertop in front of him, all brown cleavage in a white blouse and peach lip gloss. She was red-haired and he noticed that the freckles cascaded from her face, down her neck, and plunged between her breasts. "Why don't you try and tell me what I'm thinking."

"This is like something out of a movie," Blue smiled shyly.

"It would be if I did this," she said, unbuttoning her top button and licking her lips.

They both laughed then and he took a clumsy sip of his beer.

"I'm off now," she said, nodding her head backwards at the clock. "So, ah, you want to come with me?" she smiled.

It was the first night Blue had ever spent with a woman. And Faith was a woman—she was twenty-five years old and she had her own apartment and a beat-up little car without a muffler. Her apartment was full of paintings of nude women. She said they were self-portraits she'd done although none of them looked the slightest bit like her.

It was a hot night but Blue felt embarrassed to take off his shirt, even after they had tumbled down onto the mattress on the floor with their jeans around their ankles.

"What's the matter, baby?" she asked him. "You got some horrible scar under there? You got a third nipple or something?"

"Gross, no," he shuddered. "I'm just a little shy, I guess. Sorry."

"You don't kiss like a shy boy," she said, clenching his tongue between her teeth.

"It's just ..." he hesitated. "Well, I'm a virgin."

"I know, sweet pea. So am I."

CAMILLA GIBB

"You're not," he said, surprised.

"No, I'm not," she conceded. "And I have a boyfriend. But I could be a virgin without a boyfriend if that would make you feel more comfortable."

"I feel comfortable," he said.

"We'll go slow. We've got all night," she said, wrapping her leg around his naked thigh. She moved her smooth leg up and down his calf and they kissed, tongues on tongues and teeth and lips for some time before she began moving her crotch against him. He thought of Emma on top of him in the basement. This was sort of the same, technically anyway, but entirely different in the feeling department. He could feel his cock hard and thick between them, Faith positioning herself on top of it and groaning. He stared at her lips and her breasts as she moved up and down the length of him.

"Could you come this way?" she asked him after a while.

"Uh-huh. If you kept doing that," he said.

"I could come this way, too," she said so deeply that he had to moan.

He began to get braver, pushing his pelvis up into her, closing his eyes, breathing deeper, until they burst with the seriousness of themselves into laughter.

Afterwards, they cuddled and whispered in the dark. "I envy the girl who gets to love you for a lifetime," Faith said as she lay in his arms.

"Was that really okay?" he asked.

"Oh, honey." She stroked the sweat from his face. "It was so sweet. It was perfect."

He lay awake that night in a strange city on the mattress of a girl he'd only met that day and wondered if Oliver ever had moments like this.

Moments of being suspended seductively in a space between bliss and uncertainty; a place worth the risk of staying because there was nowhere else you would rather be even though there were plenty of safer places to go. She was nice to him, this grown-up girl with the beat-up car and the freckles on her breasts.

He showered in the morning and she greeted him with a towel and a protein shake. "For you, big boy," she said. "'Cause you'll need your strength today."

"What do you mean?"

"I just have a feeling."

"About my dad?"

"Just a feeling," she repeated.

He began to believe in women's intuition that day. Sure enough, Oliver walked in the restaurant around eleven o'clock that morning and took a seat in the booth in the corner. Faith raised her eyebrows and Blue turned around slowly and saw a man with thick grey hair, working intently on a crossword puzzle. Blue felt short of breath at the sight of him and the buzz of the fluorescent light above grew as loud as cicadas on a hot summer day. He took a couple of deep breaths, but he couldn't stop the light from breaking up into bee-sized bits. Suddenly, he was in the middle of a swarm of black-and-yellow hornets.

"You okay?" Faith asked him.

"Uh-huh," Blue nodded, although he felt like he was on the verge of throwing up.

"Just take it easy," she said, putting a hand on his shoulder.

He sat there for a minute as long as a lifetime with his eyes closed. He tried to remember who he was and why he was there. *You're not a fucking faggot, are you?* rang in his head. "No. I'm not a faggot. I'm

Blue. I'm a boy. I'm your son. You're my dad," he said to himself. After a night with Faith, he was sure of it. He repeated this, looked over at Faith, and the hornets began to retreat. He saw the smoke-filled sunlight around him and stood up and walked to the corner of the room.

"Dad?" he said, standing beside the booth.

Oliver looked up and squinted at him. "Blue. Huh. Well, well. Small world, isn't it?" He was so nonplussed at seeing his son that Blue wondered whether time and space had collapsed for him.

"Can I sit down?" he asked.

Oliver shrugged. "It's a free world."

"How are you doing, Dad?" Blue said, sliding onto the red vinyl across from his father.

"I'm all right. Just about done this crossword. What do you make of this: 'Cantankerous just before Christmas in Sweden.' Eight letters."

Blue just stared at him.

"I forgot," Oliver said. "You're not too bright, are you?"

"No, I guess not," Blue shrugged. He recovered just enough to ask, "So, where are you living, Dad?"

"One of the warehouses around here. Great building. Masses of space. I do odd jobs in return for rent—painting, carpentry, that sort of thing. Nice arrangement. Gives me plenty of time and space to work on my inventions."

"So you're still doing that?"

"Still doing that? It's my mission, Blue. You know, my calling. Fact is, your mother could never appreciate that. No, siree, she wanted my inventions to fail. In fact, she deliberately set out to sabotage them. If I'd built a fence, she would have been there with a pair of wire cutters in her pocket."

"She just worries a lot," Blue said.

"Well, that worry made her old. Old and ugly and a bitch," Oliver said. "Does she ever talk about me?"

"Uh, not really."

"Hmm."

"That doesn't mean she doesn't think about you, Dad."

Oliver flinched then. "Funny word, isn't it?"

"What's that?"

"Dad."

When Oliver left the coffee shop half an hour later he didn't ask Blue to come with him.

"Well, it was good to see you, Dad," Blue said as Oliver threw four quarters down on the table and stood up.

"Sure, you too," Oliver said. He looked directly at his son then, making eye contact for the first time in their meeting and said, "Listen, you better not call me Dad any more, okay? You're a little old for that. Besides," he said, looking around at the other people in the restaurant and lowering his voice, "people might get the wrong idea."

"Sure," Blue nodded, feeling hurt, and more than a little confused.

"And it's not Oliver," Oliver whispered. "It's Frank, okay?"

"Frank," Blue repeated.

"See you then," Oliver said, giving Blue an army salute.

Blue was paralysed: stuck to red vinyl and trying not to cry. He wanted more, so much more, but he didn't know what that more was. He'd felt closer to Oliver when he'd been on the receiving end of his soundless criticisms through a schoolyard fence. In the flesh, Oliver was an even more elusive entity whose words were even less intelligible.

Faith silently refilled Blue's coffee cup and patted him on the back. The tears plopped from his eyes right into his cup. He sat there with his head hung low for what must have been hours. He saw the sun move from the left side of the booth to the right but didn't remember it ever passing over him. He watched the dust dance by the window and scraped dried egg off a knife with his thumbnail.

# Anybody?

Blue went in search of more. Well into the winter he prowled around Cherry Beach with a tuque pulled down to his nose, wandering from warehouse to warehouse looking for a sign. It was weeks before he saw Oliver again. When he did, he found him in the entrance to a no-frills supermarket. But Oliver wasn't grocery shopping. He was standing there trying to get warm. There was a great big German shepherd by his side.

He looked embarrassed when he saw Blue and started yammering on about various things. Fragments. "Furnace in the building is shot ... Worried the dog might get hypothermia ... "

Blue stared at his father who was wearing the sleeveless lining of a winter coat and Adidas running shoes. He looked rough, not the least bit equipped for winter. Blue took off his tuque and said, "Wrap your hands in this." Oliver accepted, despite himself.

A Pakistani family with four children came through the supermarket doors and the mother reached into her purse and tried to hand Oliver a two-dollar bill. Oliver spat at her, "I'm not a fucking beggar." She muttered to God and put her arms around her two youngest children protectively, pushing them through the next set of doors. "Fucking immigrants," Oliver cursed.

It crushed Blue to see his dad looking humiliated. He'd seen a thousand other expressions, but never this. Oliver the Titanic, the giant overinflated ship that he was, was sinking, was sunk, and all Blue could think to do was tentatively hold out his arm. "Dad?" he said quietly. "Let's go get a coffee or a drink or something, okay? Come on." He reached out again, taking his father by the forearm.

"Okay," Oliver mumbled, allowing himself to be escorted out by his son. They shuffled side by side through grey snow and walked toward the coffee shop, the German shepherd limping sadly behind them.

"What do you want to drink, Dad?"

"Coffee."

"Sure you don't want something stronger?" he asked him. Oliver hesitated. "My treat," said Blue, realizing Oliver probably didn't have any money.

The cheap whisky warmed him into conversation. "Ever heard of fibre optics?" Oliver asked. Blue shook his head. "Transmission of light through long thin, transparent fibres. Ingenious. Limitless potential. It's the wave of the future," he said, getting increasingly excited. "I've been thinking about it a lot. Thinking that's what I should be investing in."

Blue looked at his father, trying to take him seriously, but he couldn't picture Oliver calling up a broker and saying, "Take my million out of soya and put it into fibre optics."

"I've got some capital coming," Oliver said, sensing Blue's disbelief. "Couple of cheques in the mail." Blue wondered, though, how Oliver was going to cash a cheque addressed to Frank when he didn't have any ID. "I could throw in a few hundred for you, if you'd like, Blue. You're working now, aren't you?"

"Yeah, I'm working. Sort of a stupid job. I don't really have any spare change for investing just yet."

"Well, bear it in mind," Oliver nodded.

Sure, I'll do that, thought Blue. Maybe I'll consult my accountant.

"Dad? Can I just ask you something? Are you feeling okay? You look a little rough."

"Ahh. It's a bit of a rough winter," Oliver admitted. "The heat in that building barely works and my asthma's been troubling me. There's a lot of sawdust around. And I've got a rotten blasted toothache."

"Could you see a dentist?"

"We'll see," Oliver replied. "Things will improve. It's all just around the corner."

"What is exactly?" Blue had to ask.

Oliver didn't answer him. He seemed to be searching for a word but unable to find it. All he could think of was *fuck*: I'll fuck everybody and they'll be sorry. In the powerlessness of his current existence, Oliver would find a way to exercise control. There were still people smaller than him in the world. He could still be a big man.

Blue watched Oliver leave that day, then followed in his direction ten minutes later, eyes to the ground, stepping in the prints of Oliver's running shoes. His tracks led to a long, yellow brick warehouse with dirty windows. The place was deserted, not a single car in sight and no lights on in the building. The footprints, man and dog, circled the entire building and stopped at a loading dock. Blue hoisted himself up onto the dock and rapped his knuckles against the metal door. "Dad," Blue called out. "Oliv—Frank? Frank? You in there? It's Blue!"

CAMILLA GIBB

He heard a scramble and then the metal door scraped opened a crack. "Shhh," Oliver said. "Keep it down."

"Sorry," Blue mumbled. "It's just—you forgot your change," he said, handing him a twenty-dollar bill through the door.

"So I did," said Oliver, taking the bill.

"Can I come in, Dad? I'm freezing."

Oliver hesitated. "All right then," he said, opening the door. "But keep your voice down, okay?"

"I thought you lived here."

"I do."

"Why do you have to keep your voice down then?"

"Because it's not exactly legal."

He followed Oliver down a dark musty stairwell and through a wooden door leading to a damp basement running the entire length of the building. The floor was dirt and broken concrete and there was a row of windows at ground level, all of which had been spray-painted with opaque green paint. Some of the windows were broken, letting snow into the room. The snow wasn't melting.

The low ceiling was a maze of pipes and in the middle of the room a single, weak yellow bulb hung from a wire. The bulb illuminated a pile of domestic debris: a camp cot, a blue tartan-lined sleeping bag, a row of empty vodka bottles, a bag of oranges, a bedside lamp that couldn't be plugged in anywhere, and a stack of porno magazines. "Apart from the cold, it's all right," Oliver said with what appeared to be genuine enthusiasm.

Blue was speechless, sick in fact, his stomach lurching with the thought of Oliver living here like an animal without fur or the ability to hibernate. "Sorry I've got nothing to offer you to drink," Oliver said, as if he was greeting some business colleague who'd

106

just dropped by unexpectedly on his way home from the golf course.

"Dad? Are you really comfortable here?"

"Sure, I come from hardy Scottish stock," he said, slapping his palms against his chest.

"Still," Blue hesitated, "it's a little rough. Have you thought about moving? Finding somewhere a little better?"

"Nothing wrong with this place," Oliver said defensively. "I don't need much. Got all the essentials here."

"But where do you shower?"

"The gas station," said Oliver.

"And you can't cook here or anything?"

"I've never liked cooking," he shrugged. "Jesus, Llewellyn. I've never been one for middle-class pretensions."

"I'm not talking about pretensions," Blue objected. "It's just—"

"Do you see me offering you advice about how to run your life, Blue?" Oliver said, raising his voice.

Yes. All the time. Every day. Through the schoolyard fence and in my dreams and whenever I dare to stop and think.

"This is my business. I didn't invite you in here to start telling me how to run my life. Christ, that's why I left your mother."

Blue had never quite seen it that way. Elaine maintained that she had thrown Oliver out. "I told him to clean up his act or get out," Blue had heard her tell anyone who would listen. Although Blue knew it hadn't quite happened that way, he thought Elaine's version still made more sense.

Blue muttered an apology. He left the warehouse and made his way to the bus station that night feeling bruised and confused. He didn't have the heart to go back the following weekend. Instead, he called Faith at the coffee shop and asked her if she'd seen his father.

She hadn't. Not then or the following weekend. Worried, Blue worked up the nerve to go back to the warehouse two weeks later. He took peace offerings with him: a roast chicken, coleslaw, a six-pack of beer, and a forty-ouncer of vodka.

Oliver didn't respond when Blue knocked on the door and called out so he went straight in. He found his father in a poor state: shivering with fever under his sleeping bag. He didn't recognize Blue at first, and his speech was disjointed and nonsensical. "But you were here yesterday," Oliver whispered.

"And here I am again," Blue responded. "I think we need to get you to a doctor, Dad."

Oliver shook his head. "No doctor."

Blue could see he wasn't going to be able to move him. He needed help, and Faith was good enough to respond to his call, bringing a bottle of codeine, a thermos of tea, a hot-water bottle, and several woollen blankets from her apartment later that night. Blue met her in her car by the loading dock and told her she was an angel.

"You're the angel," she returned. "I don't know if I could handle it if that were my father," she said, passing him a pile of blankets. "Do you want me to help you carry them in?"

Blue shook his head. No one should have to see what was inside. Especially a girl who didn't know the whereabouts of her own dad. "I promise I'll get this stuff back to you," he said, thanking her.

"Whenever," she said, waving out the window as she peeled off into the grey night.

Blue kept vigil that night. He put codeine on Oliver's furry tongue every four hours and made him drink it down with lukewarm tea. "My dad used to boil the tea in milk," Oliver reminisced in his delirium. Blue felt Oliver's forehead with his palm and asked him if he was warm enough. Blue had wrapped himself in a Hudson's Bay blanket that smelled of Faith. "It was warm by the fire in the kitchen," Oliver muttered. "Dad was there. And Mum used to make scones and we'd dip them into the cream at the top of the milk bottle. Where are they, anyway?"

Blue didn't want to remind him that he'd never talked about his father and that his mother was dead. He and Emma had never met their elusive granny, the woman they'd simply known as Granny who sent them a box of home-made fudge every Christmas until she died. They'd never eaten any of her fudge—it was always green by the time it arrived, having been sent by surface mail.

Oliver began to cry the hot, weak tears of fever.

"Why are you crying, Dad?" Blue asked, his voice soft, gentle.

"It's just ... I don't know where anybody is," he whimpered.

"Well, I'm right here," said Blue, trying to reassure him. As pathetic as it is, I'm right here, he repeated to himself. You might have fucked off, but I haven't. You don't know where anybody is because nobody knows where you are. You left everybody, remember? I wish it were so easy to leave you.

"But the rest of them," he muttered. "Where's Elaine?" he asked Blue.

"She's at home—Niagara Falls. She's working a lot."

"And what about Emma?"

"Emma? Well, she's ... I don't know. She thinks she's in love with this guy and she's living with him in his parents' house."

"She's left you two?"

"Yeah, Dad. She's left. You know, just like you did. She's a lot like you actually."

Oliver looked confused.

"Dad. Whatever it is—don't worry about it. You're sick. Everything will be okay."

After the wretchedness of that night, Oliver showed some signs of improvement. He ate a little chicken and sat up for the first time in what might have been several days. "You look like you could use a bath," Blue said to him.

"Can't remember the last time I had a bath," Oliver smiled weakly.

"Let me see what I can do," Blue said. "I'll be right back."

Faith gave him the key to her place and said he'd find clean towels under the bed. He couldn't thank her enough, and promised to be in and out quickly and not make a mess. "As long as you're out of there before my boyfriend gets home from work, it's cool," she said.

Oliver looked about two shades lighter after lying in the bath for forty minutes. An oily film lay across the surface of the water.

"Is this your girlfriend's place?" Oliver yelled from the bathroom.

"Nah. Just a friend."

"You're not screwing her?"

"Dad," Blue protested.

"Come on, you can tell your old man."

"No," Blue lied.

"You're not queer, are you?"

The hairs on the back of Blue's neck stood on end. It was only during the recent night spent between the freckled thighs of a woman he barely knew that he'd recovered that piece of himself that he'd lost in the schoolyard. He felt rage now—enough to storm into the bathroom and shout, "Look! I'm not a fucking faggot!"

"Hey!" Oliver said, raising his palms defensively. "Just teasing you. Good-looking boy like you should have plenty of women, that's all. You know, my old man took me to a prostitute when I was fourteen so I could get properly laid. I still see a prostitute now and then." Blue stared at the man lying naked in the bathtub: skinny and drawn, big boorish talk coming from his helpless, pathetic body. "If I had the money, I'd do the same for you. Best thing for a boy your age," Oliver went on.

Blue left the room, suppressing anger and sadness. He wondered if Elaine had ever heard this story about the prostitute. He knew Emma would want to hurl a brick at her father's head if she ever did. Blue wasn't sure how to react. Maybe this was normal: maybe most fathers found prostitutes for their sons. Maybe that was what male bonding was all about. He didn't have a clue, and there was no one he would ever dare ask.

Blue spent most of the following week lying on his bedroom floor, high as a kite, calling in sick to work. Oliver called him from a payphone at the end of the week to tell him he had a job interview. "All sorts of perks. Even a company car!" Oliver enthused. "Thing is, Blue," he said, with some degree of embarrassment, "I haven't got a clean shirt to wear."

"I'll bring you a couple of my white shirts when I come on Saturday," Blue said in a voice as grey as February. "Anything else?"

"Well, I don't really have any shoes."

"What size are your feet?"

"Thirteen."

"You'll fit into my dress shoes. I hardly ever wear them. What kind of job is it?"

"Sales manager."

"I'll see you on Saturday."

Oliver was in fine spirits that weekend, rattling on about pensions and benefits and a company car. Blue didn't have the heart to burst his bubble, but he wondered how realistic his father was being. He nevertheless handed him a bag containing two white shirts, a silk tie, a razor, and a pair of shiny burgundy shoes.

"Thanks, Blue. You're a sport," he said, slapping his son on the shoulder. "You know, I'm starving. I could really eat a steak about now. You?"

"Sure, Dad. Maybe you could even shave and wear one of those shirts. You could think of it as practice." At being of the world, being human, Blue meant.

"Great idea," Oliver laughed.

Blue couldn't help but feel proud standing beside his clean-shaven father in a white shirt at the entrance to a Finnish diner downtown. Oliver was perhaps a little too flirtatious with the waitress but Blue was glad to see him in such good spirits. Their conversation flowed easily enough at first, but in the process of drinking three gin and tonics in quick succession, his father's enthusiasm mutated, becoming progressively more aggressive.

"Who's this boy your sister's seeing?" he asked Blue.

"Guy named Andrew. University student. A total geek."

"And she's living with his family?"

"Yup. You know that massive house just past the botanical garden?"

"The limestone one," he nodded. "I delivered an antique headboard there once."

"That one. Well, that's their 'country home,'" Blue said, rolling his eyes.

Although their conversation meandered from there, Oliver came back to it after he'd downed another gin and tonic. "I wonder what sort of favours she's giving him."

"What do you mean?"

"Sexually."

"What?"

"Her rich boyfriend."

"Uh, Dad. I don't think it's like that. She thinks she loves him. I mean, it might be that she's more in love with the idea of him, but it's not what you think."

"What do you know about what I think, Blue. Huh?" he said, poking him in the rib. "Don't tell me what I think."

Blue blinked back tears, swallowed hard, and tried to change the subject to Oliver's upcoming interview. But Oliver, now that he was on a roll, could only shut his son down. "I've had plenty of interviews in my time. I hardly think you should be giving me pointers."

Blue bit his tongue, silencing himself, thinking, The last time you had an interview must have been before I was born. Instead, he resorted to saying the things he imagined Oliver wanted to hear: "You look great in that shirt. I'm sure you'll get the job. You're more than qualified ..."

What Blue refused to see, though, was that which was obvious to everyone in the restaurant around them. They saw a crazy, homeless man wearing a starched white shirt and a tie under the sleeveless lining of a winter coat, barking at some big bald boy picking at his dinner. The boy looked despondent. Uninterested in his food. His head hung down like he was used to being yelled at. The man's grey pants were stained with grass marks from some earlier season and he'd nicked his chin in six or seven places. While he looked more respectable than he probably had in years, Oliver had long ago lost the ability to pass for a well-adjusted human.

Blue was used to people staring at his father. When he and Emma were little, Oliver had already developed a few habits that invited stares from people passing by on the street. They had learned to stop asking, "Who are you talking to, Daddy?" They had learned to hear the relentless machinations of his strangely wired brain as normal speech, Daddy speech.

When Blue went to the warehouse to take a photograph of Oliver the day before his job interview, he found him crawling on all fours in the dirt wearing nothing but Blue's white shirt. He was looking for something, although he couldn't articulate what, but given the desperation of his search, it was clearly something essential. There was blood at the corner of Oliver's mouth and Blue eventually realized Oliver was looking for his tooth. It seems he'd anaesthetized himself with gin the night before and yanked out the molar that was bothering him. Only in the sober light of day, did he realize he'd pulled out the wrong tooth.

Blue had hoped to give Oliver back a picture of himself that day—posing proud and ready to re-enter the world wearing a clean white shirt and an affable expression. The potentially proud moment collapsed into tragedy and the photo Blue came away with said it all: Oliver had become animal.

Two weeks later, Blue knew he'd have to call someone. Oliver had slipped over to the dark side and lost his legs. Blue came away from his final visit with a secret, without breath, with a battered face, and without much will to speak. He'd seen something he hoped there were no words for. All he could say was that his father definitely wasn't right.

Faith cleaned up his face and suggested calling the Board of Health rather than the police. She made an anonymous call on his behalf from a phone booth and he took a tab of acid and swam back on a current of guilt to Niagara Falls. He slept for a week, burying secrets without words in hidden caves. He lost his job, took another tab of acid, and decided he couldn't afford to feel any more.

# Bitter Trail

It had been several years since Emma had had any communication with her father at all. So when he called her up a week before her eighteenth birthday she nearly choked on her own spit. "Dad," she cried. "Dad? Where have you been?"

"Em," he said gently. He almost sounded affectionate to Emma. "Just had to get my life sorted out, you know?"

"Yeah," she sighed with the irrational instantaneous forgiveness that sets murderers and rapists free in the minds of their loved ones. How he'd ever found her at Andrew's house would remain a mystery. It never occurred to her that Blue could have inadvertently communicated the coordinates. It never occurred to her that new coordinates couldn't obliterate the fact that she was still, and would always be, Oliver Taylor's daughter. Her father had done a reverse Houdini, and while she felt relieved, she was wary, and rightly so, because although the pretence for the call was her eighteenth birthday, what motivated Oliver was something less benevolent.

⟡

"I know you don't want to know," Blue said when she told him the next weekend. "But I've got to fucking tell you, it's a bad situation," he said, throwing the photograph of Oliver on all fours across the table at her.

"But it doesn't even look like him," she said, staring at the image so hard she could have burned a hole through the paper with her eyes. "What's he doing?"

"He's looking for something."

"What?"

"No idea. Maybe his mind."

"But I just assumed he was living in some apartment in Toronto and getting on with his life," she stammered. "You know—like he even had some whole new family and everything."

"Yeah, well, you didn't want to know, right?" Blue said, a tinge of bitterness in his voice. "I did what I could."

"But he sounds okay, you know?" Emma said, hopeful. "I mean, he remembered my birthday and everything. My eighteenth birthday."

"Well, maybe he got some help," Blue shrugged. "Just be careful, okay?"

"You don't want to come?"

Blue shook his balder than bald head and stubbed his cigarette out in the middle of Elaine's favourite plant.

Emma didn't sleep for a week. On the day of her birthday, she changed her clothes fourteen times and took a bus to Toronto where she met Oliver at Union Station. He was clean-shaven and wearing a brown tie with a worn navy suit jacket and he smelled like Ivory soap. In the photograph Blue had shown her, he didn't smell like Ivory soap. He gave off the odour of wild, unwashed dog. But under the fluorescent light of the train station, he smelled clean and looked like the dishevelled relative of a human.

They took a taxi to the Ukrainian Credit Union where Oliver handed over a slip of paper and got a wad of cash in return. He led her across the street by the elbow as if she was an old woman and they descended the stairs into a dark restaurant, a Finnish diner, where they ordered pork chops and mashed potatoes and gin and tonic.

"I was kind of amazed to hear from you," Emma told him.

"Why's that? I'm your dad."

"It's just—you know—I haven't heard from you in years."

"Has it been that long?" he asked.

"Kinda," she nodded, wondering if it was just that he'd lost track of time. "So what prompted you to call now?"

"It's your birthday."

"But you missed the last few," she said, confused.

"This one's special. Eighteen. You're an adult now. I thought maybe you'd welcome some words of fatherly wisdom," he smiled.

"But I could have used those years ago."

"Well, better late than never," he snickered. "So, tell me, my girl, what are your plans?"

"I'm starting university in the fall," Emma answered. "I'm going to study archaeology."

He paused, twisting the swizzle stick in his drink, and she watched as the friendliness of his expression melted away. "Now what do you want to do a thing like that for?" he said, looking puzzled. "What good do you think that will do you?"

"I think it'll be interesting," she defended. "Remember the dinosaur teeth?" she said, hoping he'd remember.

"Dinosaur teeth?" he mocked.

"Yeah, from the back of my closet."

"They weren't dinosaur teeth," he scoffed.

"But it was fun to pretend they were."

"That was a joke, Emma. Not the basis of a career."

But it was our joke, she thought. We unearthed a secret together, and you drilled a hole so I could carry that secret around my neck, and I wore it for so long—in and out of the bath and rainstorms and winter after winter—that the rope rotted and my neck turned green. I'm still carrying our secret around, Dad. Right now, under my sweater.

"Take it from me," he said. "University is a waste of time. Didn't do your mother or I any good. All it does is raise your expectations so your disappointments are that much greater. Spare yourself."

"But you can't get a job without a degree these days, Dad."

"Oh, come on. I had a degree back in the days when they were still supposedly worth something and I still had to work my ass off to support the three of you. I don't think you and your brother know what hard work is," he said.

Emma knew it would be pointless to interrupt, tell him that it was Mum who had worked her ass off. She remembered Elaine receiving a cheque from Oliver after he left. Some attempt to compensate her for the money he had drained from their joint account. The cheque had bounced so high that it had disappeared like an Indian rubber ball over a schoolyard fence.

"Do you think you're too good to work or something?" he continued.

"Pardon?"

"Where on earth did you even get the idea of going to university?" he barked.

Emma noticed his eyeteeth: long and yellow, projecting from his mouth. He was mutating into the wild, unwashed dog of the photograph. Clearly not from you, she thought. "I always had it," she said defensively. "I just never knew I could do it. I didn't think I was smart

119

enough. But then I met Andrew and he really made me believe that I had it in me."

"That your boyfriend?"

"Dad," she protested, embarrassed that he was raising his voice.

"Who is he?"

"He's this really smart guy, a brilliant scientist. And he makes me feel special. He makes me feel smart. He's the guy I'm going to marry, Dad. When I finish university."

"Did he say he'd marry you? Don't be naive, Emma. Men'll say anything for a screw."

"It's not like that," she said, shaking her head. We're in love. So in love, and we have a plan for our lives, a plan we've made together. We're going to move to California. Get married amongst palms in botanical gardens in Pasadena. There will be ivy-covered tables sprinkled with rose petals. We will be happy. We will be professors with adjacent offices in some small college and have our graduate students round for potluck suppers. We will take sabbaticals together in Tuscany where I will unearth ruins and Andrew will invent theorems over red wine and dinner on warm nights. We will be friends with people like Julia Kristeva and Umberto Eco. We'll have a rich and brainy life.

They would be just the sort of people that Oliver would despise.

Oliver just stared at her: his pupils swimming in a sea of yellow. Hepatitis, rabies, wolf-man. Possessed by something inhuman.

She said nothing more. He had ripped into every word she spoke like it was raw red meat. She recalled then what she'd tried to forget— that things that started out like normal conversations with Oliver tended to end up in some ugly place. Halfway through her potatoes, Oliver was sitting across a sea of smoke and starting to froth at the corners of his mouth. She had to force herself to remember this wasn't the only place to be. That at another table, with other parents, people listened, and she had things to say.

She left him that night feeling more depressed and disillusioned than she had in years. He'd been gone for so long and she'd been angry because she loved him and hated him and missed him, but she wondered now if she would prefer to miss him than know him as strange and cruel.

She left him that night, but he wasn't going to let her go that easily. Two weeks later, he showed up at Andrew's parents' house. She caught sight of him coming up the drive. "Fuck, Andrew. It's my father," she said anxiously.

"You're kidding," he said, pressing his face against the window-pane. "He looks ..."

"He looks what?" she prodded him.

"Well," Andrew hesitated. "Emma, sorry, but he looks like a bum."

"I know. It's bad."

"Well, what's he wearing?"

"Something like the lining of a coat," Emma said, ashamed.

"I'll get the door, okay?" Andrew offered.

"Mr. Taylor," said Andrew, greeting him. "I'm Andrew. This is a surprise."

"Emma here?" Oliver said abruptly, barely acknowledging him.

"I'm here, Dad," she said from behind Andrew.

"I've got to talk to you about something," he said over Andrew's shoulder. "In private," he added.

"Well," she hesitated. "Okay. Do you want to come in?"

Oliver stepped inside and rubbed the soles of his running shoes repeatedly against the Persian runner. "Posh," he muttered.

Andrew stood there protectively and said he would be in the library, putting a hand on Emma's shoulder.

Oliver sneered, "I'm her fucking father."

"I'm aware of that," said Andrew. "And I'm just leaving."

"Patronizing son of a bitch," said Oliver as soon as Andrew had closed the door to the library. "Who the fuck does he think he is?"

"Dad," Emma objected as she guided him down the hall into the kitchen. She put the kettle on and took a seat at the table. "So, what did you want to talk to me about?" she asked him, trying to control her apprehension.

He remained standing. "Right. Well," he said, clearing his throat. "I've got a business proposition for you," he whispered.

"A what?"

"A business proposition," he repeated. "This way, you won't have to go to university at all."

"But I want to go to university," she said. "I mean, I *am* going to go to university. It's all arranged."

"But why waste four years when you could be making money? That's what it's about, Emma. Here, look at this," he said, pulling a wad of Canadian Tire money out of his back pocket. The bills were stapled together at one end. "That's what it's all about," he said, flapping the wad against his palm.

"Thanks, Dad. I appreciate it. I do, really, but I want to focus on my education at the moment," she said, staring at his thick torn hands and wishing he would just disappear.

"Won't you just hear your old dad out?" he pleaded. "You see," he continued, undeterred, "security's a real issue these days. And with all these welfare cases around today you want to make sure you're protected ... A man's home is his castle!" he exclaimed. "Security starts in the home! And you know how many people have sliding-glass doors these days ..."

"Sure," she nodded, although she suspected that not a whole lot of people did.

"Then you see what I mean!"

"Not exactly."

"Security risk!" he shouted. "Big security risk. Which is why"—he fumbled, reaching down into his pant leg—"which is why I've invented this!" he announced, waving what to her looked distinctly like a wooden pole.

"A broom handle?" she asked, dumbfounded.

"See? It's the most simple yet ingenious thing. We could charge hundreds of dollars for this. You just place it at the base of one of the sliding doors and it prevents the other one from opening. Even if it's unlocked."

"Uh-huh," Emma nodded. "I don't really know if people are going to go for it, Dad," she said, apologetically. Better that than telling him she thought it might have already been invented. Once it was elaborate plans for global telecommunication, now it's broom handles?

"Which is why I need you as my partner!" he went on.

She nodded, bracing herself to hear that she "lacked vision," was "naive and unrealistic," or was "missing the point altogether." She stared her way blankly through his delivery.

He wanted her to make the pitch to potential customers because "marketing surveys suggest that the association of youth and femininity with a product appears to influence customer purchasing decisions." While Emma was busy wooing and seducing, he would just whip to the back of the house and install it before they'd even had a chance to turn them away. "They won't believe it unless they see it," he explained. "People lack vision. They have to be shown."

Emma retreated to her earlier stance. "Dad, you know, thanks for thinking of me and everything, but I really am going to go to university."

"You're just as bad as the punters!" Oliver shouted. "No fucking vision. No imagination. No drive. Just like your mother. I don't know why I fucking bother to try and help you."

"Sorry, Dad," was all she could say.

He stuck his hands in his pockets and stared at the floor, shaking his head. "Yeah, well, just don't come running to me when you haven't got any money," he said bitterly. "And by the way," he added. "What about that twenty bucks you owe me for dinner the other night?"

"I thought that was your treat."

"Well, nothing's for free in this world, Emma. If you haven't figured that out yet, then you're really lost. Quid pro quo. Tit for tat."

"Andrew?" Emma whispered in the dark.

"What is it, Emma?"

"I don't know if he's just crazy or whether he's really evil. He's so bitter and mean. Nasty. Sadistic even."

Andrew didn't offer any comment.

"Would you tell me if you thought I was going crazy?" she asked him.

"You're not going crazy. And you're not going to go crazy."

"But what if I've inherited it?"

"I don't know if you should assume it's a biological thing."

"But I could still have caught it somehow. I mean, maybe it was the food we all ate, or the fumes from the chemicals he used to use to stain the furniture. Maybe Blue will go crazy, too."

"I won't let you go crazy, Em," he said, squeezing her shoulder. She burst into tears then, and he repeated, "I won't."

From that point on though, Emma decided to always sleep with one eye open. And to never shake her father's hand if she ever saw him again, just in case it was contagious. She imagined her father walking away from Andrew's family home and wandering back to Toronto, leaving a trail of bitter blue blood all the way. She couldn't help but wonder if she was meant to follow. It disturbed her: I'm part of this family, aren't I? Or are they just being nice to me? Making me feel like I belong. I know I'm different. But I'm trying. I know I don't really speak their language, but I'm not as unintelligible as my dad, am I?

She was occasionally struck with the paranoid thought that she was, in fact, just like him. She was a dreamer, too, sometimes unrealistic, but those fantasies she did at least keep to herself because she knew they were fantasies rather than realistic possibilities. She could be just as pig-headed and stubborn. She wanted to do big things: unearth a mummy, be a famous archaeologist, locate Atlantis. Oliver had wanted to wire the world, send a satellite into space, dig an irrigation ditch next to Niagara Falls. Was there a difference? Or was she actually a homeless person, too? One that simply happened, however temporarily, to have a home.

## Bloated Boy

Blue was overwhelmed by the fear that he would turn out just like his father. He'd hold a job, no matter how shitty, in order to prove to himself that it could be otherwise. He saw his father everywhere. Oliver appeared to him in the way that a mother whose child has been kidnapped by a stranger must see her child in a thousand different small faces every day. He could see him in the faces of men rummaging through garbage cans, old women pushing shopping carts filled with the refuse of other people's lives, and babies who looked like they weren't quite sure they were meant to be born into the world. He could see him every time he looked in the mirror. He pictured Oliver without heat, without sweaters. Wearing the sleeveless lining of a winter coat and sleeping with his greasy head on the exhausted teats of some mutt who'd lost her mind to too many litters. He could see him everywhere but he didn't know where he was.

"He's lost it, Blue. I mean it," Emma had said after seeing him. "He's cracked. Like, over the edge. Gone."

Blue was already feeling so guilty about having let Faith call the Board of Health that he decided to seek him out again. Emma's words proved unconsciously prophetic, because when Blue went down to the beach, he couldn't find Oliver anywhere. He really was gone. Blue circled the warehouse in the vain hope of a Gone Fishing sign, but it seemed his father had wandered off into some strange darkness and vanished into his own miasma. "Dad's done another Houdini," Blue muttered to himself.

Standing there in that lonely gravel lot, not knowing what to do, his anger started to surface. "Fucker," he said. "And now I'm supposed to follow you again? Find your fucking ass? Hunt you down, sniff you out? What the fuck, Dad? What do you want from me?"

He hurled a brick with all his might at one of the windows of the warehouse. Watched green glass shatter and then picked up another brick. As he lifted the second brick over his shoulder, an angry face appeared from around the corner of the building.

"I'm gonna nail you for this, you fucking idiot!" the man shouted. He started running after Blue with a brick in his hand, threatening to smash it against Blue's head.

Blue ran across gravel and scrub toward the water. Didn't hesitate and ran straight in—Doc Martens and Levi's and leather jacket and all. All swallowed by Lake Ontario. But Blue rose to the surface despite himself: his belly a bloated buoy filled with rage and secrets.

# Family Portrait, Circa 1974

Oliver had sprinkled hot pepper on Emma's ambition. Her conviction to become an archaeologist grew even fiercer. She'd wear that dinosaur tooth around her neck until she found a mouth big enough to take it. She'd find a place for broken bones and put them back together again. She'd throw out living relations in the search for remains of value.

She was a little concerned that Oliver would be able to smell her government loan from wherever he was hiding. She could picture him begging her for a loan from her loan, or else trying to convince her that if she bought shares in his brain, they would be sure to pay off. Worse still, if she could pay for the insurance on their mother's house, he could burn the building down. Fifty-fifty split.

She left for the University of Toronto in September, hungry for her classes to begin. She'd enrolled in two archaeology courses, a class in Middle Eastern history, and one in introductory Arabic—all this to stock the arsenal that would help her blast her way out of Niagara Falls. She was drawn to the East: she could almost feel the sand between her teeth, the particles of silicone forming grit-filled words and creating mirages of other worlds.

On the way to all this glamour, though, there were a few hurdles, the first of which was enduring the ritualized torment of a week of orientation before serious learning could begin. Emma masked her shyness with derision. She called the bonding exercises "puerile" and took a moral stand on drinking. The truth was, she was awkward around people, especially people having fun, and she'd never been much of a joiner. All around her people were linking arms and shortening each other's names and throwing up in the same bucket. In three days they had abandoned old familial ties and adopted a whole new army of best friends. Not Emma. She lingered at the edges and opted out altogether where she could.

She was most resistant to the activities of the last day, which included some perverted organizer's favourite humiliation—mud wrestling. The orientation committee had dug a pit in the middle of a field specifically for this purpose and even erected bleachers for the crowds of onlookers they obviously anticipated. She could picture herself writhing there in semi-naked torment, an Amazon above her, knees pinned against her chest, the crowds screaming, "Kill her!"

She found respite under a willow tree where she leaned her head back against rippled bark and started to cry. This isolation, in the midst of throngs of happy others, was killing.

"I totally agree," said a voice from somewhere.

She looked around, confused.

"Up here," said the voice. There was a woman perched like a bird in the branches above. Emma could see her purple underwear.

"What are you doing?" Emma laughed, brushing away her tears.

"I'm hiding. Staying the hell away from this sordid activity."

Emma laughed again. "It's awful, isn't it?"

"A nightmare," the bird-woman agreed, sliding across the limb of the tree and jumping down to land at Emma's feet. She had leaves in her matted dreadlocks, a gold-capped tooth, and a mole the size of a dime on her cheek.

"I'm Emma."

"I'm Ruth. Except everybody calls me Ruthie. Or at least they did, but my mum said I should probably stick to Ruth at university because Ruthie sounds a bit juvenile."

"Oh, and everybody's so grown up here," Emma said facetiously, pointing at the mounds writhing in the mudbath.

"Let's get out of here," Ruthie said.

"Really? But won't they do a head count?"

Ruthie shrugged. She really didn't care. "You hungry?"

"A little," Emma answered.

"I found this amazing roti place."

"What's a roti?"

"You've never had a roti? Where do you come from?"

"Niagara Falls."

"Oh," Ruthie nodded knowingly. "I see. A little lacking in culture, I guess."

"Where do you come from?"

"Guyana. Well, Sarnia really. That's where I grew up anyway. Wait here. I'm going to get my skateboard."

Ruthie led the way to Kensington Market that day. Her left foot pushing the pavement, her right on her skateboard, her right hand on Emma's shoulder. She nattered on incessantly, made Emma laugh harder than she had laughed in too long. Ruthie was a rebel with a brain the size of Oklahoma and they were bound to become fast and furious friends.

By the end of the first term, Ruthie and Emma had swapped hung-over roommates in order to share a room. Emma wasn't interested in the drunken parties that took place at the end of the hall, and Ruthie couldn't afford to be because she'd had a bit of a drug problem in high school. In their room, Ruthie worked out chemistry problems and Emma memorized Arabic vocabulary and the details of potsherds. They would make dinner together in the small kitchen at the end of the hall. Emma would have to steal someone's butter because someone had finished her milk from the tiny fridge jammed with rotting vegetables and identical cartons of two per cent. Someone's pot full of burnt rice invariably sat soaking in the sink.

Ruthie spent most weekends at her sister's apartment in Scarborough, and when she was gone, Andrew came to stay. Every other Saturday he walked through Emma's door, stripped off his clothes, and climbed on top of her. They slid and ground their bodies against each other with wordless yearning, rubbing skin in lieu of speech. Emma could still smell Ruthie's sweat in the air; sense it hanging above her like a pungent wet cloud while she spread her legs beneath Andrew and pulled him inside her. In the sensuous silence between them she would fantasize about lying in a bath full of sand and warm butter. There was poetry in the silence, but there was something not quite right when they spoke. He would fall asleep, his body good and heavy, her breathing slow and suffocated as she fell into sleep and dreamt her dreams of ruins. She was migrating elsewhere, in search of bigger castles.

Over the months they became strangers to each other, looking and sounding less familiar. Outside Andrew's parents' house it seemed harder to share dreams. They needed those walls to contain them, hold their shape.

The distance between Emma and Blue was even more vast. She could feel it between them when she went home to Niagara Falls that first Thanksgiving. He was sitting there in the living room with his boots on the coffee table, flicking through the channels with the remote control. He clearly wasn't happy to see her.

By Christmas, it dawned on her that Blue resented her absence. She hadn't gone that far, but far enough that she'd begun to forget the smell of water hurling itself over the escarpment.

They'd gone to pick up a Christmas tree together and they were standing arguing in the living room.

"I told you it was too tall," Emma said.

"So we'll saw some of it off, it's no big deal."

"All right," she said. "But it won't look the same."

He rolled his eyes at her and went to the basement to get a saw. When he started to saw the top off the tree, she interrupted: "Do it from the bottom. You need to leave the top for the star."

"What star?"

"The star that goes on top of the tree."

"Since when?"

"Since forever."

"Emma, we haven't had a star since that Christmas when Mum and Dad had a huge fight about it. Why do you think Mum's not here? She hates decorating the tree. Don't you remember? That freakazoid who used to live across the street? He made this star for Mum out of stained glass one year and Dad flipped out and accused her of taking the idea of Christmas cheer a little too far?"

Emma looked at him absolutely blankly.

"Emma! Dad said, 'Where the hell did this come from? Look's like that old bugger's handiwork. Did you pay for this?' And Mum said, 'He gave it to me.' And then Dad said something like, 'What for? What did you give him?' And then he grabbed the thing and stormed outside and

132

threw it down on the driveway and ran the van back and forth over it. Don't you remember?"

"Well, I remember something about the star, but I don't think it happened like that. Like Dad thought it was a tacky piece of tin or something so they put something else there instead."

"You've got some kind of mental block, Emma."

"I think you're embellishing the story somewhat."

"Embellishing," he repeated. "Sounds like a cooking method. Sorry, but your big words won't change the way things were."

They continued to bicker about everything—Andrew, who Blue thought was a git, Emma's ambition, Blue's lack of it. Finally, Blue charged, "What I don't understand is why you can't just stay here in Niagara Falls and get a job like everyone else. Like a normal person."

"Like what? At the Donut Castle? Like Brenda Tailgate? Wear a brown polyester uniform all my life and get paid minimum wage? Besides, Blue, it's not like I'm qualified to do anything."

"Do you think you're too good to work at the Donut Castle, or something?"

"No. That's not what I'm saying. It's just that given the choice, I'd rather not."

"I can't believe what a fucking snob you've become," he said, picking dirt out of the treads of his boot with a Swiss army knife.

"Well, I'm glad *your* chosen profession has such meaning and purpose," she couldn't help saying.

Blue had recently announced that he was going to be a tow-truck driver. "It's cool. And besides, drivers get lots of girls," he had defended, thinking, It's a good job. At least I can hold one. What the fuck is it to you? "Fuck you, Em," he responded to Emma's sarcastic jab. "What are you going to spend your life doing, anyway? Digging up arrowheads? Pretty fucking useless, if you ask me."

"You sound exactly like Dad," Emma said contemptuously. She knew immediately from the look on his face that she'd gone too far. Blue walked straight over to the window, gazed out for a moment, and then punched his hand swiftly through the glass.

Emma shrieked. Blue stood stone still in a puddle of splintered glass and didn't turn around. He reached into the pocket of his jeans with his left hand, pulled out a joint, and stuck it in his mouth. He lit up with one hand, the other hanging by his side, covered in blood. Emma didn't know what to do: whether to take him to hospital or yell at him.

"Blue?" she asked tentatively.

"Fuck off," he said, quiet, not turning around to face her.

She went to the broom closet and got a dustpan and started sweeping up the glass around his feet. He didn't move. He remained by the window, the only sign of life captured in the smoke that fled from his mouth. The pieces of glass slid in slow motion from the dustpan into the garbage can. "Let's wash your hand, Blue," Emma said. He stubbed the joint out on the windowsill, left the roach sitting there, and walked out of the room toward the bathroom. Emma followed. She reached ahead of him to turn on the tap and held his hand as the water ran over it. He winced, but neither of them said a word.

He stuck his hand inside a sock and turned up the volume on the TV so that the voices in the box drowned out the rage in his head and the piercing curiosity of his sister's silence. Emma slammed the door of her mother's bedroom in confused anger. She stared at the top of Elaine's dresser. There they all were. Family portrait, circa 1974. Blue wrapped in Elaine's poncho. Oliver and Elaine on their wedding day—

white silk and pillbox, black suit and lots of teeth. Oliver framed and still in Elaine's bedroom. Oliver looking, much to Emma's horror, a lot like her. It was all just a little too eerie. All the years that had passed and Oliver still sitting there, getting dusted once every two weeks and, Emma imagined, probably yelled at not infrequently.

Emma wasn't entirely wrong. Behind her closed bedroom door Elaine did occasionally rage at his picture or slap the photo down. Sometimes she just stared at his picture and cried. Still, she never removed it from her dresser. Why? Elaine didn't exactly know. Maybe she wanted to remember that life had once been more than the sight of her two troubled children through a dirty glass. Maybe she wanted to remember herself as she looked then: with a sense of future, framed by a halo of love, however fleeting.

# Salt Water

Emma knew Blue would call her a snob if she told him the truth. She did want a life where the castles contained something other than doughnuts. She didn't want to spend her life in Niagara Falls, being fired from job after job. Become a chambermaid in a honeymoon hotel and rip cum-soaked, red silk sheets off beds shaped like hearts. Book hotel rooms for tour buses full of Japanese tourists who treated her like a lower life form the way they did Elaine.

She didn't want to stare at the Falls and see the smallness of life, the inconsequence, the pettiness of being human. Watch season after season of lone rangers come to throw themselves over the cliff in barrels. Be this close, yet worlds away from that great giant United States of America. Wear a uniform all her life. Have to smile and say, "Have a nice day," when what she'd rather say was, "Why don't you put your eyes back in your head, fuckwit, and pay a little attention to your wife," and, "Are you sure that at three hundred pounds you really *need* this hamburger and fries?"

She'd built the idea of another life with Andrew. They had dreamt so much about the future that Emma had begun to wonder lately if they actually had a present. The present seemed to be a lot of sex and a lot of fighting, and not a lot of conversation in between. They would deny the bitchy tediousness of the day to day by hinging all hopes of happiness on the future they were patching together like a quilt. One square for northern California, one for the house they would live in, one for Emma's wedding dress.

Then the reality of the present came crashing ashore. Andrew, who had applied to Stanford for graduate school, got a letter of acceptance. A scholarship even. A ticket some three thousand miles away. This piece of apparently good news, this integral square in their plans for the future, arrived carrying an ominous stench.

In lieu of words, Emma started doing strange things like throwing textbooks at him and, once, a pot full of chili. Rather than react, Andrew withdrew. He used expressions like "acting out" and Emma looked at him with narrow, cat-like eyes as he spoke with all the disapproval of a school principal. His dispassionate reasoning was like gasoline on her fire and she screamed at him in the hope of waking his soul. Nothing. No sign of heart, either angry or forgiving. No emotion whatsoever—Where's your feeling? you bastard. It's all ambition with you, and no soul.

Blue, on the other hand, was all soul and no ambition. He kept dreaming over and over that Niagara Falls was drying up, throwing less and less water over its shoulder every year. He had tried to warn people but no one would listen. Worst of all, Emma laughed and told him that waterfalls only ceased when people had given up crying—when it had become so futile that there was no more point to letting go. He left the couch and stood for hours under the great wall of spray. He stood there at least once a day that winter, convinced that every day there was less and less water. He stretched out his tongue and he was sure he tasted salt. *Tears*, he thought, thinking of what Emma had said. But it can't be. If the fresh water turns to salt, we're all ruined. But if we stop crying, the water will dry up all together. Either way, we're sunk.

Over the winter, things calmed to a dull roar. Blue's eardrums were numb from the sound of falling water and the only thing he could hear was the call of the wild.

On Valentine's Day he decided to look for love. He went to the butterfly conservatory, where he hadn't been since he was a child. The woman behind the counter looked at the boy who was six foot two and two hundred pounds and hesitated as she handed him his change. She looked at him like she was afraid he would open his mouth and spit a room full of rat poison, or pull an Uzi out of his biker jacket and hold her hostage while he let all the butterflies go free.

He wanted to reassure her. Tell her he loved butterflies, and only wanted to stand among them. Perhaps he would sketch some of them in his sketchbook later like he had done when he was a child. "I used to come here with my dad when I was a kid," he tried to explain. But it was too late, he'd been defeated by the threatened look in her eyes, and rather than enjoy his moments beyond the turnstile, he looked down at the ground in a room full of fluttering wings.

The truck seemed to be the only good thing in his life at that moment. It toughened him to sit inside steel casing, it made a man out of him when he drove. But his days as a tow-truck driver had been numbered from the start. There was a lot less cruising for chicks with a cup of coffee gripped between his thighs and a lot more arguing with people in suits than he had bargained for. He thought tow-truck drivers were cool until he realized they were only cool to themselves. Everybody else treated them like scum. Like piranhas. He wasn't quite ready to be universally despised.

He stared through glass at a crusty row of chrysalises hanging on for life. He watched a new butterfly box her way out of her prehistoric sarcophagus, emerge a hesitant, slippery beauty. He saw freedom, and resolved then and there to make like a monarch and migrate. Emma had done it. His trip might be the end of him, but he didn't care. What mattered was direction.

# Trespassing

Over roast pork in a dark, wood-panelled dining room on Easter Sunday, Annelisa was frothing at the mouth over Andrew's acceptance to Stanford. Her baby boy had a brilliant future ahead of him. "I'm so proud of you," she repeated.

Andrew blushed in silence, and Emma audibly wrestled a piece of pork fat between her teeth. Nothing felt right. Not the meat in her mouth, not the pictures on the walls, not Andrew beside her, not the words coming from Annelisa's mouth. All the pieces were the same but they just didn't seem to add up the way they once had.

She could see Annelisa was gearing up for one of those nauseating rides where she determined everyone's lives according to her own fantasies. I see where Andrew gets his ambition, Emma thought for the thousandth time, as Annelisa turned to her daughter, mapping out her life for her as well. She was keen to see Rebecca go to med school. Probably hoped she'd become a brain surgeon. Emma watched Rebecca as she arranged the peas on her plate in a straight line and sent telepathic messages to the potatoes on her plate. *Go away*, Emma could hear her saying. *I don't eat you. I don't eat much at all*. Emma kept watching as Rebecca's pupils darted back and forth and Annelisa persisted: question after suggestion after question.

Just when it looked to Emma like Rebecca was going to blow, Russell interjected and said, "Just give her time."

Emma waited for Annelisa's reaction. Watched and waited as Annelisa's knuckles turned white. "Time?" she shouted at Russell. "You sound just like her father."

Confused, Emma slumped back in her chair. She stared at Annelisa; she looked around the table at all their faces as if she were looking through a one-way mirror. Through the glass, their features were distorted and enormous, all big hair and big teeth and pupils stuck on overdrive. They looked ugly, foreign. *Foreign* was her father's word, although she'd never understood his meaning of it before. Emma had heard him use it against people she thought looked exactly like him. But perhaps this is the way Oliver saw himself in the world. Like he was the last surviving member of a species roaming around a planet populated with otherworldly pretence.

She stared out the kitchen window. She saw Oliver there, lurking in the vegetable garden, feet hovering just above the spot where lettuce would eventually grow. He rolled his eyes and Emma was relieved. At least somebody, even a deadbeat dad hanging over a vegetable patch, understood. She was, after all, her father's daughter.

"You know what, Annelisa ..." Emma began saying, much to Andrew's horror. "I don't think you give a shit about anyone's welfare or happiness. All you care about is superficial markers of status: credentials, class, material stuff. You'd like Rebecca to be a doctor even if she was prescribing herself a thousand laxatives every day." Emma touched her lower lip. She wondered if Oliver had actually said the words: poked his head through the kitchen window and blurted them out.

"Emma! How dare you. When we've given you a home."

"I'm not an orphan," Emma said defensively. "I do have parents. I do come from somewhere," she said.

"Andrew?" she said later.

"Yes," he replied, his tone terse. He still hadn't forgiven her for her dinnertime outburst.

"Russell isn't Rebecca's father?"

"He's our stepfather."

"So he isn't your father either?"

"No."

"Why didn't you ever tell me that?"

"Because it's irrelevant."

*Irrelevant?* The truth was, the more she saw, the more she realized they weren't a family at all. It was all an illusion and Emma had bought it wholesale. What's that thing they say about castles in the sand? she wondered, as she stared at the ceiling. Does it mean that one swift kick from a bully on the beach can destroy everything you think you have? Does it mean that without cement foundations your house is likely to crumble?

"You know, Andrew," she eventually began to speak. "You just can't keep building a skyscraper without scaffolding, especially when people are questioning whether the whole building was ill-conceived and structurally unsound in the first place."

"*What* are you talking about?" he asked her.

She shook her head. "I don't know. My dad lost all sense of the third dimension—perhaps I wasn't even born with it."

"You don't make any sense to me any more," he said in frustration.

"Did I ever really?"

"If you are so hell bent on ruining things, Emma, I'll leave you to it."

"Ruining," she muttered to herself. "I make ruins."

Waking up alone in the dull morning light she packed a duffel bag full of clothes and books. She tiptoed out of the house for fear that the whole building was going to come crashing down on top of her. There were footsteps in the vegetable garden. The prints of well-worn running shoes. She stepped in, bare-soled and angry, and looked through the dirty kitchen window for one last time. She had just enough sense left to put the rock in her hand back down.

# West

All men seemed to be heading west. Andrew off to California, and now Blue, who'd announced he was sick of living in a hell hole, was going to travel across the country in search of somewhere or something better.

He never said he was going looking for his father. Elaine didn't know it, Emma might have been able to guess, but even Blue wasn't sure if that was the motivation. What he felt was scattered. He hadn't given up on his father at all. He'd just lost him. He'd stayed away for too long, and Oliver had disappeared. He'd gone searching and come up with nothing. In the coffee shop he'd asked the regular customers, asked them again and again, asked them until one of them finally gave him an answer. Truth or lie, it didn't matter, it was an answer he was after.

"I think I heard him talkin' about goin' out west," a construction worker with a harelip had said. "But the guy's nuts. Always mumbling about something or other."

The spectre of Oliver hung haunting in the West, because it had to hang somewhere, and Blue didn't know which way to turn. Some cat named Fucked Up had grabbed a hold of the end of his ball of yarn and was tearing though the streets of the city leaving him thin and stretched to his limits. He felt like lime-green thread lying on cold pavement. Pointless wool spaghetti. No sauce and not enough for a meal.

As he was boarding the bus, Elaine handed her son a bagged lunch like he was a kid going off to summer camp. It was a sad peanut-butter gesture—a tragic miscalculation.

"See ya later," he said, with a wave over his shoulder as he boarded the bus.

"Call when you get there, won't you?" Elaine pleaded.

"Yeah, yeah, Mum. Don't fuss," Blue responded.

Although she was relieved he was going, doing something other than sitting on the couch as he had for the past several months, she was worried about him. It wasn't easy having an angry young man living under the same roof, punching holes in the walls, plastering over them, and then punching holes in them again. He was looking more and more like his father every day and God knows that wasn't a sight she wanted to see every night when she got home from work. But he'd stopped talking altogether lately, and that was what worried her most.

A week before, he had walked in at dinnertime and simply announced that he was moving to Banff. Elaine, nearly choking on a Brussels sprout, had said, "If that's what you want to do, Blue. But you do realize it can get awfully cold, don't you?"

"At least I'll be able to get a fucking job there. Better prospects than this shit hole," he had said.

"Tell Em she can keep my truck for me. Drive it out and see me when she gets back—that is, if she ever gets back," he had said the day before he left, tossing Elaine the keys. "But tell her not to drive it like a girl, okay?"

"Are you going to tell your sister you're leaving?"

"I don't really think she'll give a shit," he replied.

Feeling guilty, he did call her later that evening though. "Em, I'm thinking about going out west for a while. Making some money, getting the fuck out of this place."

"But for how long?" she asked, her heart sinking.

"Dunno."

"Won't you be lonely?" she said sadly. "I mean, I would be lonely."

"I'm used to it. Doesn't matter where you are."

"I guess so. But at least you've got family, people who know you here," she tried, grasping at straws.

"Right," he said, making no effort to mask the sarcasm.

She knew he was right: they were not much of a family, and she'd hardly been much of a sister to him of late. "And what about Dad?" she asked.

"What about him?"

"Have you given up on him?"

"Why are you asking?"

"Just wondering. I mean if you go, he won't know where to find you if he chooses to show up again."

"Thought you didn't give a shit."

"Just taking inventory, I guess. I don't know who's here and who isn't any more."

"Well, it depends what you mean by *seen*," said Blue.

"Don't be cryptic, Blue."

"Only in my dreams. I've gone looking, but I can't find him."

Blue didn't say he sensed this absence was different, but Emma could hear it in his voice. Up until that point she'd always expected that they would eventually hear from Oliver again. That he would call Blue from a payphone somewhere and say, "Lou! Come and have a steak with your old man." Or call Emma and say, "Telephone banking, that's where it's at, Emma," and ask her whether she'd finished her useless degree yet. In Blue's voice, though, she heard the possibility that this time he might have disappeared for good.

Emma hated to admit it to herself, but the thought of oceans and worlds between her and Oliver offered some relief. Maybe he's even dead, she thought, swallowing guilt.

"Will you write to me?" she asked Blue.

"I'm not much of a correspondent, Em. But I'll read if you write."

"But how will I know if you get my letters if you don't write back?"

"Booly boo," he said.

"Uh-huh," she nodded. She'd have to listen to him in a previous tongue. A language they'd shared before words were intelligible; one they used now when words didn't make enough sense. "Aren't you going to miss me?" she asked hopefully.

He didn't know quite how to respond. He had, after all, been missing her for years.

Blue gave his mother a peace sign from behind the green glass of the bus window. He saw her clasp her arms across her waist and start to cry. She looked sad, his mother, she looked tragic. He couldn't stand to see it. He gave her a final nod, stuck his Walkman on, threw his coat over his head, inhaled the stale smell of tobacco from the lining of his coat, and closed his eyes.

As Elaine watched the bus pull away, she replayed the sickening memory of having abandoned her children long ago. She didn't often give in to guilt, but here in the moment of seeing her child leave her behind, sadness overwhelmed her. She had put Emma and Blue on a bus together when they were small, hung signs around their necks, and left it up to fate and someone else's driving to get them to their destination.

In the most horrible chamber of her heart, she had wondered whether they would even make it to Niagara Falls. She had entertained the thought that perhaps she and Oliver would arrive in their new city to discover that they were still on their honeymoon; that the past several years had just been some awful nightmare. In that imagined reality, Oliver would be meaningfully and lucratively employed, and she would be writing some bound-to-be best seller and baking bread to soothe her soul between chapters. Children would only be a concept: a nice, theoretical subject they occasionally discussed over some civilized meal and a bottle of wine.

In that moment, years ago, she had wished her children unborn. Now they were leaving her. She deserved it, she supposed, but she could nevertheless feel her heart breaking as she was left to stand alone. A husband who had betrayed her and lost his mind, or perhaps the other way around. A daughter who had packed her bags as a teenager, adopted a new family and a whole new idea of herself. And now her son, a troubled, high school dropout, leaving on a bus for somewhere simply because it was anywhere but there. She was the only one who hadn't moved.

In that moment in the bus terminal, Elaine was more aware than ever that she was indeed their mother. She had spawned likeness: she had produced two more aliens in the world.

Blue dreamt his way to Lake Superior. Dreamt of white mountains. He was shouting across a valley at a tiny figure standing at the summit of the next peak. "Dad? It's time to come down now," he shouted. "You've been there long enough." But the figure didn't move. "Are you stuck or something?" he continued. "Do you want me to come and get you?"

At that, the figure started to run. He slipped on a patch of ice and went crashing down the far side of the mountain. Blue knew there was no way he could have survived that fall, but when the figure disappeared from sight he started to run down the side of the mountain to rescue him. He would keep running, running through centuries of snow, until he found the body.

Despite himself, Blue started scratching a letter to Emma on the back of a paper bag. She'd said, "I'm going to miss you," and the words had stayed lodged in his stomach. It only looked like he was the one leaving, really, she'd gone long ago. There was more, so much more he could have said.

He stuffed his mind with straw for two days as they crossed the Prairies. He thought of himself as a silo standing solitary on the horizon. The light in his head didn't switch on again until they stopped at the bus station in Calgary, where he stepped off the bus for a cigarette. Disembarking, he looked around furtively: this was the epicentre of Oliver's new world, he could feel it in his bowels. This was the West, where business was booming, all concrete and cars and signs pointing toward "New Communities" where houses spawned other houses and crept up hills overnight without regard for geography or humanity. He bought a stamp and mailed the letter to Emma that he'd laboured over despite himself. He had his first shit in a thousand miles, pulled his cap down over his eyes, and boarded the bus again.

The mountains rose up higher and higher on either side of him, funnelling him into bittersweet thoughts of life when there was only one road ahead. He remembered the rarest of days. Oliver had taken Emma and Blue on a spontaneous outing one fall afternoon when the leaves had started to become crunchy underfoot. Together they had picked a bushel of McIntosh apples on a farm at the base of the Niagara Escarpment. The two of them had watched in amazement as Oliver stood against a tree and ate an entire apple, including the core. He spat the seeds out and said, "This is the only part you can't eat. They'll get lodged in your appendix and sprout roots." They believed him: pictured tree branches growing out of his ears. Thought of the appendix as fertile ground for rooting badness. Blue thought that's why his math teacher died of cancer. He remembers her sitting behind her desk one day and eating an entire orange, including the peel. "She has tumours," they said later, and he pictured her face buckling in response to the orange grove growing under the surface of her skin.

# The Limits of Smell

Emma and Andrew didn't even say goodbye, they just picked up shovels and started digging a trench between them. She hurled words and accusations and he just lobbed them back into her court.

"Remember you told me to tell you when I thought you were going crazy?" he said.

"Well, I said *if*, not *when*."

"Well, you're either going crazy or you're just showing your true colours. And believe me, they're not pretty."

The hollow within was now two parts hurt and two parts guilt-tinged regret. She had hitched a ride on Andrew's satellite and breathed artificial air for almost three years, and in the process, if she really faced the truth of it, she'd sacrificed Blue. With Andrew's departure she sank down in the bath and washed him away. Underneath all the dirt she was covered in bruises, big and blue, just like her brother, the boy who'd once carved his initials into his skin so that he'd never get lost. He was moving elsewhere now, moving west, and while she could handle the scars left with Andrew's departure, without Blue, she felt battered and unhinged.

There was no map any more. She could either bounce out of orbit into some eastern fringe where the sun stank and the dust storms were blinding, or she could follow in the well-worn footprints of a man who'd gone nowhere. Otherwise, she could chart a different path, even if it meant moving like a starving dog sniffing everything she came across in the hope of finding some nourishment. Burying her nose in the backs of strangers in elevators; her tongue twisted in foreign manes of hair, inhaling sweat and licking hairspray. She'd find something human, something outside herself.

Her heart was still in hiding, though, when she received a letter scribbled onto a paper bag.

> *Dear Em,*
>
> *I said I probably wouldn't write because I'm not a writer. I hate writing. But anyway, remember when you asked me if I'd seen Dad? Well, I didn't really tell you the whole story. I'd been looking for him for a few months. The warehouse where he used to live had burned down to the ground and so I started searching for him in all the other warehouses but I couldn't find him anywhere. A few weeks ago I ran into this guy at the coffee shop where he used to hang out and the guy said he'd heard Dad talking about hitchhiking out west. I don't know. He could at least send a postcard or something.*

Blue was obviously on a quest. One that didn't include her.

# Learning Japanese

Blue's bus pulled into a fairytale-like strip of hotels and stores running through a valley in the middle of Banff National Park. A picturesque oasis at the base of ragged grey mountains. It humbled him to look up. As he stood on the main street, with his heavy knapsack cutting into his shoulders, he marvelled at the inconsequence of being human. He had always felt small despite his size. Here, his size didn't matter.

He made his way to the youth hostel, where, for twenty-two dollars a night, he could rent a shared room and pee in a communal toilet at the end of a drab hallway. His roommate was a big lug of a guy named Mitch from Montreal. Like him, Mitch had come west for some unspecified reason. Blue suspected the reason might have been criminal in nature, but he could tough it up as good as the next guy, so Mitch treated him like a buddy and gave him the alternative geography of Banff: the map that detoured around ski trails and sporting equipment stores and fine-dining establishments to the places where guys in the know could buy pot, party after hours, and find girls.

Blue liked the bitterness of Banff and the community of exiles who congregated in these hidden places. Apart from the mountains, they were the only relative constants—a small core of workers who stayed through the seasons and drank, played pool, hung out, and complained about their shitty jobs and the fact that their managers were telling them they were going to have to learn Japanese.

Within three days of his arrival, Blue had a job in the laundry room at the Ptarmigan Inn. The job had its humiliations, but it included accommodation in the basement of the hotel, so he and Mitch divided up what remained of their jointly purchased case of beer and he moved up the street and underground.

Blue had never imagined he'd have to learn a new language to work in a laundry room. He wondered if there were really words for things like fluff and fold and permanent press in Japanese. He closed the Ptarmigan Inn–issued pamphlet of *101 Useful Phrases for Doing Business in Japan*, and picked up a pen. Perched on a bar stool, eating bacon and eggs at three in the afternoon, he wrote to his sister again.

*Dear Em,*

*Banff is pretty fucking amazing. I think you'd love it. You're never gonna believe this—I saw a moose in the middle of the road yesterday. How cool is that? There are tons of elk here too. They can be pretty vicious, especially when it's humping season, so sometimes they pack vanloads of them off and send them to northern Saskatchewan. It takes them a few months, but even- tually they make their way home to Banff again.*

*The town is okay. It's full of tourists like Niagara Falls, but these ones are loaded. Lots of people here looking to make a whack of money. I'm going to save all I earn so I can start my own business when I get home. I've got a job in the laundry room at a hotel downtown. Downtown? That's a bit of joke. It's just like Niagara Falls, really—one street you can drive down in two minutes. Guys still cruise the strip. Open their windows and blare the music late at night even though there's no one on the street and it's fucking freezing. Funny.*

*My job's kind of embarrassing, but they give me a room for free. And there's no tax on beer in Alberta! And the girls are awesome. When I first got here I met this girl who was Swedish. She was all yurdy, gurdy, fletch and burdy, and I didn't know what she was on about. She didn't make any sense but she could have been a model. Anyway, I better stop now because this is probably the longest letter I've ever written in my life and my scrambled eggs look like they're covered in wax.*

God, I almost sound happy, he thought, putting down his Niagara Falls pen. He burst out laughing.

"No more coffee for you today, big boy," said the waitress.

He folded the letter like an accordion and scribbled his phone number on the back.

# Imagine

Emma did the unthinkable and reached under the lab table to squeeze the thigh of the graduate student who was the teaching assistant for her osteology course. She felt his thigh tighten instantly, and she exhaled with the relief. Somebody could feel her presence: she must be alive. He kept his eyes fixed on the tin plate of charred animal remains in front of him, but his pupils dilated, becoming black stars.

She daydreamed them into the desert. They were excavating a castle. Him in shorts, the sun beating down relentlessly, their mouths like cool water in the blessed shade of a lonely tree. She worked her fingers between the buttons of his Levi's, crawling in to nuzzle hard warmth. His black stars exploded into black holes, compelling and vast. He let out his breath and Professor Newman turned around and gave him a disapproving look.

Alone in the lab on Thursday evening they analysed the patterns of wear on a set of human teeth. She offered to bite him but he ignored her. He talked about difference in wear patterns in carnivores and herbivores while she moved her toes in his lap and his breathing became heavy.

His name was Peter and he lived with Patti Summers, the thirty-year-old wonder-child with a tenured job in the department. They had met on a dig in Jordan two summers ago, but that didn't seem to be stopping him from letting Emma crawl under the table and take him and his sweet smell of soap and pepper into her mouth.

He pressed himself against her back and pushed her gently down the stairs into the basement of the building. He lay on top of her on the hot, dusty floor by the boiler. A bigger boiler, a different boy. But when Peter looked into her eyes she didn't see anything familiar. She could feel him retreat, going limp, shrinking, and waving bye-bye: I've got to go home to Patti. "Very sexy," he said, shaking his head. "But very impossible."

Under his weight her tears began, running down her face and into her ears. Once she'd started, she couldn't stop. He pulled her into his lap like a child and held her against his chest. She buried her face in the side of his cliff and he apologized over and over again in the dust of the basement. "Very sexy," he repeated. "But very impossible." *Very tragic, really.* She was crying almost, but not quite a river.

Emma was horrified to see Patti marching down the hall of her residence at the end of that week. Patti was screaming at the top of her lungs, calling Emma things she never would have imagined a professor saying. "You fucking bitch!" she screamed into Emma and Ruthie's room. Other students poked their heads out into the hallway and stared. Emma closed the door in her face, but Patti kept on yelling.

"Holy shit," Emma said, crumbling against the bookcase. Ruthie, who was sitting down at her desk with her back to Emma, didn't turn around. "Ruthie?" Emma said weakly.

Ruthie remained still. Emma said her name again and finally Ruthie turned around reluctantly and said, "What is it, Emma?"

"I'm sorry about that."

"It's not me you have to apologize to," she said, not looking at Emma.

"What's wrong, Ruthie?"

"Nothing wrong with me," she said abruptly.

"Don't be like that."

"Emma, it's just ... what the fuck do you think you were doing messing around with her boyfriend? That wasn't very smart."

"I know."

"And you know it's not him. You're just on the rebound. You've got to chill out for a while. You know, give yourself a chance. Find your feet, don't just run to someone else. Sorry to say it, but it looks a little pathetic, you know?"

Ruthie was right, though her wisdom came like a punch in the stomach. Emma buried her face in her hands. "It's just that I feel like I don't have anything left."

"That's not true."

"Well, what's left? Seriously?"

"Me, for starters. But more importantly, your work. Why are you here, Emma? You're not here because of Andrew, you're not here because of Blue, you're here because you want to be an archaeologist. Why don't you just focus on that for a while."

Emma would have to make a choice—perhaps the first choice she'd ever made on her own. Instead of going home and finding some shitty job and being depressed all summer in Niagara Falls, Emma could spend the summer working on a dig. Archaeology and Andrew weren't inherently pieces of the same pie. It had never been something she was just going to dabble in like a dilettante while her husband was off at the lab.

This summer, she could get her hands in the dirt, dig deep, and create a new life. She'd begin with the act of ceremonially throwing all previous neuroses into the back of a dump truck headed for the sea. Like an entombed Pharaoh, she would take with her only those things that she wanted near her in her next life: the broken dinosaur tooth she carried now in her pocket, and the book of wild imaginings she and Blue had made as children. She'd recited their entries to Blue in the basement while war waged in the kitchen above them.

"Imagine that I had gills and that whenever I wanted to talk I had to stick my head in a fish tank," Emma would read to Blue.

"I'd like to be a fish," Blue would say.

"So would I," Emma would reply.

When the plates came crashing to the floor above them, Blue would quickly ask his sister to recite another.

"Imagine that there was one magic word in all the universe that could make the sky crack with thunder and I was the only person who knew that word."

"I wish I knew that word," Blue would say.

"So do I," Emma had to agree.

Those lines had offered them comfort then. Now Emma recited them to herself.

## Somebody Else

Emma had obviously taken the photograph of herself. Held the camera at arms' length and snapped off the top of her head. A dangerously slanted grey building leaned over in the background and the hot-dog buns of some vendor dominated the lower left-hand corner of the frame. Blue had to laugh when he saw the picture. She thinks she's being artistic, he thought, as he stared at the photograph on the back of which she'd written, "I am somebody else."

She was always trying to be someone else. She would make bold proclamations about who she was and what she was going to do but she seemed to spit them out of her mouth before she'd ever even tasted, let alone digested them. She would get things in her head that she didn't get in her heart. It was harmless enough when they were children—*I'll trade you my marbles, if you'll give me your life*—but the older she got, the more was at stake. *I'll give away all sense of humour—hell, I'll even give away my brother—if you'll just let me be the slightest bit like you.*

At some level he understood. There was always a sacrifice to be made. He looked at himself in the cracked mirror of his tiny hotel bathroom—saw a big, burly man with thick skin and a chin covered in

160

black stubble as rough as porcupine's quills, and thought, They think this is me. It bewildered him. Whatever was going on inside certainly didn't look like that.

He wondered if Oliver had felt that way. Confused by the fact that people looked and treated him as a single person, when he probably experienced himself as scrambled pieces of jigsaw puzzle scattered across a linoleum floor. You could put the pieces together, but there would always be several missing—critical pieces, like the bow of a ship, or California on a U.S. map.

Blue wasn't sure if all the things he felt could be part of the same landscape, let alone the same person. He'd known that the last time he visited the butterfly conservatory. He'd been reminded of it several times in his life by incidents that exaggerated the distance between the inside and outside of him.

At sixteen, making his way home on Christmas Eve, a police car had sped down the street and pulled up on the curb just ahead of him. Two uniformed men got out of either side of the car, stiffly, with their hands on their holsters. "What are ya carrying there under your coat?" one of them said, eyeing the bulge under Blue's leather jacket.

He had run out of the house in yuletide panic because he didn't have a Christmas present for his sister. It was eleven-thirty at night and the only thing open was the 7-Eleven. He bought a pink stuffed pig that said "I wuv you" when you pulled its tail and snorted when you poked it in the stomach. Emma still has it somewhere.

"A Christmas present," said Blue, perhaps a little too defiantly, because the next thing they did was throw him up against the side of the car and pin his arms against his back. One man pulled him off the car and the other one unzipped his jacket. A brown paper bag fell into the snow at his feet.

161

"Do you want to tell us what's in the bag?" the officer said, prodding the bag with his steel toe.

"It's a fucking pig," snapped Blue.

"Whad'ya call me?" the officer shouted.

"I didn't call you anything," said Blue, rolling his eyes. "There's a stuffed animal in the bag. A pink pig. It's a present for my sister."

"Pick it up," the officer barked. Blue bent down, all his leather squeaking, and picked up the paper bag. "Open it."

Blue opened the bag and pulled out the pink pig. "See?" he said angrily. He poked the pig in the stomach and it let out a big snort. The officer in front of him jumped backwards at the sound. The officer behind Blue laughed.

"Ahh, fuck off, Barry," the officer in front said to the officer in back.

Blue pulled the pig's tail. "I wuv you," the pig whined, and Blue walked off, snickering to himself. That's how he chose to remember it, anyway. In truth, he'd cried all the way home, devastated at the world's wish to strip him of his innocence.

Blue stuck the picture of his sister to the bathroom mirror. "I am somebody else, too," he said, toasting her with his toothbrush.

# Digging

Having her own tools made Emma feel like a real archaeologist. It didn't matter that they were just a trowel and a used toothbrush; in her hands they felt like the equivalent of Leonardo's paintbrushes, or Shakespeare's inkwell and quill. She was on all fours in search of native artefacts, or in her most extreme fantasies, some unparalleled discovery that would throw existing theories into doubt and cast entirely new light onto, say, our understanding of human evolution. This would lead to a cover of *Scientific American* with Emma standing parched and freckled, holding some equivalent to the Rosetta Stone in her hands, and then a tour on the lecture circuit, stopping at, say, *Stanford*, where Andrew could wither in the audience as she waxed eloquently about the limits of carbon dating and received her honorary degree.

It didn't matter that their professor, with the unlikely name of Nick Rocker, had told them this was a routine job for the government: the archaeological survey of a building site slated for construction the following spring—the site of a subdivision to be built not in Egypt, or the Yucatan, or China, or Iran, but in the blandest of the bland suburbs of Toronto. It didn't matter that Professor Rocker told them it was unlikely they'd turn up a single arrowhead, because Emma's head was deep in dirt.

In reality, Emma was squatting, as she had squatted every morning for the past couple of weeks now, with a used toothbrush between her forefinger and thumb, sweeping dust off a fragment of pottery that was meaningless in the grand field of discovery: a piece of Dutch porcelain, circa 1929. She squatted alongside fourteen other students, engaged in the tedious and uninspired motions of scraping, teasing, and flossing, most of them restraining the urge to dig tunnels to the Antipodes. From above, they looked like ants labouring in a field under the dictatorial leadership of an anteater with a clipboard and a Ph.D.

They didn't begin the day with espresso, or end the day with tequila, they began bleary-eyed every not-quite-yet-morning and finished leaden-headed by the end of each exhausting sun-soaked day. But Emma nevertheless began and ended the day with fire in her eyes, scribbling her notes on the subway every morning, oblivious to the fact that she was sandwiched between a bunch of blank-faced people on their way to jobs they clearly hated.

After six hours of digging, they would all sit down to eat soggy egg salad and tuna fish sandwiches on white bread, and moan about tired shoulders and sunburns before packing themselves up to shuffle wearisome and wordlessly back to their homes in the city.

Among them, Emma stood out, engaging Professor Rocker in conversation, questioning him about context and dating techniques. It made her a butt-kisser in the eyes of the other students, but Professor Rocker would have to give her full marks for effort. She was obviously passionate about the subject, but since this particular situation was nothing but sheer drudgery, he could see she suffered from a syndrome that commonly afflicted novices. He was charmed by this kind of naive enthusiasm, it made him feel hopeful, it made him feel young again, but he knew it was only a matter of weeks before she discovered the truth: archaeology was a fundamentally boring and predictable occupation which required patience and commitment above all else. It was much more like a marriage than a shipboard romance, and in his twenty years of teaching, he'd seen many of the most enthusiastic fling themselves overboard in the end.

But Professor Rocker couldn't know that Emma's convictions were not simply born of idealized notions about archaeology. If that were simply the case, they would be easy enough to dispel. What underlay them was a determination fuelled largely by anger and sadness. Dreams born of a need to escape, passions inflamed by a desperate desire to reinvent herself, invest life with meaning, and bury the bad of the past. Professor Rocker had no idea what he was dealing with. Her romance floated on a ship the size of the *Titanic*.

Even on her way home on the subway, Emma scribbled notes in her dusty lab book. She attempted to make an overall sketch of the site but failed, because she'd never been artistic, she'd never had perspective. Blue did, not because he'd been taught, but because he just did. She envied that. She flipped to the last page of her notebook and scribbled him a letter.

> *I wish I could show you the place where I'm digging.*
> *It just looks like boring suburbs on the surface, there's*
> *no life to speak of above ground, but if you're patient,*
> *you can find it buried in the dirt. You'd get it, if I*
> *could show you. If I could, I'd stretch a big canvas*
> *between here and there and paint you a picture large*
> *enough to bridge the distance. But you're the artist in*

*the family, I'm just the dreamer, and even that can't*
*help me visualize you out there among mountains.*

Ruthie was in the kitchen on their floor of their residence stirring a pot
of something that smelled far too exotic for the surroundings. She was
stirring blindly, reading from a textbook lying open on the chopping
block. She was studying hard all summer, determined to write her
MCATs in the fall.

"You look like you've had a good day," she said to Emma who was
looking goofy with a big smile cracking her face.

"He's really good, this Professor Rocker. He makes us sort it out for
ourselves."

"No spoon-feeding," Ruthie nodded. "Speaking of which. Open up
your grinning gob and taste this—" Ruthie held out a steaming spoon.

"That's delicious."

"Guyanese recipe."

"What's in it?"

"Coconut milk, chicken, chili pepper, coriander, and a secret
Guyanese sauce."

"What's the secret sauce called?"

"Heinz ketchup."

Emma laughed as Ruthie ladled some of the stew into a bowl for
her. Dinner. Ruthie had left it for her on other occasions. A note on the
fridge: "Green bowl, nuke it for four minutes." Ruthie had more innate
sense than Emma's mother of how to make a home.

After dinner, in her narrow, sepia-stained room, Emma tore the letter to
Blue out of her notebook, and folded it around a couple of pictures she'd
taken of herself. On the back of them she wrote: "I am somebody else."

She took her dying fern into the shower with her, and watched dirt fall into a puddle at her feet. Every night she watched a brown puddle accumulate as she shed her dusty skin. Shower after shower, the dirt under her nails remained. There was even mud in the sink when she brushed her teeth. She was so tired that minutes after she'd crawled into bed, she fell asleep. Ruthie, whose room was next door, silently came and picked her lab book off her stomach, turned off her light, and shut her door. Emma slept on uninterrupted, dreaming ribbons of dirt and burial and the dead.

The next morning, she slid the letter to Blue under Ruthie's door with a note attached. "Ruthie, I'm sorry to ask, but if you have time today, can you stick this in an envelope and mail it to my brother? I appreciate it. Have a good day. Em."

Ruthie picked up the letter when she woke up and dutifully put it in an envelope. She looked at the pictures, and decided no one would know if one them was missing. She took the prettier one of Emma, smoothed its creased edge, and stuck it in the back of her biochemistry textbook alongside a recent photo of her parents.

# The Invisible Sister

Yet another morning alongside her colleagues under the relentless rising sun where they continued to make tiny gestures with grand implications. They were almost a month of the way into it and there were those who suffered sunstroke and dehydration and those who started to lose it, muttering inane words and nursery rhymes to themselves as they mashed their fingers against rocks. They sent one young man from Australia packing after he started eating dirt. *Oy, mate. You've got gravel on your lips again.*

The tougher her skin grew, the tighter her muscles pulled, the more Emma's imagination soared. There was silence in the dirt: wide room for reflection. In the rhythm of work she found a sense of innocence and awe that she could only associate with the colour of sunshine in her childhood bedroom and the sight of Blue's face when she brought him a book on Picasso. Rare moments when the world had felt large and full of promise.

She wanted to recall that feeling, re-enact the play, draw out the middle section, the one where they laughed, and rewrite the ending so that the Oliver didn't always get the final say. There'd be no big bolt of lightning, no curtain that fell so heavily at the end that all that had come before was erased. It would be one delightful act from start to finish, with Audrey Hepburn playing Elaine, and Johnny Depp cast as Blue, and, of course, a long fought-out battle between Jodie Foster and Winona Ryder for the part of Emma. There would be no casting call for Oliver's part. Oliver would simply be a distant memory, a gravesite Audrey and Johnny and Jodie/Winona could all visit once a year on the anniversary of Oliver's final soliloquy.

If only it were that easy. If someone leaves, is it because you are really better off without them anyway? Could Oliver really have gone postal? If he were registered mail, there'd be grounds to sue. As it was, there was no regulating body to complain to or blame. There was nowhere to take it, not even a grave. If he had vanished for good, they'd have to keep it in their bodies—swallow all the unanswerable questions whole, where they would fester in their stomachs and become phantom pregnancies—swollen bellies out of which nothing would ever be born. She and Blue were bound to be sterile—the possibility of the next generation had long ago been killed.

After six weeks of work, exactly halfway through the dig, Professor Rocker took the remaining initiates to a musty old pub to celebrate. They drank pints of cold lager and ate pretzels and chicken wings and some of them stood to play a game of drunken darts. Emma monopolized the conversation between the remaining four at the table. Monopolized it to the extent that when she finally paused to take a breath it was just the two of them left there with a row of empty pint glasses between them. She kept asking Professor Rocker questions about his career and he kept denying that it was a life of glamour and intrigue.

"Come on," she encouraged. "Tell me about something that you found that made you really feel it was all worthwhile."

"I'll tell you this, Emma," he said, brightening. "I once worked on a site in Northern Ontario where we were trying to establish connections between the ancestral Huron in the area and natives in the Midwest. We had some knowledge of a historic relationship between them but no archaeological evidence from the pre-contact era."

"Uh-huh," said Emma enthusiastically.

"Well, we hadn't come up with anything after three months of excavation and, well, to tell you the truth, I was getting bored."

"I can imagine."

"So I slumped myself down one afternoon on a hillside and started to do some sketches. Hobby of mine. I was sketching the flora around the site, doing so pretty mindlessly, until it dawned on me that some of the plants might not have been indigenous to Ontario. Sumpweed, for instance, and chenopod."

"Yeah?" said Emma, not seeing the point.

"Well, sure enough, I went and did a little research on my own and discovered that these were plants indigenous to the Midwest—plants that had been of particular social and economic importance in pre-contact times."

"So you established a connection, and ...?"

"So we established a connection based on the flora. The plants had obviously been carried from the Midwest to Northern Ontario."

"And?"

"Well, that was the theory we came up with."

"That's it?" Emma asked. Surely there had to be more to it.

"Yes. It was considered an important development—establishing a connection based on flora. It hadn't been done before."

"Well, where did you take it from there?"

"I made it the subject of my Ph.D. thesis."

"Wow," said Emma, trying not to convey disappointment. "And what about after that? What else have you found that's been of interest?"

"Well, nothing that hasn't been discovered before. I'm afraid that a discovery like that is, in archaeological terms, sort of the highlight of one's career."

"I see," she remarked, crestfallen.

"Emma, the odds against finding anything bigger or more unusual than that are incredibly rare. A 'big discovery of a lifetime' would be something like finding an unusual wear pattern on stone. Finding evidence to suggest that it might be possible that people cultivated maize as early as 9000 B.C., rather than 8750 B.C. as we currently believe."

"You don't get discouraged?"

"No. Because archaeology is about the details."

"You don't dream of finding something bigger?"

"Well, of course you always have hope that you're going to be the one to make some huge discovery, but the big stuff is mostly intangible. You know, the big stuff, like religion. You're not going to discover a religion; you're going to unearth the tangible remnants of a form of worship. It's actually a lot like life. You're not going to *find* happiness or meaning. It's in the details. The petty details, of yours, mine, whoever's life, and how you make them all add up."

"That's kind of depressing," Emma said.

"All depends how you look at it," replied Professor Rocker, draining the last of his pint.

She made her way back to residence with the taste of disappointment in her mouth that night. It was as if Professor Rocker had put an aspirin on her tongue and told her to suck it. She was hoping the bitter pill would dissolve quickly even if it left a rancid aftertaste.

Her heart lifted a little at the sight of a letter from Blue. She pulled the grey envelope out of her mailbox in the porter's lodge and tore it open.

"Another love letter?" the porter said, peering up at her from his newspaper.

"Hardly," she replied, embarrassed.

She turned her back to the porter and skimmed Blue's letter. His tone was rushed, elated even, not at all like Blue. The reason? He'd apparently met the girl of his dreams. Wait a minute—Blue's in love?

"I'd shack up in Alberta, live in an igloo, become a Mormon, and grow strawberries for a living if that's what she wanted," he wrote. "It's a crazy, crazy feeling!"

She wanted him to be happy, but she couldn't help feeling slammed by his news. Blue was far enough away already, and with this declaration, he was migrating that much further. She could feel herself slipping into the distance on his horizon. He was waving to her, cheerfully, obliviously, his spirits lifted by new arms, while she was foraging on all fours in the dirt, looking for sumpweed.

Emma moaned aloud with the weight of a falling heart.

The porter looked up from his newspaper and stared at her.

"What?" she said abruptly.

"Nothing," the porter replied, startled.

"Did I say something?"

"Something about feeling blue."

The next morning, she pulled her overalls over her shorts and T-shirt, and put on a sweatshirt over the entire bulk. She rushed past the porter's desk and travelled across and out the other side of the city.

Blue's declaration of love sent her head and heart first into the dirt with renewed, nearly manic conviction. Whatever she was digging for, she was going to find it. There was nowhere else for her to go.

Later that day, Emma sat beneath a tree in the courtyard of the residence under the orange sun. Frisbees floated and sprinklers punctured holes in the humid air. A baseball game was under way at the far end of the adjacent field. She was a spectre against the backdrop of summer hoots and hollers, a stranger, a foreigner, writing field notes in her lab book, sketching a bad approximation of another fragment of pottery they'd unearthed that day.

"Dear Blue," she wrote in the last page of her lab book and leaned back against the tree. She stuck the end of the pen in her mouth then because she didn't know what else to write.

"Booly boo?" she called out, looking up. "Where are you?" The words travelled across the country, slammed into the Rockies, and came back to her as an echo: "Boo hoo." He couldn't hear her, there were giant obstacles in the way, he was too far away for telepathy, perhaps even too far for understanding.

They'd spent an entire winter trying to communicate telepathically when they were children. At home, before they fell asleep, they would synchronize their watches and agree that at precisely nine o'clock, Emma would purge her head of all thoughts and try and listen in to his. It didn't seem to work, nor did it work the other way around, where Blue went blank and invited her thoughts into his head. They just weren't conversant in the sixth sense, no matter how hard they wished or tried.

She lingered at the lonely edge of that echo. He couldn't hear her, and if that were true, was she still his sister? She wasn't sure.

173

*I used to share a life with you—do you remember? A life like a bed that was more than big enough for two people, or at least the two of us. I don't understand what happened. When did the cement that used to bind our foundations crack? I feel it, Blue—like the foundations have buckled and split down the middle and you're standing on one side of the ocean and I'm over here in some weird wasteland and I don't even look like you or me or anybody I recognize when I look in the mirror now. I can't even picture you any more. Where are you? Are we just playing hide-and-seek? Am I it? If I am, can it be your turn now?*

*Love,*
*Emma*

# The Snake and the Butterfly

His sister sounded like she was cracking up. He had just received a letter from her and the envelope was full of dirt and cigarette ash. He didn't really know what she was yammering on about in her letter, though he suspected she was in the midst of another one of her identity crises. She was asking him where he was. Saying they'd drifted apart. But she was the one who had left and moved to Andrew's. She was the one who had decided to go off to university and become an archaeologist. There was distance between them because every time she went off to try and be someone else she had thrown the baby out with the dirty bathwater of the life they had lived that far.

Now he was busy trying to have his own life and she was asking him where the hell he was. So he'd tell her. He was in Banff and he was in love with a woman named Amy. "She's amazing," he wrote. This one was for real. There had been a string of one-night stands when he first got to Banff, a couple of mistakes, including one bearing a minor, but contagious infection, but this one-night stand had lasted for two weeks already, and it was spilling more and more into the daylight hours.

Amy was a stripper, and she worked at the Heavenly Bawdy, a strip joint beneath a restaurant on the road to the next town. The official name of the place was Jingles Singles Club—for members only—a respectable front for the questionable activities that went on behind its doors. The place was occasionally raided for minors and drugs, so the manager, Larry, had a system. If the music suddenly looped from bump and grind into Billy Holiday, the strippers would sit down at tables with the clients and make like they were simply looking for husbands. A drag queen would come onstage and mouth "Summertime," and the happily pretending and not-so-happily pretending would dance cheek to cheek around the parquet floor. The Jingles Singles Club.

In and amongst the crowd on any given night there would be at least a couple of Mounted Police. You could tell, because despite being unmounted while in attendance, they still had manure on their boots. They paid like anyone else, even though what went on was completely against the edicts of the strictly guarded business regulations in the National Park.

Blue had only been to a strip joint once before. One of his tow-trucking colleagues had had a stag party at Jilly's in Toronto, and although he had been mesmerized by the long, young bodies that floated in and among their tables, he had been disconcerted by the men around him. They looked like they'd been stunned stupid. They sat with their greedy mouths open, their hands wandering, and were gently chastised by the women moving their bodies in luxurious waves before them. When the song was over and they had to be men among men again, they flipped it all over in their heads and hurled crude insults at the women who, minutes before, had so enchanted them that they'd lost all motor control. Blue had felt embarrassed. Kept his eyes fixed on a pierced belly button and tried to smile politely at the woman who finished dancing in front of him.

On a summer Saturday night as cold as winter, Mitch picked him up at the hotel and said he fancied seeing a little pussy flirting in his face.

"Enough with the language, okay?" Blue said. "Don't you have a sister?"

"Of course I have a sister."

"Well, imagine if guys spoke about your sister like that."

"Oh, come on, Lou. Relax, man," he said, pushing the accelerator and careening down the main street.

In the club, Blue gripped his beer bottle and looked for a pierced belly button to give him purpose. He stared at a woman with a snake tattoo that curled from the top of her thigh to her nipple, and when she caught him staring she asked him if he wanted her to dance for him. "I was just admiring your tattoo," he said to her, blushing.

"Yeah, well watch this," she said. "Watch how the snake moves when I dance," she said, winding her hips and torso like a belly dancer to "Like a Virgin." He watched the length of primary colours rippling up and down her body. She spread her legs, revealing a cavern of silver: rows of rings through her labia and clitoris. He leaned in, fascinated, and Mitch laughed and slapped him on the shoulder and said, "Yeah, just like a virgin."

Blue was amazed by the hardware between her legs. Sculpted and adorned so precisely he could feel the pain of it. He reached up and rubbed his bicep, remembered the pinch and then the dull ache of pulling needles through his own skin. He wanted more of that. "It's beautiful," he said to her.

"Feels beautiful when you pull," she smiled, and then tugged at the rings and threw her head back in a convincing performance of rapture.

After a few more beers, a small, lithe, blonde girl wearing a body-hugging layer of leopard skin approached Blue. "Want a dance?" she asked. "Discount for a cutie like you," she smiled. She had a pink puckered mouth and hips so narrow she could still be a child and he had to stop himself from asking her how old she was. He hesitated, catching sight of the little gold butterfly around her neck. "That's pretty," he said.

"This?" she said, fingering the pendant around her neck. "Thanks. Present from my stepdad. I love butterflies."

"Yeah? Me too," he said nervously. "I used to go to this amazing place—this butterfly conservatory in Niagara Falls," he found himself telling her. As he said it, he chastised himself: Be cool. Shut up, you idiot. He needn't have, though—she was more than willing to engage.

"You're from Niagara Falls?" she asked him.

"Yeah."

"No kidding?"

"You too?"

"Yeah," she nodded enthusiastically. "How long you been here?"

"A month. You?"

"Year and a half."

"That's a long time," he said.

She shrugged. "Guess so."

"Do you miss home?"

"Nah. It's a shit hole."

"I know what you mean."

"Listen, do you want me dance for you? Larry, the manager, gets pissed off if I'm yakking—I don't get paid for that."

Blue felt uncomfortable. "I'll pay you just for talking," he said.

"Can't do that," she said. "Looks bad."

"Hey, he can pay you for talking and you can dance for me, sweet-heart," Mitch said, budding in.

"Okay with you?" she asked.

Blue shrugged. "Be my guest." But he couldn't watch. He stared off in the other direction for the next four interminable minutes as she moved her way through Prince's whining.

"My name's Amy," she said, whispering into Blue's ear as she moved away from the table. Her breath was enough to make him hard.

"I think she likes you, buddy," Mitch said, nudge nudge, wink winking him.

"Nah. It's just we're both from Niagara Falls. Nice coincidence, that's all," Blue said.

"She's got a hot little tamale of a body," Mitch added.

"I didn't really notice."

The following Saturday he went to the club alone. He wore a baseball cap—some attempt at concealing himself—and sat down in the same seat as he had the week before. Amy noticed him soon after he arrived and said it was nice to see him back. "Do you want a dance tonight?" she asked.

He shook his head. "I just came to say hi," he said. "I was wondering, if maybe, well …" he hesitated. "Maybe you'd like to go out with me some time."

She puckered her pink lips. "That could get me into trouble."

"Is that a no?"

"Just a caution. But if you just happened to ever-so-discreetly scribble your number down on the table, I think I might take notice of it," she winked. "Gotta go now."

"My name's Llewellyn," he said over the music.

"What?" she asked.
"Just call me Blue."

She did call. Called the very next day in fact. Sunday, his day off. "Well, what are you doing today, then?" he asked her.

"Me? Going for a big long walk."

"You a hiker?"

"I love the mountains. They keep me breathing, keep me in shape. You want to come with me?"

"Uh, sure," he said through his tar-filled lungs. "But I'm not in great shape."

"We'll take it easy," she assured him.

She picked him up in a rusty old brown Ford Mustang not yet old enough to be considered retro. She was wearing a hooded Gap sweatshirt under a black leather jacket, jeans, and hiking boots. She wore no makeup and her hair was pulled back. She looked as unlike a stripper as he could imagine.

"You've been here for a month and you haven't climbed any of these mountains?" she asked him, incredulous.

He shook his head.

"I just look at them and I want to run up," she said. "Why are you here then?"

"Because it's better than there, I guess," he said. "Money," he answered, thinking it was something she would understand.

"I came for these mountains," she gestured. "Let's take the gondola up Sulphur Mountain. Then you'll really be able to see what you're missing. Those boots aren't going to get you very far anyway."

It suited him to be lifted up into the air on a clear, bright blue day, sitting in a swinging cubicle, across from the prettiest girl he'd ever known.

It was a whole new perspective on top of the mountain where the air was thin and quiet. "I had no idea," he said.

"It's amazing, isn't it?" Amy beamed. "I love it here."

They drank hot chocolate in the café at the summit and Amy talked about her life in Niagara Falls. They weren't happy, the memories she recalled. "I *hated* high school," she groaned.

"Me too," he nodded. "I didn't last very long, actually."

"I got thrown out because my idiot boyfriend left his drugs in *my* locker."

"Oh, that's bad. I just dropped out."

"Yeah, well, I probably would have dropped out eventually anyway. So many assholes at McArthur."

"You went to McArthur?"

"Only for a year."

"My sister went there too."

"Where's your sister now?"

"University of Toronto."

"What's she doing there?" Amy asked, obviously impressed.

"She wants to be an archaeologist."

"That's cool."

"Yeah," he nodded, and looked down.

"Why do you look sad then?"

"Aw, I'm not really sad. It's just my sister's going through something weird right now. You know, like trying to find herself or something retarded like that. She'd kind of disappeared a while before she left anyway. Do you know what I mean?"

"You aren't close?"

"Used to be. Used to be like glue. Then she—I don't know—I think she was mad because after my parents split up, my dad stayed in touch with me, but not her. Like she was jealous, or hurt or something. So she kind of said, 'Fuck all this,' and went and moved in with this total dweeb and started going to university."

He felt embarrassed, like words were new for him and they were tumbling out without his full participation.

"She must be really smart," Amy said, encouraging him to continue.

"I'm really proud of her, you know, trying to make something out of her life, but she's become a bit of a snob in the process, like she doesn't really want to have anything to do with us any more. She thought I was a loser because I didn't have big ambitions like her, and she hated my dad because he was a fuck-up. The funny thing is, though, she's just like him. Both a couple of dreamers at heart."

"Your dad's a fuck-up?"

"Pretty much," Blue muttered. He couldn't believe he'd just said that to someone he didn't really know. "I'm talking too much," he apologized.

"My dad is too," she said. "But my stepfather is great. You know, after my mum died I continued living with him, and it was okay for a while, but then he got this new girlfriend and she moved in, and soon it was like *way* too small for the three of us. She was so lazy—and, like, I'm going out to work and helping my stepdad pay the mortgage and she's sitting on her ass all day. That's when I said to myself I had to just start my own life, you know?"

He nodded. He was sort of doing the same thing. "My dad disappeared," he told her.

"Really?"

"He was kind of losing it. I was in touch with him, right, and I was going down to Toronto to see him on weekends and stuff, and then one weekend, I just couldn't find him. I kept looking for months, but the guy had gone."

"Any clue where?"

"Apparently he'd been talking about going out west."

"Really," she said seriously. "So is that why you came out here?"

He hesitated, wondering if he should just stop here. But her face was open, so fresh that she looked like a clear river you'd trust was safe to drink. He'd never seen such clean water and it made him incredibly thirsty. "Partially," he finally replied. "But mostly because I needed to get away. Like you—I wanted to start my own life."

Once they'd reached ground level later that afternoon, she squeezed his hand and said, "You're the first guy I've ever shared that with."

"Hopefully, I'll be the last."

"Whoa. You move fast!" she laughed.

"I'm serious. I've never met anyone like you."

That's when she planted the first of a series of big ones on his lips. They both dove in for more, their breath steaming like geysers. In a tight, furious embrace, they carried each other back to her place and made love on the floor, and then the couch, and then the bed, and then the floor again. From top to bottom to bottom to top and all over again until they were laughing like children amazed by their own strength.

Their skin stung with rug burn as they lowered themselves down into the narrow bath. They passed a beer bottle between them and grinned stupidly in the first, wordless moments of love.

"She's amazing," he repeated at the end of the letter to his sister. "P.S.," he added. "Why don't you get your stupid ass back home and come out here and see me. Can't you take a break? Sounds like you could use one. Drive my truck out. It'll be excellent. Just put your foot all the way to the floor when you change the gears and put on your mascara *before* you get behind the wheel."

# Gold

The porter could see she was headed for trouble. She had always seemed a little strange to him, muttering as she did, all that cow manure under her nails, but now she'd picked up the pace and was moving with a peculiar intensity. He wanted to give her the benefit of the doubt and believe she was just memorizing things aloud for her final exam, but he wasn't so sure.

What Emma was, was deeply preoccupied. She thought she'd found something, something big, but she had to be sure, or at least surer, before she told Professor Rocker. She had to find a way to put it into words. A large area of flat rock at the far end of the site. A long linear crevice in rock that shouldn't crack—at least not in straight lines. It was wrong somehow. It was too deliberate. A couple of centimetres wide, it looked deep, deep enough to warrant investigation.

In her knapsack that day she had packed a bread knife and a flashlight. She lingered at the site at the end of the day, as everybody collected their gear and made their way to the bus.

"Aren't you coming, Emma?" Professor Rocker asked.

"I'm just going to finish this sketch. I won't be long. I'll take the next bus," she said, waving him off.

"All right then. But try and get some sleep tonight. You look like a wreck."

She nodded dismissively and continued with the pretence of sketching.

When they'd all left, she got the bread knife out of her bag and ran it through the crevice. She plunged the knife in as far as it would reach. She took the flashlight from her bag and held it over the split rock. The beam spilled into the width of the crack and then burst like a sparkler in the dead of night. There was a cave of some sort below. The rock must have been deliberately cut and placed overtop to obscure it. Her heart beat rapidly. She knew she was on to something big.

It came to her as a vision that night. Through the crack, in the hidden cave, there were a thousand skeletons. The jumbled remains of various bodies. A burial pit—an ossuary—a massive native grave. All the smaller graves of a century dug up; bodies and pottery lifted and lowered into a communal pit where they could sing as a chorus in the afterlife. Together forevermore under blue and orange skies, under the rain of a thousand seasons. The way burial should be: rubbing femurs and fibulas with everyone you've ever known and loved.

## Strictly Leather

Blue scribbled a note to his sister on the back of a postcard of two moose mating below the slogan: "Get Your Rocks Off in Banff." "Shacked up with Amy. Getting all domestic. Hope you're keeping your hands dirty," he wrote, and then flung it in the mail.

After their first weekend together, things between Blue and Amy continued in much the same way—with big expeditions during the day, and even bigger ones at night. She showed him the magic of her world, the mountains, the ice that never melts. She had otherwise discovered these wonders on her own and felt grateful for the sweet, doting presence beside her that made them seem all the more dramatic. She loved his size. Blue was larger than life: a complicated mixture of untamed innocence and erotic danger that had hooked her from the very beginning.

Together, they bought him proper hiking boots in a respectable store and Blue laughed at his feet looking normal and conservative. "Okay, I'm drawing the line here," he said. "You won't be getting me into a ski jacket or parka."

"No way, babe," she laughed. "I know you—strictly leather or lumberjack."

"That's right. And don't you forget it."

More than just the shoes had changed, though. He was learning how to breathe, climbing up the side of mountains, scrambling after his diminutive girlfriend who leapt over boulders with the ease of a deer.

Amy moved in with Blue a month to the day after they had first met. He got a bigger room at the Ptarmigan Inn and they took all the nasty framed pictures off the wall and put up posters of Jimi Hendrix and the Grateful Dead in their place. They gave it atmosphere. Filled the mini-fridge with cheap wine and processed cheese and burned incense when the cigarette smoke became oppressive. "You're a civilizing influence," he told her.

He called Elaine with the good news. He neglected to mention that Amy was a stripper. Elaine was relieved to hear that he'd met someone and she did an uncharacteristically motherly thing in response—she sent them a case of pickled things: beets, eggplant, mushrooms, and onions. She'd actually pickled them herself. Labelled them with her own brand of humour, a humour her children had never really seen—Blue's Beets, Elaine's Eggplant, Magic Mushrooms, and Oliver's Only Onions.

Blue didn't get it. Didn't get her sense of humour or what possessed her to pickle vegetables. He wondered if she might have found herself a boyfriend. Something to have unleashed this unprecedented outpouring of affection.

Elaine was proud of the way her children were turning out in her fantasies. She imagined Emma discovering the tomb of King Tut's father and turning the world of ancient ruins on its head. She imagined Blue, well adjusted and middle class, wearing an expensive parka and making weekend jaunts to Whistler where he skied with his girlfriend among the rich and fabulous. Having first felt abandoned, she had

187

come to savour the thought of them at this distance where she could assign them good lives and they couldn't disrupt her illusions.

Her desire to make maternal contact with Blue had, as Blue suspected, come fast on the heels of meeting a man, a good-looking man who, although he happened to be married, had started paying her a fair deal of attention. She'd boasted about her children to him, and in so doing, had constructed these successful lives for them.

Blue looked in the package his mother had sent and told Amy that meeting her had changed everything in his life.

Five nights a week Amy still took herself and her hot tamale of a body down the road in her brown Ford Mustang to take off her clothes for gaping guys who gave extravagant tips. He could handle it, he told himself. A job is a job. And she was resolute about this. "Some guys can't handle having a girlfriend who dances for a living," she had said before she agreed to move in. "But as long as you remember it's my job, and I'm a professional, you have nothing to worry about."

"But you met me there, didn't you?" he asked in one of his more insecure moments.

"That was different."

"But maybe another something different will come along."

"Blue, there's nobody like you."

"But I worry about you."

"Well, you get a few creeps in there occasionally, but the management usually makes it pretty clear that they're not welcome. Most of the guys just come to talk with their buddies, hang out, flirt a little, but, you know, they're pretty respectful all in all," she assured him. "Come with me tonight and I'll show you. Just watch how I work—you'll get it," she said.

He did go with her. He stayed the whole night, but there were rules he had to follow. He couldn't interfere with her while she was working and he had to pay like anybody else had to pay if he wanted her exclusive attention. It was mostly staff from the Banff hotels who came down to the club when their shifts ended to have a few beers and watch the show. It was uncomfortable, but if he drank enough beer, it seemed relatively harmless. The borders around bodies blurred. It was like looking through the dirty glass of a fish tank. Seahorses and shimmering fish swimming gracefully in and out and around static objects with wide hungry eyes. He almost felt proud. He loved a fish that no one else could catch. The other men were motionless, fixed in place, and abandoned there when the lights came up and the fish slipped away to their hidden caves. These men's lives ended when the lights went up, where Blue's never did.

For Amy's birthday they decided to rent a room in the Banff Springs Hotel and have a proper grown-up dinner in a big, old-fashioned dining room. They played Mr. and Mrs., him in a suit he'd borrowed from Mitch, and her in a little red satin dress she'd bought in Calgary. She wore heels so high he had to carry her like a new bride across the parking lot to the hotel entrance through the cold, teeming rain. They were giggling and happy, ordering the bottle of wine that fell in the exact middle of the wine list, simply because it fell there. They knew nothing more than it wasn't cheap and it wasn't too expensive.

They were surrounded by older white-haired couples and refined Japanese gentlemen, and they toasted each other with a clink so loud that the people at the table behind them turned around. The waiter delivered the roster of specials and said he would be back in a few minutes.

"What the hell is a fennel?" Amy whispered to Blue.

"Some la-di-da vegetable," he said, drawing upon knowledge

stored in his numbered days as a busboy for the hoity-toity. "Looks like celery, tastes like licorice."

"Gross," she sneered.

"Okay, Missus. What doesn't look gross then?"

"Maybe steak," she said. "They've got to have steak, right?"

"Aw, come on. You can have steak any time. Try something exotic."

"Okay, you choose, Mister Cosmopolitan."

"How about goose with cranberry glaze and portobello mushrooms?"

"I'll try it," she shrugged. "What are you going to have?"

"Steak," he said.

"You!" she cried out, throwing her napkin across the table at him.

They blew a light bulb with the cork of a champagne bottle in their room later and Amy let out a scream so piercing he thought someone might call the police.

"You nut," he said, slapping his hand across her mouth and throwing her down on the bed. She wriggled beneath him and he tickled her so hard tears ran down her reddened face. She bit his cheek then, clenching until he was forced to say, "Mercy."

They lay there, full, drunk, and out of breath, him on top of her. He looked into her eyes and said, "Why don't I make you a real missus?"

"Does that mean I can make you a mister?"

"Technically, I already am."

"Then it's not fair."

"Since when has life been fair?"

"But I want to make you something too."

"You have already."

"What's that?"

"Happy."

"How the hell did that happen?"

"God only knows," he laughed.

The next morning, in the sultry cloud of semi-sleep, he rolled her over onto her stomach. She purred beneath him and spread her legs. "Mmm. Just do it. No preliminaries," she rumbled into the pillow.

"You sure?" he whispered into her ear, pushing the full length of himself inside her.

"Sure," she groaned.

"How sure?" he whispered, lifting up her hips with one strong arm and slowly rubbing two wet fingers against her clitoris.

"So sure," she moaned.

"So sure you would marry me?"

"Mmm. If it always felt like this ... I'd—"

"I mean it, you know."

"Only if I can make you something more than happy. More than just a Mister Happy."

"*Just?*"

"Yeah. There's gotta be more."

"You've got big expectations, my girl."

"I just never thought happy was the end of it all."

He pulled out of her, flipped her over onto her back then. Looked at her with the seriousness of a Catholic in confession and said, "You're right. It isn't the end, the middle, or the beginning. But now that I found it, I wouldn't give it up for the world."

"Not for a better life? A happy family? A father?"

"Anything."

"Then yes," she said.

"Yes, what?"

"Yes, I'll marry you. As long as you promise it will feel like this always."

"Like what exactly? What am I agreeing to?"

"To always crawl inside and tell me the truth."

"Don't know if I always know the truth."

"Promise to pretend?"

"That I can do, girly girl. I can promise to promise to pretend."

# Big Bang Theory

She was the first person at the site that morning. She had her hands hammered deep into the pockets of her overalls and she was talking aloud, rehearsing a speech she was going to deliver to Professor Rocker. Emma could picture the headlines: Student's discovery advances understanding of North American prehistory by leaps and bounds. Emma Taylor (originally of Niagara Falls, now of the world), pictured here with her professor and mentor, Nick Rocker, points to the largest and most elaborate burial grounds ever discovered in North America.

But when Professor Rocker had listened to her impassioned monologue, he didn't leap into the air and scream, "*Eureka!*" He just sighed. "Emma, it's a little far-fetched. I mean, I'm all for a little creative thinking, but you've still got to make the facts add up."

"Okay. So here are the facts. There's a cave below here. This crevice is too clean and too deep to have been caused by any natural means. Someone sawed through the rock with a high-powered saw. And they must have done that for a reason. I think someone shifted these rocks here to cover something up—something that they thought would be more hassle than it was worth. I'm sure there's an ossuary below here."

"Emma, what you're telling me is one part fact, one part conjecture, and one part pure fantasy. You can't leap to those kind of conclusions. You're not even considering any other possibilities."

She bit her tongue, wanting to tell him: I can see it. I can see the bones of a thousand bodies right through there. About ten feet beneath where we're standing.

"And besides, Emma, we'd know if there was a burial ground here," Professor Rocker continued.

"But how would you know?"

"Because the area isn't subject to any native land claims and it's also been surveyed once before."

"Well, why are we here then? Why are we surveying it again?" she asked with increasing frustration.

"Because the first survey was done in the 1970s, but the proposed construction never happened. Legally, we're required to do another survey."

"So all this is basically some bureaucratic formality?" she said, getting angry.

"Ostensibly, yes."

"Well, why didn't you tell us that in the beginning?" she almost shouted.

"This is an *exercise*, Emma. A learning exercise."

"An exercise in patronizing us? Making us believe we're actually doing something worthwhile?"

"An exercise in technique, primarily," he said sternly. "But yes, also an exercise in the sobering reality of archaeological work."

"You know what your problem is?" she said, pointing at him.

"Careful, Emma," he warned her.

"You're bitter," she continued, undeterred.

"I'm realistic," he defended.

"Well, it's possible that they missed something the first time," she muttered, kicking a rock with the toe of her boot.

"I don't think so, Emma."

Emma was exasperated and unconvinced. "You don't even want to investigate? You're not even curious? You don't even want to satisfy yourself by finding your own answer? I mean, what if there really is a burial ground here? It could offer all sorts of insights on burial customs and native history. What if they just covered it up twenty-five years ago? Thought it better not to open up a huge can of worms?"

"Because no one would be that stupid or irresponsible," snapped Professor Rocker. "And besides, archaeology just isn't all that exciting. There's not a lot of intrigue and conspiracy going on, Emma. You're letting your imagination get the best of you."

"Well, at least I have an imagination!" she charged back.

The other students, who had arrived by this point, were standing in a silent cluster behind Emma.

"Unlike me, I suppose you mean," Professor Rocker replied.

"It's just that it all has to be so literal with you. You can't even entertain the possibility of something unexpected."

"I'm a scientist, Emma. Not an inventor," he said, his patience spent. "Archaeology is a science. Not the stuff of a romance novel."

Emma was now frothing at the mouth. "I have half a mind to phone up someone who'd really be interested—like the chair of your department or the press."

"Then you'd really only have half a mind," Professor Rocker retorted. "If you start making noises about something like this, do you know what happens, Emma? It means that this building doesn't go up for years. It means five to seven years of archaeological work as we are forced to prove beyond any doubt that there is nothing here. Five to seven years of wasted effort all spent pursuing *your fantasy*. It means red tape and bureaucracy into the millennium. It means that in a case like this they'll hire a professional surveying company next time. It means they won't want to have students working on surveys. It means it will be harder and harder for students here to get any practical experience digging. It means a fuck of a lot, Emma. A fuck of a lot of unhappy people—and believe me, that will include you."

"Are you threatening me?"

"I'm telling you not to be an idiot," he shouted.

Emma heard laughter behind her. She turned around and glared at the other students who were clearly revelling in the display. They nearly cheered when Rocker hurled the word "idiot" at the class pet. "What a primadonna," she heard one of the students mutter. "Quite the little hissy fit."

"You can all just fuck off!" Emma screamed, nearly hysterical. "Just go to hell! Dig deep enough and maybe you'll even find yourself there!" Emma wiped the tears from her face and picked up her bag to leave. She was so angry she could have skewered them all though the bellies and roasted them on a spit.

Then she heard Rocker's parting shot: "And another thing, Emma. In addition to patience, the most important thing about archaeology is teamwork."

Emma emerged from the subway an hour later and walked in dazed defeat down the summer street, sticky with spilt Coke and black tar and soft pink gum. She passed asbestos-lined buildings constructed in the architectural oblivion of the sixties, hot-dog vendors with

Eastern European accents, blue-eyed women with shrill laughs and arms full of books.

She pushed herself through her door and crashed into bed, muddy boots and all. Oliver was right, she'd realized, as she stormed away from the site. People did lack vision. The thought of being like Oliver was enough to make her want to chuck herself out the window, give up altogether. She cried a bucketful of tears and took three extra-strength Tylenols and fell into a deep and disturbed sleep instead.

*Vision. Perspective. Dreams.* Under a tickertape of Oliver's words she dreamt what felt like a recurring dream, although she was sure she'd never had it before. She was eighteen years old, but she had a head full of grey hair and yellow teeth and people kept addressing her as Oliver, or Mr. Taylor. She was in the airport and she wanted to shave her legs because she was going home, but she couldn't find her razor. She was searching for it in the bottom of her carry-on luggage, but all she could find was a giant breadknife with serrated edges stained with dried blood. She didn't know where the blood had come from. Perhaps she'd killed a rat in the back seat of the taxi on the way to the airport. She hoped she hadn't killed anything else. She was sure that if she licked the blade she'd be able to tell if the blood was that of a four-legged or two-legged animal.

The airline clerk was denying her entry. The picture in her passport was the girl she remembered being—Emma just after she'd first dyed her hair black—but they were addressing her as Sir, and telling her the passport she was carrying obviously belonged to someone else—someone younger and female. She was perplexed.

Blue suddenly appeared at the check-in. "It's okay," he said, winking at the woman behind the counter. "I can vouch for her. She's legit."

"But, Blue," Emma stammered as he led her away from the counter by the arm. "I don't understand what's going on."

"Just look straight ahead and keep a low profile," he said under his breath. "And don't do anything *unnatural*."

She had no idea what he meant by that so she just kept putting one foot in front of the other. But they weren't walking. They were sliding across the waxed floor and she could feel everyone stop and stare. When Emma turned to look back she saw they had turned to stone, Oliver and Elaine among them. Their fossilized eyes remained glued to Emma and Blue.

She felt Blue's hand beginning to crumble, turning to dust in her grasp. She screamed so loud that she stirred up the residue of a thousand crumbling bodies, leaving her shoeless and blind in the midst of a black cloud. Perhaps this is what it is to spontaneously combust, she thought. Perhaps this is what they mean when they talk about the origin of the universe being a big bang. There wasn't even a single whisper in the dark surrounding her. Not a shadow or an echo. Just the sound of her heart beating. Cardiac Morse code.

She awoke fourteen hours later, unsure where she was. She could sense the existence of parallel universes and multiple pasts. Dreams spill over borders, overflow the eavestroughs of places, threaten to pollute. Dreams could remind her of places she didn't really want to revisit because they felt dangerously incomprehensible, or incomplete. Being called a lezzy at thirteen because she had a best friend named Maxine who called herself Max because she wanted to be a boy. Kissing Blue under the porch because she thought boys didn't like her. And Oliver, who sent postcards from outer space.

She picked up the phone and called her brother, the first spoken words between them in too long. It was two a.m. in Banff, and he was slightly drunk, but he did his best when she told him that she'd fucked everything up and couldn't go back. He said things like: "Come on,

Emmy, don't be so melodramatic. Don't freak out. So this dig thing didn't work out. There'll be others. Why don't you just go home? Maybe you'll discover an ancient burial ground in the backyard. Fucking acres of arrowheads and bones and fossilized racoon shit. And you can take all the credit for the discovery. Didn't the Hurons used to torture their captives by pulling out their fingernails? What could be more exotic than that?"

Emma didn't tell her brother what was worrying her most—that she was dreaming up things that didn't and couldn't possibly exist. Just like Oliver. But Blue was trying, and maybe he was right. They had plenty of ruins in their own backyard—not Huron, mind you, but their own. Maybe Oliver had buried family heirlooms underneath the raspberry bushes. Maybe Elaine had laid to rest all that they had ever shared in that patch of dirt at the end of the garden where the sun refused to shine.

# Deadlock

Amy was trapped between Blue's knees again. It was the second time that week. She was near the foot of the bed, under the duvet, and Blue had her in a headlock and she could barely breathe. He was fast and furiously asleep. Rather than startle him, she gently stroked his calf and called out his name. She had worked her way through terms of endearment—babe, baby, Lou, honey, sweetie—by the time he woke up and released her.

He started to cry. He'd done it again. He could only say that he was sorry, that he didn't mean to hurt her, that he didn't know why, that he loved her.

"It's okay," she said, trying to calm him. But it did worry her. Blue had started dreaming wild dreams, and shouting his way through them. They were epics, with casts of machete-wielding thousands raping and burning women and fields. "What's worrying you, Blue?" Amy asked every time he awoke shouting. All he could do was stare ahead blankly and shake his head.

As soon as he'd asked her to marry him, Blue had become afraid. He began having difficulty with the promise of the promise to pretend.

He worried that as much as he wanted to marry Amy, marriage might actually be the gateway to hell. The first step on a slippery slope that plunged down into a torrid sea where a man and woman yelled in a kitchen and a husband became a hermit and a wife became an alcoholic. And babies came into marriages, they couldn't help themselves. And maybe fatherhood sent men flying into strange psychotic fits where they decided to build bridges and Eiffel Towers because they couldn't seem to do anything right in the day to day.

He could hear Oliver mocking him: *You actually believe someone loves you enough to want to marry you? And what about when you fuck it all up? What happens then? You'll be forced to go into hiding. There'll be an army out there. An army too big to defend yourself against.*

Rather than think about it, he found it easier to take the edge off the night by having beer for breakfast. When Amy went to work, he drank even harder stuff. The nights when he accompanied Amy were no different, just three times as expensive. As a consequence, he wasn't saving nearly as much money as he'd hoped. And that scared him even more. So he drank even more in order to assuage the fear that he would drink his way through money that was meant to take care of them. If he couldn't take care of them, he'd lose Amy, he knew that.

In the bruised circle of his reasoning, Blue become withdrawn and sullen. Whenever he accompanied Amy to the club these days, he just sat by himself at a table downing beer after beer. He would exchange a few words with one or two of Amy's friends and sometimes buy Larry, the manager, a beer. He generally ignored the customers, which was the safest thing to do because it could make you a little sick when they started to drool out of the corners of their mouths, but one night, after a week of bad dreams where men in gas masks were killing babies, someone caught his eye.

A balding middle-aged guy sat in the corner staring at Amy, and Blue watched his buggy eyes follow her everywhere around the room. "Creep," Blue muttered to himself. He had the look of the kind of pervert who would pay a kid to bend over. He motioned for her to come over, and held out his money—a couple of bills stapled together at one end—for a dance. After exchanging a few words, she started to move her hips in time to the music and peeled the straps of her dress off her shoulders and down the little length of her body. She spread his legs with her knees and danced her way down between them, her cleavage under his nose, her hair sweeping over his head and his shoulders. He kept his hands in his lap the whole time, like he was protecting himself. His bug eyes protruded further and further. Drool trickled out of the corner of his mouth.

It took all Blue's resolve not to walk over and punch the guy in the middle of his perverted face. Most men looked at strippers like they were unreal, you could see it in their faces—they knew at some level that it was the women controlling them, not the other way around, and that it was over when the song ended. A live porn video—without the possibility of pressing rewind. Then there was the occasional fuck like this who couldn't separate the fantasy from the reality—would creep around outside the club at the end of the night, tell a woman she'd been asking for it all night long, wouldn't give it up until he erupted in violence, and left her small and broken.

Blue stared at the bastard. He saw the possession in his ballooning eyes. He could see him imagining Amy fractured, split, splayed on concrete. He bit his tongue. Drew the bitter metallic taste of blood into his mouth. Held it there like it was venom.

When the song faded into a finish, Amy climbed back into her dress. But bug eyes held out another stapled wad of money for a repeat performance. She peeled off her dress and started to perform for him again. Blue was getting really angry now. "Fucking pervert," he spat, drops of blood cascading down his chin. When the second song ended and she had climbed back into her dress, the bug-eyed bastard held out yet another wad. "Oh, no fucking way," said Blue. As soon as Amy started to dance again he slammed his beer down and stood up. Amy looked over and glared at him. Blue puffed up his chest, pulled up his slouching jeans, and walked over to them. He pushed Amy aside and said, "Time's up, buddy."

Amy stood there awkwardly with her arms folded over her breasts. "I can handle this, Blue," she said quietly.

The guy looked smugly up at Blue and said, "I've paid for this. It doesn't stop until I say so."

"You don't fucking own her!" Blue shouted.

"Well, for as long as I pay her, I do," he sneered.

"Blue, it's okay, I can handle this," Amy interjected.

"As long as you pay her, she owns your dick, asshole!" Blue shouted. "And if *she* doesn't cut it off, I will."

The man had stood up by this time, and he was doing that "oh yeah" tough-guy stuff, when Larry came over and told Blue not to interfere. "Business is business," he said to Blue. "I'll bar you from this place if you keep interfering." Blue backed down then and Larry gave the man his money back and said, "Maybe some other night."

"She can keep it," the man said, pulling on his coat.

"I don't want it," said Amy, walking off in disgust.

After a day and a half of silence between them, Blue finally said he was sorry. But she was still mad. "You just can't do that, Blue," she said. "I don't want you around me when I'm working if you're going to act like a jealous asshole."

"It's not that. I wasn't jealous. It's just that guy. That guy is a fuck-ing creep. I swear, he looks like some kind of child molester or some-thing to me. Bit of reality problem, you know?"

"Blue, so the guy looks a little weird. He didn't try and touch me or anything."

"What's with those bills he passes to you? It's creepy the way he has them all stapled together."

"How should I know, Blue? Everyone's got strange habits. Even you. Sandwiching your girlfriend's head between your knees while you're asleep?" she shouted. "It's not exactly normal!"

"But I don't have any control over that!" he shouted. "You know that," he said, his face falling.

"Well, *that* scares me more than anything! Certainly more than a bunch of bills stapled together."

After one more night of anger between them, Blue started making an effort to draw Amy close again. He apologized over and over, said he would never interfere when she was working, asked her if she still wanted to marry him.

"Of course I do, you goof. I'm mad at you, but that doesn't mean I don't want to marry you. What about when we're married and I get mad at you? Or you get mad at me? Doesn't mean the whole thing's over."

He was amazed by the things that came out of her mouth. Are we even the same species? he wondered. We might both be from Niagara Falls but we're certainly not from the same world.

Just when things seemed to be getting back to normal, though, Amy realized they were nowhere near normal at all. She picked Blue's jeans up off the floor and a knife fell out of his pocket.

"What are you carrying this around for?" she demanded.

"Just in case."

"Just in case what?"

"We need protection."

"I don't think this is the way to handle things," she said. She couldn't imagine him ever using the knife. But she didn't understand why he'd even want to give himself the option.

Blue got really angry then, yelled that she didn't understand him, that some things he just had to sort out on his own, that she didn't know what was going on his head.

"Well, I'm all ears," she said, hands on hips.

He completely clammed up then.

"I give up, Blue. You don't want to talk to me? Don't talk, then. You sort whatever it is out yourself," she said, slamming the door.

# Dirty Hands

Emma held a cup of coffee in her hand and knocked on Ruthie's door. Ruthie looked like she'd been sleepwalking through a minefield, and listlessly gestured for Emma to come in.

"I came to tell you that I'm going home for a while—just till the beginning of next term," Emma said, sitting down on the end of Ruthie's bed. She knew she had to drop the course and forgo the credit, go home and get her guts back.

"What happened?" Ruthie asked with concern.

Emma didn't really know how to explain it. "Apparently I got a little carried away," she sighed. "Thought I was on to something—still think I was on to something—but managed to piss everyone off in the process."

"That doesn't sound irreparable," Ruthie said.

"It was a bit more dramatic than that. I really can't go back," she said, shaking her head, her eyes welling up with tears.

"It'll be okay," said Ruthie, putting her hand on Emma's forearm. "I'm sorry. I thought it was all going so well." Ruthie looked down and picked at a thread on the quilt on her bed. "It won't be the same without you here."

"I'll be back in the fall."

"Well, I'll still miss you."

"I'll miss you, too," Emma nodded. Ruthie clambered out of bed and started rummaging through her dresser drawer. "What are you looking for?"

"I want to give you something."

"What for?"

"So you'll remember me."

"I'm not going to forget you," Emma laughed.

"So you'll keep me with you then," Ruthie continued, throwing receipts and hair clips and dreadlocks on the floor.

"Hey, I thought your hair was real!" Emma said, startled.

"Extensions," said Ruthie. "Here," she said, holding out a brass turtle.

Emma smiled.

"My ma gave it to me when I came to Canada."

"Ruthie, I can't accept this. Not if your mother gave it to you."

"Well, I don't have a hell of a lot else that matters," Ruthie said. "I want you to have it."

Emma rubbed the turtle's back. Rolled the cool, smooth brass between her fingers. "Does it have any special meaning?"

"We had a big tortoise in the garden when I was growing up in Guyana. My ma loved that thing. Told us it was almost eighty years old. She could tell by the rings on it's back. My uncle said that was crap, but I still believed she could tell its age."

Emma told Ruthie to hang on a second. She was going to give her something too—something she'd carried with her for most of her life— the only thing she possessed that was as significant as Ruthie's gift. But it wasn't where she remembered leaving it. It wasn't inside her winter boots. It must be in the pocket of one of her pairs of pants, she thought. She started with the clothes on the floor, and then moved through the pants in her closet, flinging them off hangers and into the pile of clothes on the floor. Twenty pockets turned inside out and still nothing.

"It must be here somewhere," she mumbled to herself, collapsing onto the bed to think. And then she remembered having taken the dinosaur tooth to the dig one day with the intention of showing Professor Rocker. He'd been surly and uninviting that day, something about a rejected grant application, so she'd kept the tooth to herself. But in keeping it to herself it seems she might have lost it. She wasn't ready to give up hope entirely, but she wondered if the last of the dinosaurs had become extinct.

The only other meaningful thing she possessed was the scrapbook of wild imaginings. She was a little reticent to part with it, but the words were indelibly etched in her brain—she didn't need a hard copy any more. She worried that it wasn't entirely hers to give, though Blue had gone without any mention of it. Wherever he had gone, he didn't seem to need it.

"But this is such a big part of your history," Ruthie said.

"I'm not interested in imagining any more lives for myself," Emma sighed.

It wasn't the easiest journey she'd ever made. It was humiliating to have to go back home—to have to return to the place she'd spent so much energy on trying to escape. It didn't begin at all well with Elaine saying, "Emma, you look ill. Have you started going grey?"

Emma's back arched immediately, and she was sure her hair was standing on end. "It wasn't exactly Club Med, Mum!" she threw back.

"Have you been irresponsible?" Elaine asked.

"What kind of question is that?" Emma barked. And then it occurred to her that Elaine might be attributing her ashen pallor to morning sickness. What could be further from the truth? She wasn't sure anything could grow inside her. It was barren ground for the miles you could stretch her intestines. "I had to come home, Mum, and it's not what you're thinking. I needed a break. It's like I told you. I had a big fight with my professor and he suggested I'd better drop the course." That wasn't exactly the truth, but it was a hell of a lot less humiliating.

"But that doesn't sound fair," Elaine remarked.

"It's not a question of fair, Mum. Listen—can we just forget it?"

Despite the rocky beginning, Elaine put an arm around Emma's shoulder and said, "Well, whatever happened, I'm sure you made the right decision. It'll be all right." Elaine's words hit Emma in some soft spot, despite herself.

That night, Emma stared at the plate of lasagna in amazement. "What happened, Mum? Did you discover your mothering instinct while I was away?"

Elaine had never been a good cook, never even remotely interested. It was all sardines and fish fingers and mashed potatoes when they were growing up, and occasionally Elaine's most experimental dish, her guess-what's-in-it meatloaf, which contained one tinned item from the cupboard—it could have been tuna, or cranberry sauce, or cream of mushroom soup—it really was anyone's guess.

"Don't be mean," Elaine called from the kitchen. "I've always tried my best. It hasn't been easy."

"I know, Mum."

"And besides," she said, entering with the Parmesan cheese, "I've missed you two."

"You're kidding," Emma couldn't help saying.

"No, I'm not kidding. What kind of mother would I be if I didn't miss you?"

Emma looked at her mother as if for the first time. Something was different. Elaine had had her ears pierced, but that was only part of it. And then she identified the change: her mother looked happy.

Emma's room really hadn't altered much since she was a child. It had only been painted that once long ago and it was looking more like a flat soufflé now than the perky custard it once resembled. The closet was full of unfashionable shoes that Elaine obviously hadn't had the heart to part with. Fond memories? wondered Emma. Dancing shoes?

Emma spent much of the first night dreaming about Elaine's lasagna—diving through the rich, alternating layers of comfort, devouring them as if she hadn't eaten in months. Comfort like the feeling of chocolate melting in your mouth in a warm river of hot tea.

She awoke sweating under a woollen blanket on the hottest day on record. Elaine came in without knocking and sat down on the end of her bed. "How did you sleep?" she asked her.

"Good," Emma nodded. "What time is it? Don't you have to go to work?"

"I quit," her mother said, smiling.

"You quit?" Emma asked, aghast. "But, Mum—how the hell are you going to support yourself?"

"I have other means."

"Like what? Lottery winnings? Did Dad suddenly start sending alimony or something?"

Elaine smiled, but mostly to herself, Cheshire catlike.

"What's going on, Mum?"

"There's a man in my life," she said with a shy smile.

"A what?"

"You heard me, Emma. Don't act so shocked."

"But what kind of man?"

"A very attractive intelligent man."

"And he's supporting you or something?"

"He's very kindly offered to help me while I try my hand at writing," she replied coyly.

"You're going to be a writer?"

"It's what I always wanted to be."

"I didn't know that."

"I know it might surprise you to hear this, Emma, but before I was a mother, before I was a wife, I was a person with dreams of my own."

"And you gave them all up for this?"

"I hadn't intended to."

"So why did you then?"

"Because somebody needed to make money, Emma. Your father couldn't hold a job."

"But why did you marry him in the first place?"

"I was in love."

"But why?"

"Because he was different. Because he was a dreamer."

"But I thought that's what you hated about him."

"Yes and no. It was exhilarating at first, particularly when our dreams were shared. But you know, you need a balance. You can't just keep floating on air. His dreams never amounted to anything, they were totally unrealistic, but for some reason he couldn't see that. In the end I felt like he'd manipulated me into supporting his flaky, far-fetched endeavours and given me very little but broken promises in return."

"So you felt cheated."

She nodded. "But ironically, he was the one who acted as if he'd been. He was always telling me I had no imagination, no vision."

Emma just about choked on her saliva.

"What's wrong?"

"It's just those words. I thought I had found something on the dig this summer, something of real importance, but my professor didn't even want to pursue it. He wasn't curious at all. And so we had this fight—and I said *exactly* those words to him." Emma felt sick and put her head to her knees.

"You must have heard your father say them before."

"But I wasn't copying him. I believed it."

"It's okay, Emma."

"But it's not! I don't want to turn out like him."

"You're not going to turn out like him."

"But I already sound just like him."

"The words maybe, Emma, but not necessarily what they mean. You're imaginative and you're passionate, but you're doing something with your life. Your father was all talk and no action."

Emma paused to take it all in but it was too much from too many directions. Elaine stood up and straightened her skirt. "I'm going to the market. Is there anything you need?"

Emma shook her head and lay back down in her bed. "What's this new guy's name?" she asked as Elaine was just about to go.

"You don't need to know," her mother said.

"What do you mean I don't need to know?"

"You're never going to meet him."

"Why the fuck not?"

"Because he lives in Ottawa, and he's married."

"You're kidding. Oh, Mum. You're somebody's mistress?"

"It's not like that," she sighed.

"It sure sounds like that."

"His name is Richard," Elaine said, closing the door behind her.

Easy enough for Elaine to move on, Emma thought. She'd only been married to Oliver, she wasn't cursed with shared blood. It didn't matter if Emma never saw her father again, she'd forgo the opportunity if it were ever presented. He was right there inside her, genes and all, he was inescapable, even if she moved to Johannesburg and had a facelift and became an anti-Apartheid activist and married a man from Soweto, he would always be there inside her, chronic, like an illness.

That night at dinner, Elaine asked Emma what she was planning on doing with herself for the rest of the summer. Emma said she might just go to sleep until September, but Elaine, for whom the memory of Oliver pulling the covers over his head for weeks at a time was still so acute, told her she might want to get herself a job, keep herself occupied rather than allow herself to get depressed.

Emma didn't have much of a history of employment. She'd been fired from every summer job she'd had. The one time she waitressed, she was fired for not wearing her shoes properly. She shuffled her way on squashed leather heels to clear tables where women wearing pantyhose in hues with names like Perfect Pearl and Crown Jewel lunched on little bits of green with dressing on the side and recorded calories ingested in little black notebooks with gold and silver pens.

Despite feeling she was inherently unemployable though, Emma knew she'd have to bite the bullet and get a job. She'd have to put herself to use. She'd have to prove to herself that she could hold a job, and tame the Oliver within.

It took Emma about a week to leave her mother's house, and when she finally did, she insisted on taking a taxi. She sat in the back seat and locked the doors on either side of her. She was feeling decidedly paranoid. The streets seemed totally unfamiliar, and she worried that the man behind the wheel was bent and determined on driving off the escarpment and down into the depths of some strange city. But what place could be stranger than Niagara Falls? Everyone's a stranger here, Emma thought. The people who live here disappear: they are pushed aside by the millions who pour through on their own quests for romance and wonder.

It was a mixed blessing. It's what allowed her to walk down a street reeking of multicoloured popcorn and into the ice cream parlour next to Ripley's Museum of Believe It or Not and tell the manager she was interested in applying for the job. She sat in the freezer and memorized the thirty-two flavours in less than ten minutes and the manager told her that was the fastest anyone had ever done it and said she'd probably look really pretty in the brown-and-pink-striped uniform. She sighed and pulled the apron over her head.

# Horizon in Her Eyes

The knife came out of Blue's pocket, swam like a samurai's sword in front of the bug-eyed bastard's face. Polygonal eyes, taunting and threatening, lecherousness replicated a thousand times over. The bastard spoke like he had mud settled in his lungs. Spoke slow and water-laden and then swept over Blue like a giant wave sending him crashing to the floor. Blurry, too blurry for Blue to remember in any detail, so blurry that he could almost pretend it had been a nightmare. But there were tangible indicators: a scar across Blue's forehead, part of his ear missing, Amy, sullen and worried.

"Don't leave me, Amy," he begged her.

"Just try and talk to me," she said, squeezing the back of his neck, holding up his sad and injured face.

He would have to win her back again. He would have to grovel and sweeten. It was easy enough to do because there was a hammer knocking so hard against his skull that he was lying prostrate on the floor. He'd been humbled flat by whatever had happened. Above all, though, it was easy to find his way back because Amy loved him. She'd been terrified by what she'd seen, but she was able to forgive the man who was a boy because she knew he was full of dark secrets and she'd rather they erupted in the light than see Blue implode like a dark star.

He promised to stop drinking, and he took to cooking extravagant meals for her over a camping stove in their hotel room. It was amazing what he could do with two burners and two pots.

"Maybe you should become a chef," Amy said.

"Yeah, right," he laughed.

"I'm serious."

"And would you be my waitress?"

"No," she shook her head. "I want my own career. And it won't be dancing. I won't be dancing that much longer. You know, at twenty-five, these won't look so perky any more," she said, cupping her breasts.

"You mean, I'll have them all to myself one day?" he said, lifting up her shirt and kissing her between her breasts.

"You have them all to yourself already, greedy boy."

"What kind of career are you thinking about?"

"Don't know. Maybe a hairdresser, or a makeup artist."

"You'd probably have to go back to school."

"That would be okay. As long as I knew there was a reason for being there, it would be okay. Are you still thinking about a tattoo shop?" she asked him.

He nodded. He had been, loosely, for a while now, thinking of being a tattoo artist. Drawing purple and green on young skin. Drawing out the bad blood and sealing the skin with art. His own. He was sketching more and more. Exhausting napkins, he'd moved on to bigger canvases. He'd flipped over the plastic tablecloth on their table and drawn the horizon across its entire length. A weak sun crept up over mountains in the distance. Amy couldn't bear to set her plate down on it. She sat instead, with dinner in her lap. "It's so beautiful, Blue. And all that with just a black marker."

"What's missing?" he prodded her

"The elk?"

He nodded and picked up his pen. He drew girl-elk and boy-elk and black bears and marmots. An eagle flew overhead, a hot-air balloon descended in a valley. Mounties rode horses in single file. He added Bambi and Winnie-the-Pooh just for her. On the table was a map of a beautiful world. Heaven-bound, he added butterflies.

Amy brought him colour. An extravagant set of acrylic paints, all housed in a cherry wood box with a gold clasp. Blue brushed tears away; he told her about Picasso and the blue faces broken up into squares. He added colour to the tablecloth, and Thumper the Rabbit at Amy's request.

Next, Amy bought him five huge sheets of expensive paper and rubbed his shoulders as he sat and ran his palms in circles over the paper in gratitude. She was formulating a plan in her head, thinking about their futures. "Babe?" she whispered in his ear. "You know, maybe we should take a break and go back home for a while."

"To Niagara Falls?"

"Yeah."

"But you hate the place. And I'm not going anywhere without you."

"It's a shit hole," she agreed. "But I could handle it for a while. I could handle it with you."

"But what would be the point?"

"I just thought maybe you needed some family around you. Some familiar scenery. Something. Maybe it would help."

"But you're family. You're familiar."

But I'm tired, and I'm worried, and I can't be everything, she thought to herself.

He walked down the main street in the late afternoon, walked right to the edge of town and blew smoke rings in the direction of home. They floated out of his mouth and travelled east, dissipating in the distance. He took that as a sign. If the wind had carried them back west, he'd have had reservations.

When Blue heard that Oliver had gone west, he knew in his heart that he would eventually follow, even if he didn't really know it in his head. He thought he might just find him. That he would walk into a bar one day and the guy would just be sitting there as if he'd been waiting for years for Blue to walk in and say, "Hi, Dad, how's it going?" He'd come in search of his father and he'd found true love instead. True love that felt like everything. Amy couldn't be everything. He understood it because he often wasn't sure whether he could be anything, let alone everything, for her.

"So what are we going to do in Niagara Falls?" he asked her over pork and beans that night.

"I don't know," she shrugged. "Pretty much the same as we do here, I guess. Work a lot, drink a lot, fuck our brains out," she laughed.

"Guess that doesn't sound so bad," he smiled.

"Well, what about getting your business started? It's what you want to do," she encouraged him. "Why wait?"

"Could," he said, nodding his head. "But there is a small issue of money."

"So you work for someone else for a while. And besides, I'll help you."

He blushed, pulled up his sleeve, and then said, "First tattoo I get is going to cover up these lame-ass initials." It was his last chance of becoming another boy.

# Wings

Emma and Elaine are waiting for Blue at the bus station. He's come home alone to set things up for when his girlfriend arrives at the end of the month. Emma is alarmed by her brother's appearance. He's wearing a tuque pulled down to his nose and he's obviously covering something up, because although he might think it looks cool, there's no way he can really see. She hugs him and gingerly pushes his tuque up over his eyebrows. He's got a big scar across his forehead and his ear looks like a dog's breakfast.

"Oh fuck, Blue," she winces. "What the hell happened?"

"Oh, don't worry about that," he shrugs. "What the hell happened to you? Did you lose it this summer, or something?"

"Come on," Elaine says, separating them and taking them each by the hand like they are four and five years old. They seem like children again. She's not sure she can handle it—she didn't do well with it the first time. In the distance she'd inflated them into adults with happy independent lives. It was much simpler than the reality that has arrived home.

Blue picks away at his food that night with idle distraction. "What do you call this?" he whispers to Emma.

"It's called moussaka," Emma tells him.

"No kidding," he nods. "You know, she sent me pickles."

"She sent you what?"

"Pickles. With fancy labels and stuff."

"That's weird."

"You're telling me."

Emma stares at Blue with her fork suspended in mid-air.

"What?" he says. "What are you staring for?"

"No reason," she shrugs. "Just haven't seen you in a while." She's taking him in and he's uncomfortable being scrutinized. His face has become harder, less baby, more square, and there's a twisted line so deep between his eyebrows that Emma imagines slipping a quarter through it, pretending he is a parking meter. His mouth hangs open. His jeans are too tight and sit just underneath the belly he proudly calls his "Miller muscle." He has a shaved head, a scruffy goatee, and sideburns on his face. Her baby brother is disguised as a biker daddy. If I didn't know you, she thinks, I would cross the street if I saw you coming.

"What are you thinking?" he asks, a little annoyed by her silent stare.

She says, "I was saying 'booly boo' to you, telepathically."

"We've been trying that for years—you know it doesn't work. It's not even cute any more, Em. It's stupid. Meaningless."

But it used to mean everything, she thinks, feeling hurt. "Too grown up now for baby speak, are you?" she asks him.

"It's a little embarrassing, Em."

"You sound like somebody who's ashamed of his native tongue. You know, you lose your language, you lose your identity, your origins, your culture."

"Thank you, professor," Blue says snidely.

He thinks about it later. If it were that simple, as simple as changing your language, he'd be fluent in everything but English. But he is gearing up to defect. He's headed for initiation into a new tribe—a band of tattoo artists, where it's all about survival of the fittest, and he's being groomed for Alpha Male.

It begins with a systematic survey of tattoo shops in Niagara Falls, not a huge deal, considering there are only two and a half. The survey leads him straight through the door of the Artful Dodger. The owner, Billy, is the only artist in town who categorically refuses to do "I Love Mom" tattoos, and it is this display of defiance and originality that stops Blue there.

He soon ingratiates himself. First, he has Billy stencil a Celtic dragon over the initials he's been embarrassed by for years. "No worries," Billy says. "We'll fix it for you, man." He then proceeds to punch needles into Blue's arm. Blue watches in fascination as his skin bubbles with pinpricks of blood and childhood's lame attempt is suddenly masked with an image of the fierce.

In gratitude, he buys Billy a six-pack of Molson Canadian. They drink it together on a Friday night while Billy is finishing up a nine-hour stretch on a man's shaved back. Blue asks if he might be able to hang out and watch Billy work. "I really want to learn how it's done," Blue says.

"It's a strange job," Billy tells him. "You've got to have artistic talent, real patience, people skills, and business sense. You've gotta be fearless and smart." He hasn't exactly said yes, but he hasn't said no either.

The next day, Blue brings his sketchbook. Billy flips through it quickly and says, "Yup. You got talent. No question about that. But what about people skills. Have you got those?"

"Like what?" Blue asks.

"Okay. What are you going to do when a twelve-year-old girl comes in here wanting a tattoo?"

"Um … Ask her if she's got her parents' permission?"

"You're going to say *no*. Even if she has her parents' permission. You tell her that she hasn't finished growing yet. That whatever she does, that tattoo's going to grow with her."

Blue knows that only too well. He's got a mess on his arm to prove it.

"It's going to distort," Billy continues. "Like if you draw a heart on some little girl's butt, it's gonna look like some old guy's testicles by the time she's forty. You know what I mean?"

"Okay," Blue nods, getting it. "So give me another situation."

"Say a guy hates the tattoo you've just given him."

"Um … Try and convince him it looks really good?"

"First of all, you always make sure they choose the design, not you. If they hate the design in the end, they have no one to blame but themselves. You make a stencil of the design and rub it down onto their skin. You get them to approve the stencil. If they're at all hesitant to begin with, send them away and tell them to come back only if and when they're sure. It's a lifetime commitment—they've gotta be prepared. That's their responsibility, not yours."

"Okay," Blue nods. "Next?"

"You've just done a big piece of work on this guy. He tells you he doesn't have any cash. He offers you drugs as payment."

"Just say no?"

"That one," he winks, "is your call."

By the end of the following week, Blue is officially Billy's apprentice. Apprenticing seems to involve wiping down counters and answering the phone, and when he isn't busy cleaning, punching needles into grapefruit. "Resembles human skin," Billy had explained, dropping a bushel full of them at his feet. Blue laughed, and covered dozens of grapefruit a day in black ink for the next week.

By the time Amy arrives a couple of weeks later—having driven that brown Ford Mustang straight across the country to Niagara Falls—not only does Blue have a job, but he's managed to rent them a furnished bachelor apartment above a dry cleaners. Elaine, who seems happy to have her son back, gives Blue a Sears gift certificate with strict instructions to spend it on a shower curtain, cutlery, and towels before his girlfriend arrives. The apartment is just a dull white box with grey industrial carpet full of cigarette burns, but thanks to Elaine it is stocked with the things she has told him a girl would like to come home to.

"The fumes are excellent here, man," Blue jokes with Amy. "Even the roaches like them."

"At least they're legal," says Amy, putting her arms around his neck and jumping up to straddle his waist. "I forgot how beautiful you were," she says, kissing his face.

"Beautiful is for girls," he blushes.

Amy has no trouble getting a job. She gets the lunch shift at Ye Olde English Pub and buys a dozen white shirts from Sears. She isn't going to make a fraction of the money she made stripping, but there is no way she is going to take her clothes off in her own home town.

"Disgusting," she shudders. "Imagine—my father could walk in, or my grade six teacher, or some guy I used to date. It'll do for now," she says, but what she really hopes to do is go to hairdressing school the following spring. As soon as she returns to Niagara Falls, she starts acting out the fantasy by doing a lot of dramatic things to her own hair. It's not long before she is as bald as Blue, thanks to a few too many experiments. Billy gives them a gift of his-and-her tattoos: spiderwebs for the backs of their bald necks.

After three weeks of tattooing fruit, Blue is bored. One afternoon, when Billy goes out to get supplies, Blue decides he is ready to do the real thing. The next unsuspecting customer, a blue-haired girl with a pierced eyebrow, walks into the shop and asks him what he'd charge to draw a ring of thorns around her neck. He guides her into the chair, talks to her about the sensitivity of the neck, and asks her to consider having it done somewhere else because, in time, the skin on her neck, like all necks, will sag.

"But I'm not planning on getting old," the girl says, startled.

"No, no one plans to. It just happens."

She says maybe she needs to think about it some more and thanks him for his patience. Blue is a natural.

In walks the next unsuspecting customer. A tough little man with a goatee, asking for barbed wire to be drawn across his shoulders. Into the chair. Blue sketches barbed wire, makes a stencil of it, disinfects the man's skin, and rubs the purple ink from the stencil down onto his shoulders. Blue shows him the new needles, dons his latex gloves, says, "You all right, buddy? You're turning a little green, there."

"Yeah, I'll be okay," the man says, although he looks like he might pass out.

"Just remember to breathe," he reassures the man. "It'll take about forty-five minutes. If you need me to stop, try to tell me rather than show me. Okay, buddy?"

The man inhales deeply and closes his eyes. The needle whistles and sings and he runs it over the man's back as if he were skating on ice. Blue doesn't blink for half an hour. Half a beautiful hour where he loses himself in a river of black ink.

At that moment, Billy walks in. "What the fuck?" he says over Blue's shoulder. Blue turns and glares at him, and Billy takes a step backwards. He nods then, and raises his eyebrows. "Nice work, man," he says.

When he is done, Blue holds up a mirror and the man looks at his swollen back, saying, "Fuck, fuck, fuck, that's so cool."

Blue snaps a Polaroid and sticks it up on the mirror. His first official job. An undeniably beautiful piece of work. The man hands over a hundred bucks, Blue hands Billy forty, and that is that.

He is good, better than good, and better every day. They trust him, this stream of strangers. Despite his size. Despite the scars on his face. Perhaps even *because* of his size and scars. It's a heady, powerful feeling.

He puts his money away, stuffs it into an old army boot, and dreams and schemes with Amy about the shop he wants to open. With Amy's savings and the loan Elaine has agreed to give him, he'll have his own shop sooner than he'd ever imagined possible. He'll call it Dyeing Arts and he imagines that Amy can have a hair salon in the back when she's done her course. He's found his calling.

He tattoos Amy. A big monarch butterfly on her bum. One wing on each cheek. She squeezes her cheeks together and the butterfly flies.

"Thank you for giving me my wings," she says, rubbing her naked body against his chest.

He replies, kissing her with the redness of his full lips. "I love you, girly girl," he mumbles into her neck. In that moment, life is better than it has ever been. But no matter how good, Blue's moments have never lasted long.

# Slipping

Emma is on her way to meet Blue's new girlfriend and see their new apartment. She has a head full of ambivalence. In her jealousy, she'd been quite prepared to pass scorn on Amy because she was a stripper. She wanted to hate her for something. But when Blue had put Amy on the phone to "meet" Emma, Emma had to admit that she sounded really sweet, open, even deferential.

Emma climbs up the fire escape at the back of the dry cleaners. Someone's made a lame attempt to plant some geraniums in a plastic container hooked onto the rails. Emma's on her way home from work, still in her brown-and-pink-striped uniform, with at least half of thirty-two flavours splattered across her shirt. She's carrying a bag of books she picked up en route from the library. She's back to reading trashy novels, back to life-before-Andrew, and what a relief it is.

"I'm really happy to meet you," Amy says, opening the door. She gives Emma a big hug like she's known her all her life and then picks up Emma's bag and says, "Blue's told me so much about you. Brags about you all the time—you know, going to university and all. He calls you 'my sister the professor.'"

226

Emma is surprised. It was only last Christmas that Blue was telling her it all sounded completely useless. She takes Amy in—all five foot one of her. She seems to have remarkable strength for someone too small to change a light bulb as she hoists Emma's bag full of books over her shoulder. She looks young enough that it wouldn't surprise Emma to hear her say she's got to be back by curfew.

The apartment is overheated and smells of stale cigarette smoke. The television is on and the ashtray on the table in the living room is overflowing. Amy picks it up to empty it, embarrassed. "Sorry, it's a sty. We've both been working lots."

"Wanna beer?" Blue asks Emma, closing the door behind her. "Amy brought a Mustang full of stash back from Alberta."

"Sure," Emma nods.

"You know, I'm glad you're back here," he says, collapsing onto the lumpy brown sofa.

"Me too, Blue," Emma sighs. "It's been a pretty fucked summer." She's been feeling flat: now that she's settled into the routine of her boring job, she feels the full weight of the truck that ran her over.

"You said it," he nods.

"So are you going to tell me what happened to your face or do I have to guess?" she asks him.

"Aw, it's no biggie, really. I just got done for D and D."

"D and D?" she asks, confused.

"Drunken and disorderly," Amy says. "More than once."

Blue is silent. He crosses and uncrosses his legs.

"Things weren't going so well," says Amy. "That's why we decided to come back here for a while," she explains.

"What happened?"

Amy looks at Blue and Blue looks at Amy and lowers his eyes. "So go ahead and tell her if you want." Blue's willing to let Amy do all the talking because she seems to have a need to tell the story, where he does not.

"Down at the club where I was working," Amy begins to explain. "Well, a lot of the guys from the hotels in the area would come down there when their shifts ended and have a few beers and watch the show. Blue was great—he came down all the time and waited for me to finish so we could go home together. I know it can be hard on some guys, watching their girlfriends dancing up there and everything, but it's just a job, like any other job, and I'm good at it and it pays way more than I could make doing anything else.

"There was this one guy, though. He was a little older and kind of strange, and he would come in once in a while and sit by himself and usually pay me for a couple of table dances. I don't know what it was about this one guy in particular, but Blue just didn't like him. Just took an instant dislike to him. He never touched me or anything like that, but yeah, he was kind of creepy."

"Fucking child molester," Blue mutters.

"Blue's got some idea about this guy ... Well, anyway," Amy continues. "This one night a while back, Blue's there getting drunk and the old guy comes in, parks himself in a chair, and hands me a hundred dollars to dance a song for him. Once that song's over, he gives me another hundred. And then he tries to do it again. Usually you only dance two songs, you know, max. But the guy's paid a lot of money, so I start dancing for him, and then Blue walks over and shouts, 'Time's up, buddy!'

"It's a little weird for me, because, you know, I'm working, and the guy just looks at Blue and they start fighting.

"I'm like, 'Blue, it's okay, I can handle this.' You know, I've dealt with creeps before, but Blue won't leave it alone. He says he's going to cut the guy's dick off. Then Larry, the manager, comes over and tells Blue not to interfere when I'm working. You know, Larry's a good guy and everything, but business is business. He says he'll get Blue barred from the place if he keeps interfering. So Blue backs down and Larry gives the guy back his hundred bucks and says to him, 'Maybe some other night, buddy,' and the guy skulks off.

"We were both pretty stressed out by the whole thing, but I thought we were okay until one night I found a knife in Blue's jeans. So I asked him, 'What are you carrying this around for?' and he's like, 'Just in case.' So I'm like, 'Just in case what?' And then he says, 'Protection.' I knew what he was thinking. And I got all upset because I just didn't think that was the way to handle things. It never is. Anyway, then he got really mad at me and said I didn't get it, and so I'm like, 'So tell me, I want to understand,' but he just clams up. Not a word."

Emma and Amy both look at Blue then, but he's just silent, staring down at the carpet. He takes a giant swig from his can of beer.

"So I let it go," Amy continues. "Fine, he's got to make his own decision about this. I mean, I didn't think he'd use the knife or anything, but things can get rough in there, and like, why even give yourself the option?

"So, wouldn't you know it, the guy does come back a couple of weeks later. And he sits in exactly the same place and fixes his eyes on me and hands me two hundred dollars this time. What am I supposed to do? The guy's paid, it's my job, he might be a lech, but as long as he's not touching me he's not really doing anything wrong. Blue walks over toward me then, and, of course, he absolutely freaks. He pulls me by the hair and tells me to get out of the way, and starts shouting at the guy. Says he's been waiting for him to come back so he could do what he promised. He pulls out the knife and says, 'I'm going to slice your fucking dick off!' I'm pleading with him because I know he's going to get thrown out, and sure enough, there's Larry saying, 'Blue, I warned you the last time.'

"God. Then the guy grabs the knife out of Blue's hand and takes a swipe at his ear. Holy fuck, Blue was bleeding and then the bouncers are on top of the both of them, pounding the shit out of them. I'm scared out of my mind, and then we've got the cops in there and there's a fucking ambulance waiting to take them to the hospital.

"It's me and Blue and this creepy fucking guy together in the back of the ambulance. Can you believe it? These two guys have to go to hospital together. And the whole time, the guy's staring at me and Blue's saying, 'I'm gonna fucking kill you.' You know, and his head's like pouring with blood and everything."

"So what happened?" Emma begs.

"It was awful. After they get all stitched up, then they have to go down to the police station. They both get charged with D and D and the guy wants to charge for attempted murder. I'm like, 'Blue, let me just talk to him and see if I can get him to drop the charges.' You know, like I can just say, 'Sorry about my boyfriend, he gets a little jealous sometimes, especially if he's had a few beers,' but Blue says, 'No way. You have no idea what guys like this are capable of.' I'm not really sure what he means, but he won't say any more."

Amy lets out a big sigh and shakes her head.

"Blue?" Emma prods him.

"Em?" he says, shrugging. He has nothing to add. He doesn't want to be having this conversation. Amy can go ahead and tell the story, because when she does, it doesn't sound like him at all. It sounds like some angry young man, some guy he's not sure if he wants to know. He doesn't remember it exactly this way. He doesn't actually remember much about it. He remembers the guy walking by him and saying something provocative along the lines of "jailbait pussy." He remembers the guy's eyes and he remembers slow motion and then a surge and the whack of the floor and then blood and an ambulance.

The guy Amy's describing isn't him. But he can't always keep that guy at such a distance. He's stopped looking in the mirror lately, because occasionally he can see evidence of him lurking in the reflection.

"Is there any more?" Emma asks Blue.

"Nothing to tell. Guy dropped the charges."

"Well, thank God for that."

"He was scared of getting busted."

"But why? You're the one who pulled a knife on him."

"Yeah, but my record's clean."

"Do you know the guy?"

"I know his type." Blue sits motionless for a moment, and then goes to the fridge to get another beer. He opens the fridge door and stares at the cans distractedly. He begins to rearrange them into the shape of a pyramid. A precarious balancing act.

"Is he okay?" Emma whispers to Amy.

"He's up and down," she says. "But it's been better since we came back here. Blue's really doing well with this tattoo thing," she enthuses. "Right, hon?"

# ID Me

The next time Emma sees Blue he looks about a thousand times happier. She, on the other hand, is feeling like shit. She grits her teeth through work. Her job seems so pointless she thinks about quitting at four-thirty every day, but point or no point, she knows she has to continue.

Amy is making pasta in the kitchen and Blue passes Emma a beer and starts talking about his plans. "I really want to establish a reputation with my shop—you know, for quality work. Billy's done a lot. He's got himself a reputation, but he's more like a mechanic than an artist, if you know what I mean. So anyway, what I'd like to do is maybe open up a bunch of other shops, and maybe one day I'll even have a chain of stores across the country," he beams.

His plans are so big they sound familiar to Emma, not the details, but the sheer magnitude of them. He's got it too, she thinks. He's got Oliver's vision, but she can see there is a critical difference. Blue's dreams seem to be coming true.

Elaine had said that there were similarities between Emma and Oliver, confirming her worst suspicions. But when she said it, she had tried to give it a positive spin—she'd fallen in love with Oliver *because* he was a dreamer. When Emma looks at Blue, luminescent as he describes his big plans, she can see how attractive it is. He's found a space to rent and he's going and picking up equipment from dental supply stores, and he has a business card of a naked woman on her stomach with a snake crawling out of her ass. Not quite pornographic, but not exactly something Elaine is going to want to carry around in her purse.

He's among the first of a new tribe of tattoo artists in Niagara Falls. His work appeals to the newlyweds from small Canadian towns who come to honeymoon and cement their union with snapshots of falling water and his-and-hers tattoos. He does cops and cocaine dealers in adjacent chairs. He pierces the nipples, clits, and labia of all the strippers in town, and then at night, the cops and cocaine dealers sit in strip clubs and admire Blue's work on their own bodies and the bodies of women dancing for them.

Blue seems to have found some sort of salvation through punching needles full of ink into skin. He's not at all New Age about it— he doesn't use words like *healing* or *spirit*, but rather, speaks in tough monosyllables which pop out of his mouth like cherry pits onto hot pavement.

"Show Emma that piece of work on your arm," Amy encourages, peeling a wet string of pasta off the wall.

Blue pulls up his sleeve and Emma moves in, searching for the initials that once branded him; close enough to brush her lips against the hair on his arm and catch the scent of his patchouli-and-tobacco-infused skin. The initials are obscured now, lost in a sea of overlapping blues and greens. That doesn't seem to matter to the boy disguised as a biker daddy who is Emma's baby brother. He pulls up his other sleeve to reveal an airbrushed Jesus—all blood and thorns. The tattoo begins just below his elbow and swims laps around a fleshy, undefined bicep.

"He's reading a porno," Blue tells her proudly.

"Charming," snorts Emma. Although she finds the tattoo tacky, even offensive, she's nevertheless impressed by the large boy in front of her. The ability to dream is apparently a talent or a curse, it all depends on what you do with it.

Blue just thinks he's being resourceful, and he sees Emma as someone who is much less sure of her own resources, and always has been. She's had more success disguising herself in the lives of others than creating a life of her own—a pattern Blue has noticed, but has never fully understood. He just knows that whenever she's eventually expelled from whatever universe she's been trampling through, she lands belly up on his doorstep in the tattered remnants of some costume that never suited her. He sees her that way now. Wasted and spent from a summer digging in vain and standing here wearing a tacky uniform, looking like a fish out of water.

"Come down to the Artful Dodger on Saturday," he says to her when she leaves with a belly full of beer and pasta. "Let me do some ink on you."

She hears: *That'll fix you. Pin you down. Make you my sister again.* She's been serving ice cream, reading mysteries, and dreading going back to school in the fall. She needs to belong somewhere. She needs to be a sister again.

Emma goes down like she's promised, and does her utmost to look cool in the presence of her brother's command. The shop is full of guys loitering, smoking, hanging out in the loud, tight space thick with stale sweat. The tall, lanky one who looks like he has hamburger for brains is Billy, the shop owner. Blue's usurping him now, and Billy's getting less and less friendly. He knows he is only a technician;

Blue, on the other hand, is an artist, and he is rapidly outgrowing the place.

Emma still calls her brother Blue, although he finds it a little embarrassing. He winces when she says it in front of the guys in the shop who otherwise know him as Big Lou. They're not his friends, he doesn't have any friends, never has really, except Amy, and if you can count your sister, Emma. It's kind of a family tradition. These guys are admirers—people who mill around the shop because it's cool to have a buddy who's a tattoo artist, although they're all a little bit scared of him and he knows it. That means "respect," he tells Emma, pronouncing it without the *t* and punching a clenched fist against his chest.

He's pierced his tongue and he sticks it out to provoke her. She recoils because it looks to her like a hook caught in some prehistoric fish. He flicks the silver ball against his teeth then and says it gives Amy enormous pleasure. He knows that will get a reaction out of her. He wiggles his tongue, licks the air.

Blue likes to be crude and provocative here because it fits and fuels his tough-guy image. He obviously aspires to be white trash, and he does a fairly convincing impression. His tattoos have started to creep up his neck, past the collar of his black T-shirt, threatening to strangle his face like jungle vines wrapped tight around a tree. But somewhere in that dense mess of colour Emma can still picture Blue as small and tender; treated badly and misunderstood. She can still see them crouched beside the furnace, or holding hands at school; catching rain on their pink and vulnerable tongues stretched out under an ominous, brooding sky.

She can picture them when they were little, but she's the one who feels smaller now. She imagines herself a barnacle stuck to his leg; a fly on the brown back of a wildebeest. She imagines Blue carrying her around like that, around and around the shop where he is posturing and tattooing and piercing and avoiding paying government sales tax and doing the occasional drug deal on the side. Emma watches him operate. She marvels at the way he talks savvy and lucrative street talk and uses just the right combination of charm and intimidation to develop a reputation for being the maker of cool in their sleazy summer town.

"Dude, that's my sis," Blue yells at the greasy-haired biker standing at the counter. "She's doin' her fuckin' B.A., asshole, so treat her with a little respect," he says protectively.

Emma's happy to let him play the big tough guy because the whole place scares her. She's sitting in a purple plastic dental chair, fiddling with the lever and clasping a Diet Coke between her thighs. "Do you think I'm making a mistake pursuing archaeology?" she asks him. She's obviously having her doubts. She just doesn't feel the sense of hope or motivation she felt a year ago. She feels disillusioned, almost betrayed. She still doesn't know that there's a compromise to be made between a dream and a reality, a distance to be navigated and negotiated; that it really is those petty day-to-day details, the good, the bad, and the ugly, that add up to make the dream. She cannot see the failure of the earlier summer as a china doll that simply needs its arm gluing back on: she sees it as a Ming vase that's been thrown onto concrete and shattered irreparably into a thousand tiny pieces. The end of a dynasty.

"That's not for me to say." He's not going down this road with her. She seems depressed, and this is usually a sign that she's going to run off and do something totally unpredictable. "You'll get it back," he tries to reassure her.

"Whatever *it* is," she drones.

"Well, if it's what you really want, then maybe it will come back to you."

But she's not sure how much she cares any more. All she cares about at this moment is the fact that Blue's going to give her a tattoo. She's relieved he's here, and she wonders if all that has happened has happened for this reason: to bring them back together.

"Let me ID you," Blue's been saying. She's never outright refused, it's just that she hasn't put her mind to designing anything. "I haven't got a brain left to produce an image," she tells Blue.

"Come on, Em, get a grip, okay? Just concentrate," Blue says, his patience fading.

It has occurred to Emma that if she does this, she will be giving up the right to die anonymously. She will, with a tattoo, have an identifying mark on an otherwise unremarkable body. If she chooses to disappear or do herself in, she will thus be branded as herself rather than one of the more glamorous selves she invents in some of her most elaborate fantasies. A sacrificial virgin who has just escaped near death at the hands of her tribesmen. A minor movie star who's meteoric rise to fame and fortune is struck down with the prognosis of a fatal illness. With a tattoo, her death will never provoke a nationwide search, her death will never be an unsolved mystery. She will never be able to disguise herself again.

"Okay," she finally says. "How about a cool Celtic band just above my bicep then."

"Not cool," Blue says, shaking his head. "Stupid cliché. And besides, it's gonna look *real stupid* when you're an old lady and your arm is all saggy. It's not going to look like a circle any more."

It's never occurred to Emma before that she's going to be an old lady one day. She can't really imagine racking up enough birthdays to technically be considered old. But Blue is saying, "Remember the old lady next door? Remember the underneath bit flapping like chicken skin?"

"Okay, Blue. So do whatever. Okay? Whatever."

And so Blue tells her about the band of thorns he's going to draw around her wrist. She doesn't care really. She doesn't care what he does. It's sort of not the point. The point is she is his sister and he's going to mark her in his particular way, he's going to give her a permanent identity, take away her anonymity and her transience, and pin her down in the world. He's going to carve his initials into her arm; give her a life where she is forever branded as the tribe of Blue.

# Capital D

She has her band of thorns, at least she has that, and that gives her guts enough to let Blue drive her back to Toronto in his pickup truck and help her move into her new single room in residence. They dump all the boxes in the middle of the floor. "You going to be all right?" Blue asks her as he's leaving.

Emma nods, but she doesn't want him to go. It has taken considerable effort to come back to the scene of humiliation, particularly this late into the start of the term. She hasn't dared to look anyone in the eye, she's heard only grunts in response to her attempts to say hello. She's avoiding strict archaeology this fall, focusing on related subjects taught by unrelated professors—physical anthropology, evolution, osteology, disease.

"You're depressed," Ruthie tells her, ten minutes after being reunited. "You're a casebook classic. All the signs are there."

"Depressed" sounds like an awfully bland description for what Emma is feeling. Like a hollow carcass. Like roadkill. Stuck somewhere between nightmares and daydreams. Like the world keeps dividing in two. Into discrete halves. Split like apples by a swift axe. Intimacy becoming repulsion. Lies becoming truths.

She feels as if she's lost any conviction that archaeology can provide answers, but she's still reaching out for ruins, not out of discipline, but out of fear.

"You've got to pull it together," Ruthie tells her. "Fuck what anybody else thinks. It's your life."

What precisely she is supposed to do with that precious pearl of wisdom escapes her. She tries her hardest to conjure up suicidal thoughts but she's not particularly good at it. She gets distracted. There are the remains of a chocolate cake in the fridge down the hall still to be eaten; there is the appointment to get her wisdom teeth out the following week.

In her room, she paces back and forth trying to memorize terminology. It seems to be the only way anything will stick these days. If she pounds out terms with her feet, or sets them to music, she has a rhythmic association, which is better than no association at all. But the terms exist in isolation. They don't seem to amount to anything. They don't contribute to a big picture, they don't even seem like parts of any whole.

She used to have a goal. She was going to be something. Now she can only dream of being a headless horseman or a pumpkin carved out for Hallowe'en. Somebody seems to have emptied out the contents of her head and either baked them in the oven, mashed them into a pie, or just thrown them, ever so unconsciously, into the garburator. Maybe she really is destined for a life of scooping ice cream. Maybe Oliver was right all along.

Her fantasies are getting the better of her. Her doctor prescribes Prozac and tells her she might think about taking a little trip. "Sure," she nods. "I'm sure there's a hotel room available in hell," she says to him with all the sarcasm she can muster.

"Just try the drugs," he says, not amused. "And come back in a month."

# Wired

Blue is finishing up the last of the drywall. He who could never get a grip on a circular saw seems perfectly competent when it comes to building his own empire. With the help of a small business loan he's transformed the tiny, dank basement shop into something colourful and inviting. He cranks up some metal death thrash, cracks open a beer, and toasts the acoustic tiles of the ceiling. It's his big day.

Amy arrives after her shift, carrying a giant pumpkin and bundles of flowers.

"We're not girlifying the place, okay, baby?" he says to her.

She gives him a mock sulk, and he's forced to relent. She arranges bunches of dogwood in clay pots while he tattoos the pumpkin.

Blue's got the same metal death thrash in his truck. Emma can't stand it, but she turns up the volume anyway because the music reminds her of Blue on those rare occasions when he's happy. She's driving his truck to the brewery to pick up beer for the grand opening of Dyeing Arts. She doesn't drive like a girl, despite what Blue says, but she admittedly doesn't drive well. She chain-smokes in order to calm her nerves.

Blue's giving away beer and condoms and free tattoos as door prizes that night. The place is smoky, booming, and Elaine is there, sporting the blackest clothes in her wardrobe, doing her maternal best to cope with the situation. Her son is turning out to be a bit of a local celebrity. The *Niagara Falls Herald* ran an article about local artists on the weekend, and among them they featured her son—spray-painting "Dyeing Arts" across the window of his shop. She is proud, but she's a little alarmed by the sight of Blue's new friends. His friends are new, and so is his confidence.

Blue is soaring above the crowd, waving his arms in the air and laughing as if he's just discovered how good it feels to do so. Emma is too naive to realize this is not just the exhilaration of the opening, but a good two hundred dollars' worth of chemicals. Amy is playing cocktail waitress in a transparent black tank top and army fatigues. Her hair has started to grow in and is an altogether arresting shade of orange.

At the end of the night, Amy and Emma pick up plastic cups and mop the floor while Blue stands on the dental chair and tells them his theory of earth's place in the universe. All they catch is something about cupcakes. They're ready for bed, but he's still wired. He's off with Billy to an after-hours club to drink tequila.

Amy sprays disinfectant on the countertop and says, "You know, it's getting kind of heavy."

"What's that?" Emma asks her.

"The coke."

Emma is stunned. Feels like an idiot. Wonders what else she's been missing. "Seriously?" she says, looking at Amy.

"It's not good. I mean, it's okay at the time because he's on top of the world, but then he gets so depressed the next day. Beats himself up, oayo ho'o worthlooo."

The word kicks a hole in Emma's stomach. "Worthless" was a word Oliver was fond of using—a vast, catch-all word like a pit into which Blue often tripped and fell.

"And things are really just beginning to happen for him," Amy sighs.

# Far and Wise

The drugs help—they lay down wooden planks over the gaping abyss beneath her. The drugs help, but bigger help comes in the form of vindication.

"Courier dropped this off for you earlier today," says Ruthie.

Emma's never seen herself as someone grown up enough to receive a courier package so she thinks it must be a mistake. But no, that's her name there, and the return address is somewhere in Peru. Could Oliver be in South America?

"Why don't you stop agonizing us both and open the sucker," Ruthie says.

Emma tears the envelope open. It's a handwritten letter and a map. The letter is signed Nick. "It's from Professor Rocker," she tells Ruthie.

"Oh no," Ruthie groans.

"But listen to this—he's writing to apologize."

"Get out."

"Here," Emma says, starting to read.

*After you left, I was never completely satisfied that
there wasn't, in fact, something there. I knew it
couldn't be an ossuary, and probably wasn't anything
of archaeological interest, but it continued to bother
me. So I took a look at what techniques had been
employed in the original survey. They were, as I
suspected, the most basic.*

*Then, because I was still unsatisfied—and now,
Emma, I'm telling you this in the strictest confidence
because they'd throw me out on my ass for not following procedure—I hired a private company (my own
money) to come in and do a scan with ground-
penetrating radar when the course was finished.
And wouldn't you know it—they found something—
an old well, and the rocks had obviously been moved
to cover it up, probably for safety purposes.*

*All this is to say, I owe you an apology. You were
correct—at least to some degree. There was something
there that had been missed on the first go around,
although it's not really of any relevance. But you were
right to raise the question. Where you were wrong was
to jump to conclusions—and they were pretty far-
fetched conclusions, you have to agree. I do think
you'll make a wonderful archaeologist if you take that
curiosity, that ability to raise questions, and temper it
with a greater degree of caution and patience.*

*Finally, I owe you some thanks. As you can see,
I'm sending this from Peru. I'm here, in part, because
of you. You were out of line to imply that I was bitter*

*and had lost my ambition—but you weren't entirely wrong. What this whole thing has taught me is that it's much more about the search than it is about the find. I had resigned myself to the reality that it's unlikely I would ever find anything of value in my career. What I lost in the process of that resignation, though, was the belief that the search itself has intrinsic value—that that is where the real rewards lie. And so I've come here, on a one-term sabbatical, to do something I've always wanted to do—work on an Incan site in the Andes. Gracias, Emma.*

*Nick*

# Red Button

Blue seems to be retreating from the material world. There is material all right, and money, but what he doesn't spend in the dental supply store he seems to be spending on coke. The more success he is having with the shop, the more whacked out and inaccessible he's becoming.

He doesn't see it that way. He's floating on chemicals and relative success. It's a disembodied reality: Big Lou and Baby Blue and the angry guy in the middle who disagrees with them both. But the guy in the middle's got his finger poised on a red button. He's ready to blow them all up. He's waiting for the right moment. He's waiting until Blue's got more plates stacked up before he trips him. Blue never looks in the mirror now. The image he sees is a fireball of nervous energy, electric yellow, emitting bitter shocks like bee stings. "Fuck off, man," he says to himself.

At night, Blue brags that people all the way across the country have heard of Dyeing Arts, but during the day, he is irritable and withdrawn. When Emma visits him on weekends, she tries to talk sense to him, but it only seems to make him more sullen. Mentioning the drug use just makes him angry. He tells her to get off his back, stay out of his business, chill out, get a life. It's not easy holding it together. He doesn't need the added pressure of his sister's moralizing. What does she know? The drugs are part of the territory. Using, selling, tattooing, it's all one and the same.

To Emma, though, it seems like Blue doesn't care about anybody but himself at the moment. There are the depressing daytime visits with him, but there are also the wild nights. Nights when he calls her at 3 a.m., coming down from whatever planet he's just visited, and cries, "Em, Em, I love you so much, I'm so awful, everything's so awful," into the phone. She tries her best to comfort him, tells him he'll feel better in a few hours, but he drones on and on without interruption; without the possibility of taking in anything another human could offer. It usually ends up in the same place, with Blue talking about Oliver, calling him a fucking bastard and coward.

Emma agrees.

Blue even turns up at her residence more than once in the middle of the night—having run or flown or however he gets there from Niagara Falls—laughing or crying, or most often both, prattling on, sad and angry. It's monologues he spews. They're all in his own voice, but in his head there's a three-way conversation happening. His father telling him he's a loser and a fuck-up, the baby boy who's cowering under his blows, and the angry guy in the middle who tells Oliver he wants to kill him but turns around and punches the baby boy instead.

Blue needs an audience, but he won't speak when he's sober.

"Blue," she has to say to him more than once, "please don't smoke that joint in here. Come on—you know I could get chucked out for that."

The third time she says it, he puts his steel-toed boot straight through her door.

❦

"That brother of yours is a fucking asshole," Ruthie says in no uncertain terms when she sees Emma taping a pad of paper over the hole in the door the next day.

He may well be, Emma thinks, but that doesn't give Ruthie the right to say anything. That's Emma's right—family privilege.

"He needs some help. He's gonna blow," Ruthie continues.

"Ruthie!" Emma shouts from the floor. "Quit it, okay?" she says in exasperation.

"Well, you're the one who's going to end up with a whole lot of lava in your lap," Ruthie says.

"But what am I supposed to do? You mention getting help, you mention the drugs, and he goes ballistic!"

"Don't indulge him."

"Indulge him?"

"Tell him you won't listen to his shit."

I can't do that, thinks Emma. If I did that, I might lose him. But what else can she do? She can't force him to get help, she can't threaten him. She can't get Elaine involved because Elaine's busy having her own crisis. Seems things with her man Richard weren't as peachy as Elaine made them sound. Seems he cut off the support he was giving Elaine because he was going to have to pay alimony. Seems he's leaving his wife—but not for Elaine.

"You can take your lousy money and buy yourself a hooker for all I care!" Elaine had screamed into the phone. Emma knew that much, because her mother had slurred it over the phone to her. She was back on the bottle and she was making it sound like *she told him, she told him good.*

Emma didn't know the most tragic part of it all. Elaine had called Richard up at work because she hadn't heard from him in nearly two weeks. She'd just finished her first short story. She thought it was pretty good. She was really excited, wanted to fax it to him, but rather than enthusiasm she got the big kiss-off instead. She ended up slamming the phone down, shredding the story, and throwing it into the garbage disposal. "What's wrong with me?" she screamed at the acoustic tiles of the ceiling. "Why does it have to be like this?" she sobbed into the sink now clogged with paper pulp.

Amy calls Emma from Niagara Falls one Monday night. She sounds despondent when she tells Emma that Blue didn't show up at work that day. "He's never done anything like this before," Amy sighs. "Do you think you'll come down this weekend?" she asks. Emma would prefer to avoid it, prefer to keep some distance. "I think he's really depressed," Amy continues. "Maybe it'll help to see you. You know how it feels to be depressed. And you feel better, right?"

"I doubt it'll help to see me," Emma says. "He thinks I'm being preachy and moralistic. Last time I saw him, he punched a hole in my door."

"He promised me he was going to stop doing shit like that," says Amy. "We've been through this over and over again. He's fucking up," she sighs. "It's always like this—whenever things start to go well, he starts to lose it."

The next Saturday morning Emma heads back to Niagara Falls. She doesn't really want to, she has made a pact with herself to wait for an apology from Blue, but because Amy sounds so flat, so uncharacteristically helpless, she has agreed to go.

In their apartment, Emma changes into one of Blue's sweatshirts and crawls into their bed. While Amy cleans the apartment, Emma looks around their bedroom, waiting for Blue to get home. His teddy bear—one he made in home economics in seventh grade—sits atop two books on a broken chair: *Everything You Need to Know About Growing Mushrooms Hydroponically* and some self-help guide on anger management. She doubts he bought the latter for himself.

It's late when Blue gets back and Emma is snapped out of sleep by the sound of his footsteps. Towering above her, he says, "Emma, I don't want some heavy moral thing."

"What do you mean?" she asks him.

"Like something about drugs or self-sabotage. That kind of crap."

"We're just worried about you."

"Don't waste your energy, Emma. Spend a little more time worrying about yourself so we don't have to."

"You don't have to worry about me," she says defensively.

He bites his tongue. I always have to worry about you, he thinks. I've spent my whole life worrying about you. I'm just waiting to see what you do next. "Just look after yourself," he says. "Mind your own business and I'll mind mine."

"Blue," she pleads. "I'm not your enemy."

"Well, what are you then? Who are you?"

# The Art of Being Alarming

Amy and Emma walk arm in arm down six rain-speckled blocks to an apartment in the north end of town. Amy has called her friend Nina to ask if they can stay the night because it's too late for Emma to catch a bus back to Toronto. Blue had walked out after yelling at Emma and Amy doesn't really want to be there when he gets back. She needs a break.

"But are you *sure* she won't mind?" Emma asks again.

"She's not like other people. She's sort of a hippy, she won't mind a bit."

Emma's not sure if Nina's a hippy or what, but she's definitely something else. She is a tall lean woman who seems to have gone the way of the cat people. She's got four cats, long black wavy hair, a pierced nose, and an apartment full of rather alarming art.

"Are these yours?" Emma asks Nina, pointing to the ceiling.

"Nina's an artist," Amy says. "An amazing artist."

"And a student, and a waitress, and a mother of four—cats that is," Nina says.

"Jesus. That must keep you busy."

"I'm a Gemini," she says, laughing. "And that boyfriend of yours," she says, pointing at Amy, "has got to be a raging Scorpio."

"Well, he's raging anyway," says Amy. She sinks into the couch, pulls her knees up to her chest.

"He's certainly one angry young man," Nina says.

"It's himself he wants to hurt. He keeps going out and provoking these fights with huge guys and then just letting them beat the shit out of him. He doesn't even try to fight back."

"Did your father ever hit him?" Nina asks then, turning to Emma.

"Not that I ever saw," she answers.

"There was this one time," Amy offers hesitantly.

"What's that?"

"He'd kill me if he knew I was telling you this."

"I won't say anything," Emma reassures her.

"Well, it's just this one time. It's really weird, actually. He only mentioned it once, and when I brought it up again, he flipped out."

Emma nods in encouragement.

"You know, your dad used to see prostitutes occasionally."

"*See* them?"

"Well, you know, *pay* them."

Emma groans. "It wouldn't surprise me. Not much would now."

"Yeah, well, I'm afraid it's more common than you might think. At least where I come from. Are you sure you want me to tell you?"

"I want you to tell me, but I don't want it to be awful."

"Well, it is awful, Emma," she says seriously. "And I think it really fucked him up."

Emma waves, *go on*.

"Okay. Well, your dad was always borrowing money from Blue. And then this one time Blue walked in on him when he was living in that warehouse and he saw him there with this girl—Blue said she was just some kid full of crack—and he's got her there on all fours and he's like, well, you can imagine the rest."

Emma's face was starting to collapse in on itself.

"I know, it's sick. Really sick. He was wearing this white shirt Blue had given him and he was behaving like a total animal. Then Blue says to your dad, 'I thought I told you that the money was so that you could eat.'

"And your dad says something like, 'Don't worry, this one's only ten bucks.' He didn't have any money, right, so he was just taking what he could get, but this was a *kid*. A *fucking kid*. And Blue just flipped. He wanted to kill him. I mean—he saw him doing this to some kid. So he went straight up to your dad and pulled him off her. Then, of course, your dad went nuts and they ended up pounding the shit out of each other."

"Jesus," Emma sighs, staring at Amy. "Blue came home with a black eye a couple of times. I just thought he was getting into drunken fights. I don't mean *just*, but you know ..." she trailed off.

"Well, after that, Blue didn't see him again."

"You mean, that was when he left?"

"Seems to be. I don't know if he was scared Blue would report him or something."

"It's no wonder he's so angry," says Nina. "You know, he really should see somebody."

"*We know*," Amy and Emma reply in unison.

"I mean sooner rather than later," says Nina. "Before he's forced to, or behind bars."

"Remember that guy he threatened with a knife in Banff?" Amy asks.

"Yeah."

"Well, you know what Blue said?"

"What?"

"He said the guy reminded him of your father. The way he kept his money the way he folded the bills or something."

"Because of the way he kept his money?"

"Yeah," she nods. "So can you imagine if he ever did see him? It's why he came out to Banff in the first place, although he doesn't really admit it. I think he was hoping to find him. Some guy had said he thought your dad had gone out west—to Calgary or Vancouver or somewhere."

"But he could have gone anywhere."

"That's all Blue had to go on," Amy says.

Nina offers them her bed. Insists in fact. Emma is grateful although she's unsettled. Their family secrets have just been revealed in the presence of a stranger. Things she had never even known. *Poor Blue.* How is it that she never knew? How is it he remained so quiet? Danced a strange fucking tango with their father and not said a word.

Emma stares up at the ceiling. Some of Nina's art is almost worrying and it's all rather three dimensional. Bits of metal welded to frames nailed into the walls. Metal sculptures hanging from the ceiling and jutting out over the bed. "Watch this," Nina says, turning out the lights. She flips another switch and the sculptures are alight with white Christmas lights. Amy and Emma laugh. For those few moments before sleep Nina offers them a view of an enchanted world. The right questions from a stranger have brought something critical to light. It is a twisted way to get to this small gift, but Emma is glad to be here of all places.

Emma sleeps beside Amy with three cats between them and a fourth at their feet. Four snoring feline lumps. They are a comfort in this apartment which feels like a home. Not a residence room like hers, or a trash bin like Amy and Blue's, or a depressing haunt like Elaine's, but a home.

Nina brings them cappuccino in bed the following morning. Two cups and a bowl with a marigold floating in it on a large silver-plated tray. She sits at the end of the bed and tells Emma the names of her cats: Mirabel Airport, Raindrops Keep Falling on My Head, Sweet Smell of Summer, and Somewhere Over the Rainbow.

She tells Amy she is more than welcome to stay for a while. She insists, and after they talk it over, Amy decides that she will. She'll only go back to Blue on the condition that he agrees to get some help. Nina recommends someone. A therapist a friend of hers sees. It seems like a sensible plan.

Blue, of course, is livid. He tells Amy she is being manipulative and slams down the phone. At least the seed has been planted, Nina and Amy agree. Now they will just have to see how long Blue can hold out. "Don't hold your breath," says Nina. "He *is* a Scorpio."

There is a message from Blue waiting for Emma on her answering machine when she gets back to Toronto. "Stay out of my fucking life. You're ruining everything. Now Amy has left me."

All she can do is leave a message on his answering machine: "Amy hasn't left you, and neither have I."

Emma hears from Nina the following weekend. She's in Toronto for a welding workshop and asks Emma if she would like to meet for a drink. They meet in the rooftop bar of the Park Plaza and spend six hours talking over a bottle of red wine. Emma is fascinated by her. Nina is slightly older than her and about a thousand times more together. She studies fine art, talks about it passionately, and applies the same artistic sensibility to her wardrobe. She's perched on a bar stool, wearing big black boots that look like exclamation points at the end of her long skinny, striped legs. Amy's right. she is a bit nuts, but she's got a good heart. When it comes to Blue, though, she's more of the tough-love school than either Amy or Emma. Says you can't rely on the past as an excuse for the havoc you wreak in the present.

With Emma's family history out in the open, they share an intensity, an immediate intimacy. When there are no secrets, there is no need for omissions or lies. There is no script for this. There is no gradual, hesitant revelation of facts, no fear that someone's not going to like you when they discover who you really are. It's too late, and Nina still apparently likes her. Emma likes her back—likes the way her fingers run up and down the stem of her wineglass. Likes her chipped front tooth and her hearty laugh. Keeps inhaling her perfume, and each time she does, her stomach quivers as if it contains a school of fish.

Nina is from P.E.I. "My dad was a draft dodger," she tells Emma. "He met my mum in Atlantic City. He was on his way to Canada with only a hundred dollars in his pocket. He thought he'd try his luck in Atlantic City on the way and, God, well, he probably shouldn't have bothered because not only did he lose all his money, he ended up with my mum. She had been in Atlantic City for a couple of years trying to get a job as a dancer. She still tells people she was a Rockette, even though it's nowhere near true. Wrong city, wrong era, wrong legs. Anyway, she must have thought it was very romantic or something, running off to Canada with a draft dodger. But my dad had his own romantic notions. He had this idea about growing tobacco. He thought he was going to get rich. Can you imagine? In a province where all they farm is potatoes? Needless to say, he didn't get rich and it wasn't nearly as glamorous as my mother must have thought it was going to be, so she went and ran off with an antique dealer named Fred. *Fred.* Can you imagine?"

"Do you still see them?"

"Not a lot. My dad's okay, although I don't see him often. He lives in Halifax with his second wife and her kids. My mother's a bit of a pain. I try to see her at least once a year. It's a chore. The antique dealer's a freak. And I have a brother and a sister too. Twins. Scott lives in Rochester and Paula lives in Thunder Bay with her kids. I'm the runt of the litter, and, I guess, the mutant."

Neither of them wants to end their conversation, but the waiters are stacking up chairs on the tables around them, vacuuming the carpet. They agree to meet over an early breakfast the next morning. In the elevator down to the sidewalk, Nina says, "It's a strange set of circumstances, but I'm really glad I met you."

"So am I," Emma blushes.

The iceberg shows some sign of melting. It's cold when you're alone out there in a shark-infested ocean. "Okay," he shrugs in response to Amy's repeated suggestion of therapy. "So I'll think about it."

"That's a good start, Blue," Amy says. "I really hope you do."

"Okay, okay. Don't push me," he snaps. But later he says, "Do you think maybe you could come with me?"

"Of course," she sighs with relief. "However you want to do it."

"I really miss you," he says, beginning to cry.

He's still pretty resistant to the whole idea of therapy, but he does think the lady they go to see is nice. That's the word he uses when Amy asks if he likes her: "Nice." What he means is: *I could hurt her. I'm big and abrasive and she's little and soft-spoken. I don't want to hurt her. I don't want to hurt you.*

Amy accompanies him on that first visit, but after that, he goes alone.

"And what does that voice say to you?" the nice lady asks.

"It says I'm a loser and a fuck-up," Blue replies. "It's crazy, isn't it? To hear voices in your head?"

"Crazy's not a word I use," says the nice lady. "We all have voices in our heads to some degree. Internalized voices. Some of those are helpful, they help us to be good to others and ourselves. For instance, we know it's wrong to steal. How do we know that? Well, usually our parents try and teach us right from wrong, and society reinforces that. So when you think about stealing, you hear those internalized voices saying, 'It's wrong to steal.' But then there are the unhelpful voices, the voices that say, 'You are a loser and a fuck-up.' It doesn't mean those voices are right, it just means they are loud, sometimes too loud to defend yourself against."

"So loud that you can't hear yourself think?"

The nice lady nods.

As long as he can distinguish between himself and those voices, he'll be okay.

# Solder

It's an uncharacteristically hot Saturday afternoon in fall and Nina is lying on her stomach on the kitchen floor, legs wide apart, propped up on her elbows. It's an unusual posture for welding, but it seems to work for her. "Do you want to try?" she asks, sitting up and handing Emma a pair of goggles.

Emma pulls the goggles down over her eyes and takes the iron. It's not as easy as Nina makes it look. It's fussy, particular, but undeniably sexy. She watches the solder melt. She massages it into place. It feels delicate and slightly illicit, like having your hair lightly brushed by the kid in the seat behind you in second grade.

"Not bad," Nina says, watching over Emma's shoulder.

Emma can feel Nina's breath on the back of her neck. Feel it in her stomach. She can't move. Nina, though, seems focused on the task at hand. "See," she says, picking up the object in her hands once Emma finishes. "If you welded a hook onto the back here, you could hang it on the wall. So let's get a hook for Emma's first piece of sculpture. This is the best part," she says excitedly. "Treasure hunting." She pulls Emma to her feet. "The municipal dump," she explains in response to the blank look on Emma's face. "Why else would I live in this shitty part of town?"

She doubles Emma down the street on her rickety old lime-green Schwinn. Emma on the seat, forced to wrap her arms around Nina's waist, does so hesitantly, feels Nina's stomach warm and flat and has to resist leaning her face into Nina's back. It would be so easy. So easy despite everything it brings. Being called a lezzy by kids at school. Oliver would opt for harsher words like dyke: *My daughter's a goddamn dyke.* A world of people shouting: *she just needs a good fuck.* But with her arms around Nina's waist it doesn't seem to matter. Nothing does in that moment except the thought of kissing the length of Nina's spine. Filter out the world and suddenly all this becomes possible. Travelling without a passport. Navigating without a map. Trusting the instinct to run your tongue down the back of the woman in front of you. Emma thinks all this as they churn uphill and sway from side to side. Nina pushes the pedals up and down, brushing the insides of Emma's thighs.

The dump is a rusted field of the discarded, disused and forgotten: a shore where you can't see the beach for the shells. Nina and Emma comb metal mountains like they are archaeologists of the next millennium. Emma is looking for something that resembles a conventional hook, Nina, less literal-minded, picks up a flat round disc, like the blade of a circular saw.

"It's okay," she says, cupping Emma's find. "That's great. We can use them both. Now what else?"

"What about these things?" Emma suggests, picking up a rusted pair of clamps. "They look like antiquated stirrups or something."

"Great! So we take those and some other brutal-looking objects and we make some installation piece about women as guinea pigs in the examining room."

261

"And we give it both historic and futuristic dimensions," Emma says, eager to show Nina she can join her in this game. "Like this thing," she suggests, holding up a radiator. "It's an artificial womb!"

"We can have an exhibition called From Room with a View to a Womb with a Screw!" Nina exclaims.

"Or, Without a Screw!" Emma adds.

"Hilarious!"

"Make room for the industrial nightmare," Nina calls out, pedalling them down the hill with a basket full of junk. "It's not junk," she has corrected Emma. "It's art waiting to happen." A nice philosophy, thinks Emma. Nina sees the potential for beauty in a dump; the humanity in her brutish-looking brother.

"You're so ... I don't know ... urban," Emma later says self-consciously. She becomes clumsier the more time she spends near Nina.

"Well, that's a joke," Nina laughs. "Considering I was born in a barnyard amongst a bunch of pigs and cow shit. I grew up on carrots and chicken giblets."

Emma finds herself reaching to pull Nina's hair away from her face. A wavering, breathless gesture. A hand stretched across the silently guarded space between two bodies. Nina closes her eyes. Emma runs her fingertips over her eyelids and angular cheekbones, down her chin and neck. "You have the most interesting clavicle," she tells her.

"You mean ugly," Nina laughs. "I've always thought it was so ugly. I flipped off my bike when I was about fifteen and broke it. It didn't heal properly," Nina says, fingering it delicately. It's Nina who seems nervous now.

"It's beautiful," Emma says. "Twisted and beautiful."

Nina inhales deeply and runs her hand through Emma's hair. Emma leans her face against Nina's chest, closes her eyes, and listens to her breathing. Nina's chest is soft and solid, her sweet smell emanates possibility; her being yields to curiosity. Nina's breathing becomes heavy as Emma's hair falls from behind her ear and tickles her neck. She leans over Nina's face and moves slowly to brush her wet lips with her own. She parts Nina's lips with her tongue.

"Take my tongue," Emma whispers. Nina pulls Emma's tongue into her mouth. Tastes sugar on her teeth, salt on her upper lip. They breathe heavily, with gently tangled tongues, and Emma is sure her heart will stop. "Remember to breathe," Nina giggles.

Imagine that this is Emma, a girl in the moment of finding her courage; taking the lead down a road less travelled, and trusting herself enough to take someone there with her. Somewhere Over the Rainbow sinks his claws into Emma's back, but somehow, she fails to notice.

# Roadkill

The idea is to reconstruct an animal. Strip it down to the bones and build it back up again. Label every one of the bones and analyse their wear. Look for osteological indications of how and at what age the animal died. It's the term project for Emma's faunal archaeo-osteology course—an exploration of the weird and wonderful science of looking at animal remains in archaeological context—taught by Professor Melville Savage.

Nina offers to help Emma with the project. "That is so perverse!" she shrieks when Emma tells her she is going to have to locate a dead animal. "Like roadkill?" she asks hopefully.

"Could be. As long as the bones are relatively intact."

Professor Savage is the last of his kind. He's continued teaching the course into his late eighties because there is no one else who can quite do it. Initially, he expressed considerable excitement about having Emma in his class—with her background in Middle Eastern studies, surely she knew how to embalm. Emma had read books, but she couldn't exactly say that she'd had any practical experience. This disappointed him and Emma became just another student—that is, until she volunteered to take on the ostrich.

Where everybody else was keen to do their neighbour's dog, the python at the pet store, and the bird that had smacked itself unconscious against their window one morning while they were munching their muesli, Emma had bravely stuck up her hand when Professor Savage asked if anyone was willing to tackle a flightless bird he had been fantasizing about for years. Why the hell not, she thought. She kind of liked the idea of being an integral part of some old man's fantasy.

The ostrich was lying frozen in a giant freezer in the basement of the Royal Ontario Museum, and had been, apparently, for the better part of seven years. So one particularly cold morning in mid-November, Professor Savage picks Emma up in a rusty truck and they drive up the street to the loading dock at the ROM. Professor Savage squints over the steering wheel. In that moment, Emma questions the wisdom of accepting his help, but she knows no taxi driver is going to agree to transport a hundred-and-fifty-pound bird. All five feet of it are stuffed into a canvas bag. It looks like a corpse. It certainly doesn't look legal. It takes the combined strength of Emma and two men to lift it into the back of Professor Savage's truck, and two more men at the other end to haul it up the three flights of stairs to the lab at the top of the decrepit, asbestos-lined building. "It's small for an ostrich," Professor Savage says helpfully, taking up the rear.

In the dust-filled attic, they begin the unveiling. With the aid of a hair dryer they unwrap and unwrap the gauze layered around its sizable girth. Professor Savage makes a noise like he's got a potato caught in his esophagus. "The toes!"

Emma isn't sure what he means, but it's obviously something important given Professor Savage's reaction.

"It's got three toes on each foot!"

"Is that, uh, unusual?"

"Christ, woman!" he shouts. "An ostrich only has two toes!"

"Well, what is it then?"

"You tell me. Grab that book and look it up."

Emma flips through the various pictures of flightless birds. "An emu?" she says tentatively.

"What makes you say that?"

"Two toes. The size of it—smaller than an ostrich."

"Good girl," he says. "This is indeed *Dromaius novaehollandiae*, not *Struthio camelus*, as the label suggests."

"Not even the same family?"

"Surprising, isn't it? They must have labelled it incorrectly. Now *this* is exciting," he says, stroking his chin in delight. "This is cause for celebration."

Emma can hardly refuse his invitation to go and have a pitcher of beer for lunch in the Faculty Club. Be it ostrich or emu, a hundred and fifty pounds of flightless bird isn't going to thaw over lunch.

There are only men in the dark, smoky club—with the exception of one animated woman holding court at a table otherwise exclusively surrounded by men. When Emma walks in, this woman looks over immediately and gives her a venomous stare. "Shall we join them?" Professor Savage asks, gesturing toward Patti Summers and her graduate students.

"I'd rather not," Emma mumbles awkwardly.

"Fine by me," he shrugs. "I just suggested it out of departmental collegiality. Personally, I can't stand that woman."

Emma looks at him with surprise.

"Poor Peter," he sighs. "One of the finest young archaeologists I've ever known. Didn't get tenure here because of that one there."

Emma thinks of Peter and his vanishing erection covered in dust and sweat in the boiler room.

Over beer and chips, they are back to the matter at hand—how to proceed with the ostrich that turns out to be an emu. Two hours later, both of them slightly drunk, they are at it. Up to their elbows in subcutaneous fat. They slice giant frozen slabs of fat off the girth of the bird and toss them into a double-lined garbage can. Six hours later they have cleared away enough fat and tissue to lay the bird down in a giant copper bathtub suspended over a heating element. It will simmer there slowly for the next three days, filling the air in the lab with a smell of musty, evaporating blubber so thick they can feel it cling to their clothes and hair.

They leave it over the weekend, a weekend Nina comes to spend with Emma in Toronto. Nina arrives on Friday night, and they chat nervously for a while—talking one thing, thinking another, Emma sitting on the edge of the bed, Nina perched on the windowsill, wondering who is going to make the first move—and then, somehow, all their civilized intentions of having dinner and seeing a movie seem to be forgotten. Emma stares at the ripeness of Nina's mouth, trips over her words, walks over to the window ledge, and stands, too close for friendship, in front of her. Smells her like honeysuckle, sees her nipples through her shirt, kisses her neck and her clavicle and her ear and her cheek and her upper lip, and then, with the fullness of her lips parting, they begin to suck and pull each other's tongues, over and endlessly over in that rolling, compulsive way that could go on forever, mouths melting while your hair turns grey and your bones start to shrink and the world is no longer the world as you once knew it until you eventually stop, sore-lipped and still hungry.

The bird is happily bubbling away in an attic down the street and Emma and Nina are busy getting naked. A bird and two girls stripped down to their essence, discarding all former lives. Nina is fluid and languid despite her bones and length. Emma is stronger than she knew. And braver. She reaches up from the bed to take Nina's hand and pull her down. Nina lies still on top of her. "Breathe," Nina whispers, and then pushes her pelvis into Emma. Emma feels Nina from her feet to her neck and arches her back in lieu of moaning. Nina buries her wet mouth in Emma's neck, grips her around the waist, and slides her way to Emma's nipple. She lingers there with a delicate tongue, bites gently, while Emma grips the back of her neck.

Emma pulls Nina back on top of her and rolls her over onto her back. She grazes her lips across Nina's shoulder blade and moves her mouth along the length of Nina's body. She brings her weight down and runs her hands through Nina's hair as she kisses her, rocks against her. She feels Nina's stomach breathing into hers, like one giant, undulating wave. Movement slows to heartbeats over hours, lulling them to eventual, partial sleep where limbs are entwined, lips are close, and bodies burn with the ache for more.

Emma wakes under Nina's weight. Nina rocks against her like seaweed in slow water, until Emma sits up and takes her nipple between her teeth. Her hands reach and crawl under the twisted sheet to grasp the dark wet hair between Nina's legs. A strange curious confidence in her fingers. She slides down to spread Nina's lips with her tongue. Nina moans as she pushes herself into Emma's mouth. Emma licks her saltiness as Nina floats up and down over Emma's tongue, and Emma is lost for a thousand days and nights in the rhythm of a beautiful woman until Nina cries out, shudders, and freezes. Emma pulls Nina down, pulls at the good weight of her. She wishes Nina could melt into her as her hands run delirious circles over Nina's back. Nina buries her mouth in Emma's hair.

They don't actually get out of bed until Sunday morning, and they only do so then because Emma is a little concerned about the simmering emu. They are silent as they walk to the lab together. Not shy, not embarrassed, not regretful, but mesmerized with each other and themselves.

When they arrive, the bird is still happily bubbling away in its own juices. Professor Savage is asleep in a chair beside it, apparently keeping vigil. Emma puts her hand on his shoulder and he awakes, startled, and mumbles something about an angel in the bathtub. Emma has the sudden, horrible thought that if Professor Savage should die before the term is over, she will be stuck reconstructing this giant, flightless one, alone. She looks alarmed.

"Oh Christ, woman!" he scoffs. "I'm not losing it! I mean, it's like a godsend! I've done an ostrich before, but never an emu!"

Nina laughs, and introduces herself. She and Emma can't refuse when he asks, half an hour later, if he can take them out for a liquid lunch.

Nina charms the pants off Professor Savage with all her knowledge about birds.

Emma looks at her with surprise. Nina is endlessly surprising. "I grew up in a house full of dead birds," she laughs, explaining. "Fred— he's a taxidermist. Not professionally, but it's a hobby of his."

"The antique dealer?"

"Yeah," she nods. "Thing is, though, my mother can't stand to have the things in the house. That's what she calls them—'the things.'"

The things, Emma thinks. The wild things. Where the wild things are. "Where does he keep them, then?" she asks.

"In the garden shed, or sometimes in the deep freezer. My mother defrosted one once—she was a little hammered—little, that's an understatement—anyway, she thought it was a turkey."

"What was it?" asks Professor Savage, curious.

"A cassowary."

Emma doesn't want to admit it, but she's never heard of a cassowary.

"How fascinating," muses Professor Savage. "Where on earth did he get a cassowary? I think they're an endangered species."

Nina shrugs. "Through the Internet somehow. He's always on the Internet—usually downloading porn—it keeps him occupied so he doesn't have to deal with my mother. He belongs to some discussion group for taxidermists and they hold an international symposium every year in New South Wales. Must have been through that somehow."

"Fascinating," Professor Savage nods.

And on they go—birds of a feather, flocking together, Emma amazed and delighted with all that they share. When Emma tells Professor Savage that Nina is a sculptor, he becomes quite animated. Nina says she would be very interested in following their work: she'd like to replicate it by erecting an emu out of scrap metal. Professor Savage thinks it is a wonderful idea, invites her to sculpt alongside them, and Emma can feel herself go so red at the proposal that she has to stare at her shoes for the next ten minutes.

Emma hates to admit it to herself, but she thinks she might be a lesbian. She and Nina are doing stuff that certainly makes it look that way—and not just once, but repeatedly. She's slipping and sliding body first, with abandon. Laughing without restraint. Crying without provocation. A head on her shoulder, a nipple between her teeth, a tongue down the length of her. A compulsion, an ache, a belonging so normal that she doesn't feel the slightest bit weird about it, although she can't stand the thought that some terrorists in grade seven knew her better than she knew herself.

Being with Nina is giving her a history. A context for interpretation. Like any archaeological find, a kiss is meaningless in isolation. No wonder she couldn't stand the purple peanut-buttered tongues all the girls in her classes seemed so hungry to swallow. It seems to be making a whole lot of sense, unravelling some of the confusion, simplifying things.

In the euphoria of it all, Emma feels like she actually wants to tell Elaine. "I think I'm falling in love," she longs to say. She never spoke to Elaine this way about Andrew. She hadn't used words like "love" when she told Elaine about the brainy boy in the library. She had said: "intelligent," "educated," "big house," and "big dreams." And she had moved out of Elaine's house with the announcement that Andrew's world just seemed "more conducive to what she wanted to accomplish." Those were the words she actually used. Jesus Christ, she thinks. How pompous, how desperately unromantic.

"I've met someone," she tells Elaine when she's back one weekend visiting Nina. "And, uh, I thought maybe you'd like to meet her too."

Elaine is surprisingly calm about the whole thing—so cool, in fact, that Emma is disappointed. Elaine continues plucking her eyebrows in the bathroom mirror. "Uh-huh," she says, without batting an eyelash. She's getting ready for a date, another date with some guy who Emma knows she's "met" through a personal ad. Emma pictures a man with halitosis and white shoes. Pictures his false teeth clattering when he laughs.

"Mum? Do you hear what I'm saying?"

Elaine takes a swig from her Scotch glass and puts it down on the counter and quips, "Emma, you're always looking for a reaction!"

"Well, just a sign of life. A heartbeat or something." It had always been this way. Whenever she or Blue told their mother anything of significance they were accused of being deliberately provocative, when all they really sought was the slightest acknowledgement that they had been heard.

"I'm pleased," she says quickly then, pouting to apply her lipstick in the mirror.

"Pleased?"

"Well, at least it means you won't go and get pregnant."

Emma takes what she can get. At least she's not displeased, even though she's not displeased for the strangest of reasons.

"I just want you to be happy," Elaine admits.

"You do?" Emma can't help saying.

"Of course I do! Both of you. I just want you and Blue to be happy," she snaps, making it sound much more like a command than a wish.

# Truth and Lies

Emma's got hundreds of bones to deal with, all scattered in front of her, none the slightest bit like another. One by one, Emma brightens and disinfects each with bleach, lays it down, identifies it, and labels it with black ink. Each vertebra, each rib, each digit of a six-year-old female bird, slowly and painstakingly, cleaned, identified, and labelled.

Beside Emma's table of bird bones, Nina has accumulated a scrap heap of tangled metal. Nina picks a piece of metal for each one of the thousands of parts of the bird—welding certain pieces together, filing others to shape, bending flexible bars of a mattress for ribs, creating a cascading wave of increasingly larger bolts for each vertebra of the bird's spectacular spine.

At night, Emma retreats to the library to do research about the emu's habitat and diet. In one series of photographs, an emu bounces freely across the desert terrain of the Australian outback. In another, it's presented on a plate as carpaccio-red, raw, and sliced over Boston lettuce and drizzled with honey mustard dressing. *Mmm, mmm.*

She's copying down the recipe for Nina when she notices the cover of the latest issue of *Scientific American*. A major breakthrough in quantum mechanics. Some physicists have apparently found that elusive quark named Truth. She secretly hopes that Andrew has totally missed the boat on this one. Curious, she picks up the magazine and flips through the article in search of Andrew's name. She doesn't find it, only the revelation that the discovery of Truth wasn't an end in itself. A team of scientists had located the quark only to discover they had ten thousand new problems to solve. Truth was apparently full of secrets and lies.

Blue's been talking about truth lately, talking about Oliver, about finding him, speaking his mind, putting an end to all this. He and Amy use the word "closure"—new to their vocabulary thanks to the nice lady he continues to see. Emma suspects that if they found Oliver, the truth and reality of him, they would find that, like Truth, he concealed thousands of other secrets. Tip of the iceberg, can of worms, that idea but stronger. More like the killing fields of Cambodia where the discovery of one skull assures you there are ten thousand more.

While Emma busies herself with the resurrection of the holy flightless one, Amy and Blue plan their journey. There are all the practical considerations to do with money and the shop, but things are slowing down naturally with the colder weather—people forgetting their skin as they cover up for winter. He'll direct his few booked appointments to Mitch and take a commission for doing so. He'll close for an extended Christmas holiday. He'll think of this as a long-term investment.

Although no one's been asked for their opinion, everyone seems to think it's a good idea. Nina thinks it will be cathartic, even Elaine seems to buy it, whatever "it" really is. She's given Blue an envelope for his journey. A note wrapped around a photograph of a wild-haired man in a poncho. "Your dad," she's penned. "In the good old days." Emma, seems to be the only one who has any doubts.

*Imagine*. Just imagine. Imagine you could shrink at will. Imagine that the world was just one big jigsaw puzzle and you heard that the last piece was lying on a beach on the West Coast. Imagine that you hitchhiked out west with a knife down your pant leg and called that the Quest for Closure. Your girlfriend, unknowing and well intentioned, her head on your shoulder, sleeps through Manitoba and wakes up in the Prairies, pasty-mouthed and confused. She's had a dream that the two of you have just adopted a black Lab from the Humane Society, but in one of those horrible moments where you wish you could just turn the clock back by two minutes, you've driven the Jimmy over the dog's front paws. You comfort her in the only way how—kisses followed by sick jokes. The two of you are dying to get out and have a cigarette.

Blue and Amy do hitchhike. Not the wisest move, but Blue seems to want to make the journey in the roughest way he can. A tortuous emotional journey requires an equally dangerous mode of transport. They ride all the way to Vancouver in the back of a pickup truck, wrapped in sleeping bags, rubbing cold noses, Blue's hands buried underneath Amy's sweater. She is full of love for him on this journey. She loves his courage. She loves his innocence. She loves him because he is the first guy she's been with who doesn't treat her like she's a weak little girl.

She remembers when she first met him and they went camping. He was determined to catch her a fish, and when he had no luck with the rod he even stood in the stream and tried to spear one for her. She waded into the river and put her tongue in his ear and convinced him to give up. They swam upstream instead, where they spawned like horny salmon.

"In the winter, I'll dig a hole in the ice and catch you a whole school of fish," he told her. He had wanted to ice-fish ever since he'd first watched Red Fisher—the guru of the Canadian fishing world who littered his Sunday fishing show with passages from the Bible. They had never been believers, but Blue begged Elaine to write a cheque for Red Fisher's book of religiously inspired poetry about fishing. It came in a brown paper wrapper and was inscribed to Blue. He kept the poetry under his pillow and he carried the slim volume with him to the Sportsman's Show at the CNE where they had heard Red Fisher would be a special guest.

Blue's whole body trembled when he saw Red Fisher. "Go up and say hi," Emma had encouraged him. Blue practically kneeled at the towering giant's feet as he mooned, "You're my hero."

"That's just fine, son," Red Fisher bellowed largely, patting him on the head without looking down and walking on by.

Blue just stood there in bewildered silence, willing himself not to cry. Red Fisher had just come ashore and landed like a beached and bloated whale. Blue was nothing more than an inconsequential minnow—too small to even consider frying for breakfast. And all that talk about brotherly love.

So much has happened since. Red Fisher was the first of Blue's heroes to betray him.

# Somebody's Father

The salt of the Pacific tastes like sweat to him. The taste of fear. Reminds him of standing in front of his father, not knowing how to anticipate his reaction as he held out offerings, like a pilgrim visiting the shrine of some unpredictable God. Some days, Oliver would be grateful. Take the sweater Blue offered him and say he was glad it was wool because acrylic didn't breathe. On other occasions he would bark, "Do you think I'm a beggar?" and throw back the used item of clothing in disgust.

Blue had kept trying, though; trying to make him happy, proud. Trying to find himself a father: to locate a paternal pulse in the unpredictable mass of Oliver in front of him. The man who once built him a bicycle. Gripping the handlebars of a familiar yet dangerous beast. He'll never let go: he's still holding on for his life.

Blue and Amy are staying with Amy's ex-stepsister-in-law in Vancouver. It's a long and complicated story that no one can keep straight, but it seems Jolie was once married to Amy's stepbrother, Michael. Michael apparently went and moved to Israel and enlisted in the army and blew his own head off with an Uzi somehow. But that was after he and Jolie had already split up. Nobody was ever sure if it was an accident.

Jolie knows what Blue is going through; she knows that nothing hurts like a heart. What Blue seeks is reunion, and letting go. He seeks an end. He knows that ends are supposed to involve forgiveness, at least in Hollywood, but the fantasies of meeting Oliver are often full of revenge. He'd like to be able to say, "See, Dad, I'm not a faggot. And I'm not a loser, or a wimp. I'm tough, tougher than you could ever be. I've got a girlfriend and I'm running my own business. Successfully. Can you see me? This is me. Not you. Not a byproduct of you." He'd like to be able to say that and believe it. He'd like to see himself reincarnated as nobody's son, but try as he might to disassociate himself, the toxic residue of past life continues to contaminate, and that's why he's here.

He carries a picture of Oliver around to all the homeless shelters, asking anyone if they know the man. There's a lot of shaking of unwashed heads. He does the rounds every other day because there's a near-daily turnover of staff and he wants to be sure to ask as many people as possible. Amy doesn't accompany him on these visits. Sometimes, if he gets chatting with the staff, he stays for lunch. Eats a bowl of dusty soup and breaks bread with a bunch of foul-smelling men and asks them, "Are you anybody's father?"

"Not just anybody's," one old man says, shaking his head. "I'm Isabel's father."

"And where's Isabel?" Blue asks him.

"She's in jail for murder."

"She killed someone?"

"Yeah, me," he nods. He seems to be serious.

He hears story after story. Meets hundreds and hundreds of ghosts. Everybody has a story, a past life, it seems. Everyone's dying to tell someone. But none of the men he meets ever ask him what his story is. Only Amy asks him questions. Asks him every night how the day went, where he went, what he saw, how he felt. He doesn't know whether he is speaking truth or lies: the stories are all getting tangled, lives are crossing like bad wires.

Blue calls Emma from Jolie's apartment. He tells her he's been visiting the homeless shelters, carrying around Oliver's picture. Emma knows the photo, it's more than fifteen years old, but she supposes it doesn't really matter because she really doubts Blue is going to be able to find him.

"Em, why don't you come out here for Christmas?" Blue asks her. "It's really beautiful, and you've never even been west of Niagara Falls. Imagine, if I find Dad by then, it'll be like a family reunion."

"Blue, I, uh … kind of already have plans for Christmas," she stammers. "I'm going to spend it with Nina." Elaine wouldn't be around, she was planning on going to Cuba with some new boyfriend. Even if this weren't true, Emma's not sure if she could stand the heart-break of witnessing Blue's fantasy come to an end.

"Nina?" Blue asks.

"Blue"—she hesitates and swallows—"we're kinda seeing each other."

"What do you mean?"

"Like it sounds."

He falls silent.

"Blue?" she prompts.

"Yeah."

"Are you okay?"

"Fine," he says plainly.

"Well, I mean, so what do you think?"

"About what exactly?"

"Well, about me being in love with a woman?"

"Dunno. What do you want me to say, Emma?"

"Just something, I mean, anything."

"It's a little unnatural. Kinda creepy," he says, his voice shuddering.

"It's not so unnatural."

"Sure it is. I mean, how would you feel if I called you up and told you I was a fag?"

"I wouldn't mind at all."

"Well, that's because you're a lesbian!"

They're getting nowhere.

"I'll pass you to Amy now, she wants to say hi. Just be careful, Em, okay?"

"Okay," she says, although she's not sure what, in particular, she is supposed to be careful about.

"Gay bashers," explains Amy. "He worries about you. Now he'll worry about you even more."

"But I'm kind of worried about him," Emma replies. "Amy? Does he really think he's going to find our father?"

"Seems to need to at the moment," she replies.

But what's he thinking? A family reunion? Does he think he's going to find Oliver, and that if he does, he'll say something like, "Glad you could make it home for Christmas, son. Call up your sister and we'll roast a bird in the oven and celebrate." A dead pigeon on the hot tin roof of a car maybe. That he'll say, "Thought you might like this, Lou. Picked up a little Christmas present in the L.A. airport for you last year," and hand him a tightly wrapped shiny package containing a portable CD player.

"Ah, thanks, Dad. How'dya know this is exactly what I wanted?"

"I know my boy," Dad would blush. "Now give your old man a hug."
Whatever he's looking for, he's not going to find it, Emma thinks.
Least of all a hug from Oliver.

Blue goes for a drink that night with Amy and Jolie at the bar around
the corner. Amy and Jolie talk about the guy Jolie's dating. "I just don't
get it," Jolie sighs, exasperated. "Some kind of different internal clock
or something," she says, speaking as if men are a different species. She
turns to Blue to ask him his opinion. Blue is sullen and withdrawn that
night, and he doesn't appear to hear her. After his ninth bottle of beer
he says he's going for a walk.

"Let me come with you," Amy says, but he's not in the mood for a
romantic stroll. He wants to pound his boots against pavement and
thunder his way around the block. He wants to punch holes in the
thick air and mutter profanities to himself.

When he leaves the bar, he is ready to kill. His fucking sister. He's
been protecting her all her life—all the sordid truths he has had to absorb
in order to spare her pain. She has no idea. No fucking idea at all. Someone
had to take care of the two of them. Someone had to become tough.

His fucking sister. He had stood between her and his angry drunk-
en father—the buffer between Emma and the man who squatted on the
floor and threatened to kill Andrew. The man who frequented prostitutes and molested children when he couldn't pay. When his father said
that Emma was an arrogant cunt, he defended her and took blows to the
head. She was trying to create a new life for herself, and even though
Andrew was a wimp and the rest of his family was a bunch of stuck-up
snobs, Blue wanted her to believe that she could.

His fucking sister. After all that, she goes and turns out to be a
dyke. He wonders why the hell she wants to fuck it up and make it so

complicated. He's worried she's going to get her head bashed in by a bunch of homo haters. He's tried to make life smoother for her, but she insists on complicating it. Nobody wants to be gay. He knows that.

"Don't be such a pansy," his father used to say. "I'll show you what you'll get if you're a fairy," he said, making a crude gesture with a broom handle and biting his lower lip. Blue's sure he only ever cried once after that fateful day at McDonald's and that was when they asked him in hospital if he'd been having anal intercourse. They thought he was a fucking faggot and he wanted to kill them. He hasn't let anybody make him cry since—hasn't let anybody touch him either. It's not surprising he grew from small and scared into large and scary. His leather, his tattoos. He's built an armour of ink around his body and soul and fallen in love with a woman a third of his size. No one would dare call him a faggot now.

When he crashes into bed late that night he reeks of beer and rain. "What's eating you?" Amy mumbles, stroking his forehead.

He's silent. Doesn't want to talk. Eating me? he thinks. Something like arsenic. What if I told you the truth, Amy? That sometimes I am so angry I could kill. That I love you, but loving you doesn't change the fact that my dad's somewhere out here wandering around with my intestines in one of his hands. Dragging my guts through the streets. That Emma seems to think she can get off scot-free. Walk away, call herself Oksana, or Mrs. Franklin, or a lesbian, and leave it all behind. Leave me to search. Leave me to take care of it all.

"Don't worry, Amy," he says, pulling her into his shoulder.

He lies wide awake much of that night with his tiny bird of a girlfriend breathing erratically in his arm. He sees her eyelids flutter like a butterfly, and wonders if she dreams of animals. Through the open window, he picks up a familial scent. It's lingering there in the damp streets of Vancouver, Oliver's out there somewhere, he can smell it in the air.

In the morning he follows the scent straight to the Salvation Army.

"No luck yet, eh?" the same staff member he encountered the day before says to him at the door.

"Nah," says Blue, shaking his head.

"Well, I'm keeping an eye out for you. In the buildup to Christmas you get lots of new faces. Worms crawl out of the woodwork. It's a hard time. Even the ones whose memories are totally shot seem to get upset by the season. He could turn up yet."

"Yeah, I've just got this feeling . . ."

"Instinct's a good thing," the man nods. "Sometimes it's all you have to go on. You stayin' for lunch? It's a special day. We've got beauty contestants serving today."

"You've got what?"

"Delegates from the Miss Pacific Rim contest are here today to rack up some good karma points."

"You're kidding."

"Nope."

"That's sort of perverted."

"It's a hoot. We get a kick out of it and they feel holier than thou."

They walk into the dining hall where Miss Fiji and Miss Vancouver are standing behind the metal food wagon in full goodwill ambassador regalia. They are wearing their Miss So-and-so banners over their matching sweaters and full C-cups, and ladling stew into green plastic bowls. Miss Siberia is on doughnut duty, and Miss Japan stands at the end, pouring coffee.

A group of dazed and oblivious men stand in line and hold out their trays, taking little notice of the temporary change in staff. Blue and the staff worker take a place at the end of the line. Blue reaches into the box for a plain doughnut.

"I'll get that for you," says Miss Siberia, pushing his hand away.

"I can do it myself," Blue says, annoyed.

"We're here to help you today," she coos.

"No," he shakes his head. "You don't get it. I don't need your help. I'm only here because my buddy invited me." His explanation falls on deaf ears, though. "You don't seriously think I'm like these guys," he says, nodding over his shoulder.

"Hey, take it easy," the staff guy behind him says, putting a hand on his arm.

"But she thinks I'm one of these homeless guys," Blue says.

"So what if she does? What does it matter?"

"I just don't want to be mistaken for something I'm not," he says. Being mistaken brings him one step closer to being there. He wants to find Oliver; he doesn't want to walk in his shoes.

# She Flies

Nina comes to Toronto most weekends now—long weekends, which last from Thursday night to Monday morning—and continues to work alongside Emma. They're growing, both the birds—Nina's from the ground up, Emma's down the length of the lab table. At night, Nina listens to her, teases her as she waxes on passionately about the distal region of the emu's pelvis.

"Sounds sexy," says Nina, slipping her long legs into the bath. They sit there with their knees to their chests, Nina's back against the drain, her head against the hot tap.

"You lezzies just about done in there?" Ruthie says, knocking on the door. "D'you forget this is a communal bathroom?"

Nina toasts Emma as quietly as possible with the rim of her wineglass. Passes her the soap. "You reek of bleach," she says. "Hurry up. The old man's waiting."

They have a ritual now, the three of them. On Saturday nights, Emma and Nina get cleaned up after a day in the lab and join Professor Savage back at his old house on Markham Street. They share a bottle of wine while they wash the week's dishes in his kitchen, and when the kitchen is clean, they cook for him.

"Nothing too fancy, now," he calls from the sofa in the living room, although he's mentioned more than once today that he wouldn't mind a little portobello mushroom sauce with his steak. That's Nina's fault. She buys expensive and exotic vegetables at Longos and tells him organic is better for his sperm count. He finds that very convincing and often asks for a second helping of arugula.

Nina and Professor Savage swap stories about various wars—so convincing you'd think she'd lived through the whole century. They are stories passed down to her from her grandpa, a man whose wife only married him because he promised her he'd buy her a refrigerator. "What do I want with a useless ring?" she had apparently said when he appeared at her parents' doorstep on bent knee. "Offer me one of those newfangled appliances, though, and I'll say 'I do' faster than you can say 'Spit'!"

She got the fridge before she got electricity. When electricity arrived in their part of the country, she thought it must be a sign of the Second Coming. She believed the fridge had the power of granting eternal life: hence the five-year-old butter, which Nina still fondly remembers as something like Stilton for country hicks.

Emma is determined to have the emu standing for the Christmas party. She wishes it could wear a tux and pass around a tray of hors d'oeuvres. Nina's welded a stand for the bird, measured it perfectly, so all that remains is to lift the entire thing off the table and lower it down gently into its cradle—its manger, Emma wants to call it. She lets Nina and Professor Savage do the honours while she stands back and watches, her hands covering her heart in her mouth. She holds her breath. They count to three, lift the bird slightly, and suddenly, there she is, winged and upright, flying for a moment, bounding across the outback, smiling, and then coming back down to earth to land in her manger. As soon as her bones touch the metal stand, Emma lets out a huge sigh and bursts into tears.

"Honey!" says Nina, her face a collage of pride and compassion.

"Oh!" says Professor Savage, not knowing what to do, not understanding girls and why they always cry at moments like this. "My dear. It's okay. It's perfectly intact. It's … beautiful, Emma."

She continues sobbing and Professor Savage reaches into his pocket for an ink-stained handkerchief. "You'll have to come and get it, dear," he says, one hand still on the emu's neck.

Emma laughs and reaches out to take it. Nina is adjusting the emu's spine, balancing it's wings. "It is so beautiful," she says, standing back. "You did it, Emma. You really did it."

Emma can't quite believe it's true. She did do it. "Look at that," she says, pointing at her bird and laughing.

Professor Savage shuffles off to the corner of the room and Nina kisses Emma with all the pride of someone who completely understands what it is to take the risk of creating something life-like out of the discarded and forgotten.

A flood of things comes clattering out of a cupboard as Professor Savage yanks so hard at a door that he pulls it off its rusting hinges.

"Melville? Are you okay?" Emma asks, separating herself from Nina.

"I'm all right," he declares, wiping a shower of dust off his front. "There it is," he says, bending down with a hand on his knee for support. "My wee box of Christmas decorations," he says, standing up, one hand against his back, one holding a flowered hat box. He throws off the lid and extracts a tiny wreath made of pine cones.

He carries it across the room in his outstretched hands and stands in front of Emma's bird. "I crown thee, queen of the emus." He pats the pine cones down onto the bird's skull.

The day of the Christmas party, Nina's sculpture—distinct, yet familiar—stands tall and beautiful beside Emma's emu. Nina's is more whimsical—"I can only parody real life, I can't recreate it like you," she says to Emma. From between its legs hang six ostrich eggs painted gold, strung on a thin piece of fishing line. She and Emma plant a seventh golden egg inside the rib cage of the bird of bones.

They put votive candles on the heads of the raccoons and pythons for the Christmas party. It is a small and special occasion in the hallowed lab room. Former students and favourite colleagues stand around Professor Savage as he stirs mulled wine in the copper bathtub with a yardstick. Emma has to refrain from making jokes about the non-yuletide uses of the tub.

The emu is the object of considerable attention. "That's a remarkable specimen, Melville," says a lisping forensic anthropologist. Professor Savage points at Emma, with pride in his gesture. "Tell that to its creator," he says. She blushes and the forensic anthropologist walks over and takes her by the elbow and leads her to the bird to engage her in a discussion about the particular challenges of reconstructing a bird of this size.

Emma surprises herself with her revelation of details, her exacting osteological comparison between the emu and the ostrich.

"Any interest in dinosaurs?" the lisping professor asks.

"Lifelong," she has to admit.

"You're well prepared," he says, commending her.

In the slightly drunken headiness of it all, Emma excuses herself for a moment. She wants to call Blue. She's not exactly sure what to say: "I built an emu" doesn't really capture it.

She's thrown off course by the sound of him, though. He doesn't sound right to her. His words make sense but his tone rings false, almost menacing. "I'm close to the source, Emma, I can feel it," he says cryptically, allowing Amy to translate.

"Guy at the Salvation Army says someone matching your father's description came in for dinner yesterday," Amy explains. "Shoved chicken and potatoes into the pocket of his coat and stumbled out of there. The guy wasn't a regular, but apparently that's nothing to go on because the Christmas season isn't exactly a regular time."

Indeed. It's a premature thaw that brings comatose flies to life for an afternoon.

Even if it is Oliver, Emma thinks, does Blue really want to see him leaving the Salvation Army with mashed potatoes in his pocket saying, "I was just going to put this on my Visa?"

"They're gonna contact us if he comes in again," says Blue.

"Do you think he's being realistic?" Emma asks Amy later.

"About what?"

"About the possibility that this guy might be our father?"

"It's unlikely."

"And besides, what would he do if it was?"

"Don't know. One moment I think he just wants to know that he's alive and the next, I think he wants to blast the guy. He'd probably just give him fifty bucks and tell him to buy himself some new clothes and that would be about it. He just wants it to be over. He needs to say goodbye."

"He's just setting himself up for more heartbreak. He's searching for something he's never going to find."

"Maybe it's the search that he needs more than the finding," Amy says, considering.

"Maybe," Emma can't help but agree.

"To know that he tried his best," Amy adds.

"But he did that a long time ago," Emma says.

# Christmas

It's a relief to be spending Christmas with Nina this year rather than going through the charade of festivity that is usually Christmas. Last year, Elaine got too drunk to remember to put the turkey in the oven. Emma and Blue had stuffed it in at dusk and incinerated it within the hour.

"I couldn't agree with you more," Nina says. "Christ. You should have seen my mother last year. Scott and I pulled up to the house and she was standing on the porch waiting for us in this getup like she was a nineteen-fifties film star at cocktail hour on holiday in the Caribbean. It was like, minus twenty, and she was wearing this sleeveless yellow muumuu thing and drinking a martini. Scott told her she looked like a drag queen. It could only get worse from there."

"So did it?"

"Big time. First, there's always the issue of her getting drunk and saying she used to be a Rockette—she's always screaming, 'Look at these legs, damn it!' And then she's always telling me I look scruffy and am never going to get a man and it doesn't seem to matter that I'm a lesbian—she knows perfectly well that I am—she still always says these things—'A little lipstick wouldn't go amiss.' And then, Christ,

Scott's dog tries to hump her leg and Fred skulks around like a creep, and then my sister shows up—and she's a born-again Christian—with her husband and their three kids, and then there are just *way* too many people and way too much going on and we all have to sit down and open presents. Fred always gives me some kind of stuffed animal—I mean an animal he's stuffed—and my mother has a complete fit because she can't stand 'those things' in the house and the kids start bawling and she just gets more and more hammered and then she starts crying and invariably ends up completely missing the big meal we've spent way too much time and effort planning. It's always a fucking mess."

"Why do we bother?" Emma sighs.

"Because we keep hoping. We keep hoping it's going to change."

"I guess you're right," says Emma. It's just part of the contract of being born and related. You don't choose your family, it's true, but you can't really choose to unchoose them either, no matter how much you might want to do so in your head. Even when you haven't seen them in years. Even when most of your memories are of being insulted and criticized. Even when you know they must be homeless, insane, dead, or possibly some combination of all three.

Her father may well have spent Christmas Day alone in some gutter, without a sweater to keep him warm. Might have spent the last few Christmases like this. Dirty and decrepit, with a tangled mass of hair full of nesting earthworms and nuts squirrels have buried there for winter.

Are you still here, Dad? she wonders. Do you even care if you are? I think Blue does, even if you don't, and I can't any longer.

Out of necessity, it seems, she has chosen to stop worrying, but she will always harbour the fantasy that had they lived some other life, he would have offered her pearls of wisdom, walked her up the aisle, said to someone, "Take good care of my daughter," and handed Blue the responsibility of running the family business. In another life, Oliver would have retired, received a pension, taken up oil painting, and grown into an old and kindly man adored by his grandchildren. There would have been grandchildren, instead of children who change their names and reconstruct dead animals rather than perpetuate lineages.

The problem with never having had something, though, is that you dream it in its most conventional and clichéd sense. You ingest the romance portrayed in movies and long for chance, albeit Brief Encounters in train stations, meetings that will change your life forever. In truth, given the choice, we are too afraid to let our lives change forever, however brief, wherever the station. But Emma and Blue haven't been given a choice. Their lives are about to change forever, whether they know it or not.

Emma and Nina spend the day before Christmas on a snowmobile. It feels nearly holy to float on white with your arms wrapped around your lover's waist. All these hidden talents, Emma thinks of Nina, as they fly off a small hill and land in a dip with a thud, and then a rev, a rip, and another rise, and they are flying again. Everything you discover in another: every day the person in front of you becomes bigger, and rounder, fills the holes in you with things that are different, unexpected. Not only does Nina know how to drive this thing, she knows the trails through the trees. She sight-reads vast and endless fields of white without hesitation and they shriek as they fly under a heavy dark winter sky.

Emma tries driving. Cautiously at first, but it quickly comes to feel safe, solid and easy, as Nina grips her thighs. Emma turns sharply and they lean into the ground as the skidoo slides out from underneath them and they skate across ice on their backs. Neither of them can stop laughing—they are on the edge of a frozen lake, sheer ice, fun and danger.

They drive back to Nina's apartment in Blue's truck, Emma's head in Nina's lap the whole way, Nina trying to get Emma to join her in botching up the words of various Christmas carols.

"What's wrong, babe?"

"Nothing," Emma says. "At least I don't think so. A little preoccupied maybe. It's just a little disconcerting being apart from Blue. I don't know what he's thinking. I hope he's okay."

"He's doing what he needs to do, Emma. And he's got Amy with him. And she is really solid."

Solid, yes, but strong enough? He's got *storm* written all over him. It's not her job, or anyone's, to predict his weather, to batten down the hatches, see everyone else has cover.

There's no answer at the apartment in Vancouver, but Amy calls a couple of hours later. "Merry Christmas, big sister," she slurs. "We're all a little fucking wasted."

Emma can hear the music blasting in the background. "Where the hell are you?" she asks.

"Bar," Amy burps. "Here's your brother," she says, passing him the phone and crashing off her bar stool.

"Hey," he says.

"Hey back. So, you having a good Christmas?"

"Guess so. I went by the Salvation Army again."

"Any luck?"

"Nah. Guy didn't come back," Blue says offhandedly.

"Blue, I don't know if you should get your hopes up," Emma says. "It's not very likely that the guy is Dad. So they saw a six-foot balding homeless guy with a Scottish accent. Could be anybody."

"I showed them the picture, Emma," he says, a little irritated.

"Right," she says, but without any enthusiasm in her voice.

"You could at least be a little supportive," he says angrily. "I mean, I'm doing this for both of us."

"Are you, Blue?" she snaps.

"Well, he's your fuckin' father too."

"But you've never even asked me if I want to see him again. You've never even asked me how I feel."

"Well, you don't know how I feel."

"You know what, Blue? You know what I think? I think, So what. We're adults now. We can make choices about who we have in our lives. I just mean that as much as I might miss him, he really brought us nothing but misery. We don't owe him anything."

"What the fuck do you know about misery? At least the guy didn't use you as a punching bag."

"What am I supposed to do, Blue?" she says defensively. "Okay, so he hurt you more than he hurt me. Is that what you want to hear? Do you want me to say I'm sorry? To say I'm grateful you took it instead of me?"

Blue smacks his bottle against the bar then. "Fuck you!" he yells into the receiver and slams the phone down.

Two thousand miles away, Emma can hear the bar fall silent. The bartender approaches and tells Blue to put the bottle down. "Time to go, buddy," he says.

"Fuck off," Blue says, shrugging a hand off his shoulder. "I was just going."

Amy sits there with her forehead in her hand and shakes her head.

"You coming with me?" Blue shouts.

"No," she says quietly.

"No?" he says, looking at her intensely.

"No," Amy repeats.

"Well, you can just fuck off too then! You can all just fuck off!" He shouts and storms out of the bar.

Amy puts her forehead down against the bar. She rolls onto her cheek and reaches up and sticks her finger in her drink and fishes for an ice cube. Scoops it out and places it against her eyelid. Water trickles down her face. I give up, she thinks. I give up.

# Deliverance

When Blue leaves Frank's Bar that night, he's ready to kill. His fucking sister. He's spent his whole life trying to protect her and she turns on him. The only reason he is here is to find their father and put an end to it all. To put an end to the ever-present threat that lingers when you know a man who despises you is still hiding somewhere on the planet—so close sometimes that it's as if he's in your head. You cannot rest. You live in absolute terror that he will reappear at some unexpected moment with a broom handle or a machete to mutilate and murder you. It's only a matter of time.

Being alive is like standing in a cornfield in summer during the middle of a war. There is nothing but the empty row in front of you, but you know there are a million armed soldiers hidden and waiting to attack. The threat surrounds you even though you cannot see it.

You live like that until you can stand it no longer and you decide to pick up a gun and engage in war where you are finally on the offensive. By then you know where your enemy is. Winter has come and he is just one armed soldier in full view in front of you. He is only one man, not an army. In summer's cornfield, even if you kill one soldier, you know the others are out to get you and you can feel them encroaching, like swarms of ants from every side. In the armed winter, you can aim straight and kill your enemy and know then that you are safe. Although you have to live with the sickness that you have caused injury, you at least have the assurance that he was a lone gunman and he is now dead.

Blue's got his hand on his pocket and he's walking toward the Salvation Army. "It's your lucky day," the guy at the door says, recognizing him. "Your man's just hobbled in here for dinner."

There is a train of men standing in line, gripping trays in grubby hands. Blue squints and sees him—a bearded man in a grey hat stooped over a tray.

"Think I could have a word with him?"

"You can try. He's not much of talker, though."

Blue walks up the side of the line and moves in behind the bearded man. "Hey, buddy," another man behind him says. "Wait your fuckin' turn."

"Yeah, get to the back of the line," another one shouts.

"I'm just delivering a message," Blue shouts back.

The bearded man turns his head around to see what the commotion is about. He stares right into Blue's eyes and Blue stares back. He pulls a knife out of his pocket, and in one swift gesture, he stabs the man deep in the stomach.

"Holy fuck!" the man behind him yells. "He just fuckin' knifed the guy!" The crowd moves backwards and the bearded man falls over without making a sound.

Blue is surrounded by hostel workers who wrench his arms behind his head and throw him to the floor. His head and legs are pinned to linoleum with steel-toed boots. Blue's head is flooded with images of red blooms—poppies in some foreign field of dying men. He lies there in that field and feels the wind move through the swishing sea of opiates. He doesn't know whose country he's in, or whether he's still alive, but he knows he's won the war. He smiles and breathes in linoleum.

When the telephone rings in the middle of the night you invariably wake up with your heart racing and flip through the catalogue of potential disasters in your head. The only possible hope is that it's someone calling from a different time zone. When the telephone rings in the middle of this night, Emma knows it means that Blue is in trouble. He's using his one phone call to reach her.

"Blue?" Emma says sleepily into the phone.

Amy opens her mouth to speak but nothing comes out. "He stabbed your father," she finally stammers. "He's in custody."

## Grandpa Mel

Professor Savage insists on picking Nina and Emma up from the bus station. It's very kind of him but his eyesight really does concern Emma. He doesn't seem to be registering the line in the middle of the road, but she's too much of a mess to mention it. They sit three astride in the front seat of the cab, and when Emma starts to cry, Professor Savage gently puts his arm around her and pulls her up against him. "Ah, pet," he says gently. "Why don't you tell Grandpa Mel what's going on."

The affection in his voice just about kills her and she breaks into heaving sobs. Her new grandpa has one hand on the steering wheel and one arm around her and his truck is not an automatic. "Grab the gear stick, will you, Nina, dear?" he says casually.

"Ah, sure," she agrees, a little startled, and reaches for the gear stick.

"I'll tell you when," he says to her. "Now, then. You tell me what's going on," he says, squeezing Emma's shoulder.

It all comes out in a blurry torrent punctuated by the occasional sigh. He lets her blurt on interrupted about her father, Andrew, her brother—all the men in her life. "Why is it that they end up disap-pearing or trying to kill someone? Is it men or is it me? I seem to be the common denominator in all these disasters," she splutters.

"Ah, pet, it's neither," he says, trying to comfort her. "You're broth-er's clearly an angry young man. Unfortunately he's gone and gotten himself into a whole lot of trouble. That's not your fault, dear. He's old enough to figure out a way of handling these things without ending up in jail. Hopefully he'll learn."

"But it's too late now," she says.

"It's beyond your control, Emma. It always has been," says Nina.

"Your girl's right there," says the wise grandfather. He starts to tell her a story about his own son—a son he's never mentioned before. He stares at the road ahead and begins talking.

"When my son Kevin was a young boy, we used to catch him throwing stones at the cats next door," Professor Savage says, telling them something he hasn't told anyone in years. "I should have known then that we had trouble on our hands. When he was about eleven he bludgeoned a dog to death with a two-by-four. Now here's a boy who had been nothing but loved and protected by his mother and me, show-ing a real propensity for evil at a young age. Of course, I questioned everything we had ever said to him—I wondered what we could have done to make him become so malicious and sadistic. The thing is, Emma, I doubt there was anything we could have done differently. It's that old question about evil—nature or nurture."

"But Blue was never cruel when he was young. It wasn't like that."

"That makes it an even greater tragedy," Professor Mel sighs. "But it also means there might be reason for hope. That there's a motive other than cruelty. Kevin just went from bad to worse."

"Where is he now?" Nina asks.

"He's dead," Professor Savage says matter-of-factly, not offering any more explanation.

# Implication

Blue's being charged with attempted murder and Amy's the only one he will talk to. The police, on the other hand, want to talk to all of them. Emma's in shock—the only word she can use to describe the feeling that all the vegetation on earth has just withered and died overnight. There's nothing growing any more, just vast tracks of flat earth from here to the horizon. Maybe this is the end of the world. Maybe every single family on the planet has undergone some simultaneous catastrophe and this has nothing to do with domestic order at all, but has some much bigger cosmic underpinning. In moments of crisis you selfishly wish it were so, and then, remembering yourself human, immediately wish it back.

The officer interviews her at length about Blue. She in turn probes him for details but he can tell her nothing about the man Blue attacked except that Blue maintains it was his father. If the man is their father, Blue might actually have some legal recourse. He can claim it was aggravated assault, a defensive measure against years of systemic abuse. The officer asks her a lot of questions about her father's disappearance, and yes, it seems to all add up, but still, the likelihood that Blue actually found Oliver seems next to impossible to her.

The first step toward clarifying this involves Emma on a plane going west, at the end of which there will be an escorted visit to a hospital. She offers to swim there instead. She thinks it might be safer. It would definitely be slower. Instead, she drugs herself with Ativan and cheap white wine and dreams she and Blue are floating on a dark lake. Lying on pieces of driftwood so thin they can feel the waves lapping against their backs. It's a haunted lake with a spiralling eddy, and it's pulling her and Blue in different directions and sending them down tributaries that spill down opposite sides of a hill. Emma floats downriver and spills out into the sea. She doesn't drown, but she doesn't know if her brother has survived.

Amy meets Emma at the Vancouver airport, a police officer not far behind. They collide into an embrace and Amy shakes with tears. This is an escorted visit. Amy and Emma hold hands in the back seat of a police cruiser and pull up outside the Vancouver General. Here, Emma is asked to look through a small square of glass at a sullen and silent stranger and tell the officer that this man is definitely not her father.

Would it be better to lie? she wonders. To push her way through the door and say, "Hi, Dad. So how are you doing?" and then explain away the fact that he doesn't recognize her or recall having any children with some reference to progressive dementia or Alzheimer's. Because she chooses not to lie, it's now her word against Blue's. She is guilty of implicating her brother in an attempted murder it will be nearly impossible to defend.

The only other person who could verify that this man isn't Oliver would be Elaine, and nobody wants her involved. "Not a good idea," Emma tells the officer. "She hasn't seen him in about fifteen years and she's practically blind as a bat," she lies. "Besides, he owes her about a million dollars in child support. She'd probably say the guy was my father just so she could nail somebody," she says. "She's not the sharpest knife in the drawer," she adds, realizing she should just quit while she's ahead. She knows that they'll have to speak to Elaine.

Amy and Emma go to the Y. It's the only place Amy thinks she might be able to relax. In the steam room, Emma wishes she could turn up the heat so high that she would become liquid. She's nervous about seeing Blue. She keeps holding on to some earlier memory of him in the belief that his essence remains. She had thought he simply needed the right loving hands to peel away the ugly veils and reveal his spirit, but she's no longer sure if she believes in the idea of some essential core, some aspect of self which remains relatively stable and true. If enough worms eat their way through an apple, they will get to its core: they will gnaw away its pithy centre and the whole structure will ultimately collapse, decompose, and become dirt. He might look the same, but then again, you can bite into an apple and find it full of maggots. You can kiss a princess and she turns into a frog. You can fall in love with an illusion that crumbles before you in some unexpected moment—through a simple gesture, a smell, or a misplaced word. You learn that earth is actually heaven, which means that your only options after death are purgatory or hell. A sweeping tour of all the major religions leaves you disillusioned, and suddenly you cease to be a believer in anything at all.

As they walk back to Jolie's apartment, Amy squeezes her arm and says, "You don't have to feel nervous about seeing Blue."

"But he must be so angry."

"Actually, Emma," Amy hesitates, "he doesn't want to see you right now."

"Blue doesn't want to see me?" she asks, stunned. What happened to us? she wonders. All of us. It's like the four of them in the family were only ever joined by a suicide pact. Strangers perched on top of the same building, agreeing to jump all at once. Instead, one jumps before the signal, one loses his nerve, one slips or sees God, and the other one survives. Is it just her imagination that they were related once? Other families, for all the differences between them, still seem to be governed by some mysterious magnetic force which pulls them to eat, drink, bitch, and be merry and miserable together at least once a year.

Maybe Emma's family was just bits of fluff stuck together on the head of the same dying dandelion which became permanently scattered when somebody, or something bigger than all of them, sneezed. They've taken root in other people's gardens. They've planted seeds in other countries and grown up looking like unrelated species. If she is a dandelion, Blue is a thistle, Oliver deadly nightshade, and Elaine a petrified herb from the Pleistocene era fossilized in stone. In some taxonomist's wet dream they are related—according to the same kind of meaningless logic that calculates six degrees of separation between Brad Pitt and Lady Di.

# Haunted

The RCMP does interview Elaine. They have to—they have to interview virtually everyone who ever knew Oliver. This doesn't prove to be such a monumental task because Oliver only ever knew about half a dozen people, not including all the people who wish they'd never met him and pretend they never did.

Elaine denies just about everything as a regular matter of course. She'd like to be able to deny she has a son at this point in time, but that she cannot do because two officers are sitting across from her taking notes. They're asking whether Llewellyn has any history of violence, about his relationship with his father, about his school record, emotional stability, friends. After an hour of questioning she breaks down, uttering broken fragments instead of sentences. Her son is not a sociopath, but she can't say he was easy, or like other boys.

"And the way he coughed—Jesus," she cries. "Just like his father. In the morning, always clearing his throat. Sent shivers down my spine," she shudders. "Can you imagine?" Her nightmare of an ex-husband reincarnated in the body of her son. Now haunted for the rest of her life.

She uses words like "stubborn" and "uncontrollable" and she admits that she did feel threatened by him on occasions. "But that was when he was younger," she defends. "He seemed to have calmed down, matured so much since meeting Amy." She offers the officers a drink and they say, "No thanks. But go ahead, Mrs. Taylor," and flip to the next page of their notepads.

Everything Emma and Elaine have said only seems to drive another stake into Blue's potential pardon.

Emma knows Blue will blame her. She is, after all, the one who stands up in court and says, "No, he's not."

"Can you just repeat that for me, miss? You say the man you saw in the hospital that day is not your father?"

"That is correct. That man is not my father."

"You are quite sure."

"I am positive."

"Did he bear any resemblance to your father at all?"

"No, he didn't."

Emma can't look at Blue; she hears him shouting "traitor" in his head.

But Blue doesn't feel betrayed at all. He is calm. He knows that man wasn't his father, but that doesn't matter, that's not the point. Whoever he was, Blue doesn't feel he's losing his mind any more. Whoever he was, his father is dead. He did it for both of them, she'll probably never understand that, but even if she doesn't, her life has at least been spared.

"And we have evidence to suggest in support of this, Your Honour," continues the prosecutor, "that Mr. Taylor, in fact, died earlier this year."

Emma looks over at Amy. Her face collapses. It's too easy, Emma thinks, shaking her head. It would be easier for all of them if it were true. It's quite possible, but far too simple and not altogether fair. Does this mean that Blue's been running paranoid across the country in search of a dead man? How could he get away so easily? How could he drop off the planet and leave them wondering?

It's worse to spend years searching in vain and torment than to know he is dead. Death is more understandable than the purgatory of disappearance. This place they've been asked to wait, between life and death, good and evil. Emma realizes she's been living in dread of him ever returning; Blue, on the other hand, has been agonized by his absence. Emma sitting in purgatory waiting for Dad the Maker to arrive and read the list of her bad deeds aloud so he can banish her to hell; Blue, somehow hoping his father will appear as an angel to set them free. They've been looking in entirely different directions, praying for different endings. She looks over at Blue. He is motionless, expressionless, his irises have mutated from green to black. He sees no point in getting maudlin, no point in tears. It's over, and whatever the outcome, it's better to be relieved. He wants it this way.

Emma cannot read anything from his face. She closes her eyes, presses her fingertips to her temples, and tries to speak to him silently. *"Booly boo?"*

*"Give it up, Em. It's too late for that,"* she hears him reply.

According to the prosecutor, Blue's name turned up on a report made by a police officer in New Brunswick eight months before. Blue had never been to New Brunswick to Emma's knowledge, she didn't think he'd ever been east of Montreal. The West was always his calling. The scent of Oliver dribbled along a trail from the Falls to the Rockies.

But then Emma remembers something. Blue had bragged that people had heard about Dyeing Arts all the way across the country. He'd never told her how he knew that.

Just after Blue had opened his shop, the police came to ask him some questions. They wanted to know if he could identify a man who had been killed in New Brunswick—someone who'd been run over by a truck when he jumped over a meridian on the highway.

"But I don't know anybody in New Brunswick," Blue had said defensively.

"Well, he could have been on the move. Thing is, this guy didn't have any ID on him. He didn't have much of face left, either," the officer had explained. "But he was carrying this," he said, pulling a newspaper clipping out of his folder. There was the picture of Llewellyn (Lou) Taylor spray-painting "Dyeing Arts" across the window of his shop the week before it opened. The newspaper headline read: "Local artists explore new canvases."

"We're contacting everyone featured in the article in the hope that there might be some connection," the officer continued.

"Could've been someone I tattooed, I guess," Blue had said.

"Do you keep records?"

"Uh, yeah," Blue hesitated, because his records didn't include those transactions involving drugs.

"This individual did have a tattoo of some initials on his arm," the officer said.

The initials didn't mean anything to Blue, nor did they look like his work, so Blue couldn't help them. Blue did wonder for about thirty seconds whether there was any possibility that it could have been his father, but he had dismissed the thought just as quickly as he'd entertained it. He was sure that Oliver was out west, and his father would never have a tattoo because he'd always said tattoos were only for criminal elements and devil worshippers.

After the blanks they drew from all the other young artists mentioned in the article, they had closed the case.

It is the RCMP officer who spells it out. The initials on the dead guy's arm were "LOE." LOE? Lowlife is Emma's first association. Maybe the guy couldn't spell. Feeling low? Lo and behold there's a dead guy on the road?

"What about Llewellyn, Oliver, and Emma?" he suggests. "Coincidence perhaps?" he asks, turning to the jury.

Marked and identifiable bodies. Blue's initials on his arm, Emma's wrist, a dead man's body. They might change their names, cut up their plastic cards, and dispense with living in houses altogether, but they are not completely alien and mysterious—they can do everything *but* disappear. Their bodies remain standing: silent witnesses to relationships and rebellion.

Oliver disappeared, but he did so with a trace, a trace that suggests he didn't completely disassociate himself from his children. He might have tried: he might have left them and forgotten them, but he handed over memory to his skin because memory cannot be lost, only relocated. Purging his head left visible reminders.

They are not altogether invisible. And that is something, isn't it?

# Dripping Faucet

Nina tells Emma that all they need is time, but she doesn't really know what it is to live in a family like Emma's, where people can walk away forever and stop life's clock. They have a fine role model, their father, before them. They have the potential double burden of genetic predisposition and learned hostility and capacity to abandon. If she doesn't reach out to her brother, she'll lose him forever. She doesn't know who they are in relation to each other any more, but if she doesn't even ask the question, then they'll both have to live with another unsolved mystery. They will always wonder about each other. They will drip into each other's sinks like water from leaking taps. And then one day, after turning each other into idols or monsters, they might come looking for each other because they can't find washers big enough to stop the dripping. The sound of water will keep them awake forever.

There is a good thick inch of paper piled beside Emma and Nina's bed—each page beginning, "Dear Blue," most going no further. It's a ritual Emma has developed since she and Nina moved in together. Every morning Nina disengages from one or other of the cats and gets up to put the kettle on. She brings Emma a cup of tea and Emma props herself up against the pillows, thanks her, and pulls a fresh sheet of paper across the bed. Those are the only words between them in that first hour of the day. They live well together, she and Nina, moving in and out of words.

"Dear Blue," Emma writes in black ink, and stops and pauses. Sometimes she holds her pen poised over the paper and stares at those two words for the rest of the hour. This is the hour a day she spends with Blue. Perhaps it is prayer, she doesn't know. She's never known what it is to pray, but she does know she would rather pray for the living than the dead.

It doesn't end there, but with death comes a new beginning. She feels her shape now where she used to feel like nothing more than liquid: clear substance flowing in and out of the holes in other people's lives. She doesn't know when she first became aware that she had a body to contain her, but she knows that initially she didn't resemble anything more than an amphibian. She had grabbed hold instinctively and crawled ashore; her gills desperately sucking in short painful breaths of toxic air; her body, slippery and unformed, naked in the presence of the unfamiliar creatures who call earth their home. Slowly she began to mutate and trust the feeling of ground beneath her. She built her skeleton out of a thousand bones. She built wings and feet and began to feel calmer in this brave new world. There's no Oliver any more, threatening to come and rip the ground apart and suck her back into some ugly unformed magma-like existence.

Six months later, Blue still doesn't want to see his sister. Emma gets this news from Amy who flies out and visits him in Vancouver every couple of months. He's been given the option of relocating to Kingston Penitentiary, much closer to home, but he's not interested in being incarcerated in familiar landscape. He wants to keep his new life one step removed from the world he used to inhabit. Preserve it in oil.

Amy will join him. She will finish her hairstyling course and move out to Vancouver. They both know that the love between them hasn't changed, but the life between them has, and will continue to do so for at least the five years of his sentence for attempted murder, before he's eligible for parole.

Emma resists the urge to send Blue a thousand pieces of paper that say "Dear Blue" and nothing more. She changes the ritual, knowing Blue still does not want to see her, by crawling into the bathtub in the early morning while Nina is still sleeping. She puts a sheet of paper flat against the porcelain. Still, all she manages to write is "Dear Blue." She can find no other words. She doesn't understand. I was just beginning to like my life, she thinks. She thought he was too.

She wonders if he will write because she can't. If neither of them does, they could be lost to each other forever. Maybe they already are. Ends are just as arbitrary as beginnings. You just pick some salient marker, like you do with a lover to mark an anniversary—was it when I first saw you? when we first kissed? when we first made love? when we had that awful fight and you broke down and said you didn't want to live without me? when I turned your favourite white shirt green and you told me you liked it better? Pick some instance that signifies the start and the finish. You never know whether you have done the right thing—the unanswerable questions—the if-I'd-stayed-longers and the if-I'd-tried-harders still wash over you periodically like guilty waves.

But waiting to see whether he writes becomes slow death. Each day she doesn't hear from him is like plucking another one of his hairs off her sweater. Soon her sweater will be free of his hair and there will be no evidence of him ever having rested his head in her lap. She has become untwinned from the notion that she and Blue live a symbiotic existence, but she has no idea that her life and her liberty are a result of his partial extinction. In a world of limited love, one Siamese twin is separated so that the other can live and breathe.

Blue could tell her as much, but to him, it's not the point. She will probably never know, and that is the truest form of sacrifice. Blue sits on a leaden mattress in a room off a lonely corridor with the certain knowledge that he has been victorious. He has single-handedly wrestled the guy with horns to the ground and, in so doing, restored some partial sanity for himself and spared Emma. He feels regret for the pain he caused an innocent man, enough so that he admits it to the prison psychiatrist and considers the chapel on Sunday mornings, but it was the unavoidable collateral damage in a war that needed to be won. He reminds himself of this. He has to draw solid lines because otherwise he'll never be able to walk straight. He writes to his sister:

*Em,*

*I just want you to know that I don't blame you for what happened in the courtroom. So it wasn't Dad. What were you going to do? Lie? I wouldn't expect you to do that. So it wasn't Dad. But that's not really the point.*

*At some level I knew Dad was dead. I knew it earlier in the year when the police came to question me. I guess I knew it on what you could call a technical level, but not on any other. I mean, how the fuck could he get away with it all so easily? Guy just fuckin' dies? It just seems so unfair. So you hear he's dead and you*

*just want to fucking kill him even more. Do you know
what I'm saying? I still wanted to kill him. He was
haunting my fucking head and it was only getting
worse. Can you imagine what it feels like having someone crawling around on all fours taking big bites out
of your brain? I thought I was going mental, Em. So
the guy I stabbed wasn't Dad. It was still the only way
I could kill him. And you know, as soon as I did it, I
didn't feel like I was going mental any more. And that
made it worth it. I'd do it all again if I had to.*

*You just don't seem to get it. That's why I'm mad
at you. Not because you said the guy wasn't Dad—but
because you didn't understand. He's dead—I'm
relieved and you're safe. This is a happy ending. So
don't feel sorry for me or anything. It's not all bad.*

He's straightening lines that are forever twisted; doing his best to create order, box any uncertainty, prevent spillage.

Amy passes Emma the photo of the wild-haired man in a poncho.
Pushes it across Emma and Nina's kitchen table. "Blue wanted you to
have this."

"What would I want this for?" Emma asks.

"He's giving you a gift, Emma," Amy says, almost annoyed.

"Some gift. This, in lieu of Blue."

"We haven't lost him."

"But he sounds dead. He stabs a guy, the ghosts leave his head, but
then down falls a heavy iron curtain."

"He's not dead at all," Amy defends. "He's alive—in the here
and now."

"Yeah, well, some life."

"He's says it's not all bad. He gets to do his tattooing, gets dope, smokes. He doesn't want a whole lot more right now."

"Like I said, some life."

"But he did it for you, Emma. Don't you get it? So that at least one of you could be free."

"But I never asked him to," she says.

"You didn't have to."

# Postcard from Hell

Oliver sends a postcard.

*Dear Kids,*

*Marie and I are having a fabulous time on Salt Spring Island. You wouldn't believe the scenery. Blue—you would kill to see fish like these swimming alongside each other—it's as if they were family. Emma—my God, the girls ... like your mother at twenty-five. If I were your age, I'd be in heaven, but as it is, I'm in hell.*

*Love lots,*
*Daddy O*

# Acknowledgements

With thanks to Martha Kanya-Forstner, Maya Mavjee, Ravi Mirchandani, Louise Dennys, Jen Shepherd, Suzanne Brandreth, Dean Cooke, Anne McDermid, Gary Crawford, and Anne Shepherd, and to my family and friends, Heather, Sheila, Stan, Alex, Annie and Vibika.